YULETIDE EMBRACE

It seemed the most natural thing in the world that he took her hand and led her back into the Great Hall. She need not have agonized over the means to catch him beneath the kissing bough. It was where he took her of his own accord.

Their gazes locked, they stood beneath the bough of greens and holly berries and mistletoe.

"You did not win the wager," Elizabeth said softly.

"But I'll get my prize. Didn't I tell you I was looking forward to claiming it?"

He swept her into a crushing embrace, which Elizabeth returned with fervor by clasping her arms around his neck. She raised her face and knew this was the moment she had been waiting for since she saw him stride toward her on that rainy day of her arrival. . . .

ZEBRA'S HOLIDAY REGENCY ROMANCES CAPTURE THE MAGIC OF EVERY SEASON

THE VALENTINE'S DAY BALL   (3280, $3.95)
by Donna Bell

Tradition held that at the age of eighteen, all the Heartland ladies met the man they would marry at the Valentine's Day Ball. When she was that age, the crucial ball had been canceled when Miss Jane Lindsey's mother had died. Now Jane was on the shelf at twenty-four. Still, she was happy in her life and accepted the fact that romance had passed her by. So she was annoyed with herself when the scandalous—and dangerously handsome—Lord Devlin put a schoolgirl blush into her cheeks and made her believe that perhaps romance may *indeed* be a part of her life . . .

AN EASTER BOUQUET   (3330, $3.95)
by Therese Alderton

It was a preposterous and scandalous wager: In return for a prime piece of horse-flesh, the decadent Lord Vyse would pose as a virtuous Rector in a country village. His cohorts insisted he wouldn't last a week, yet he was actually looking forward to a quiet Easter in the country.

Miss Lily Sterling was puzzled by the new rector; he had a reluctance to discuss his past and looked at her the way no Rector should *ever* look at a female of his flock. She was determined to unmask this handsome "clergyman", and she would set herself up as his bait!

A CHRISTMAS AFFAIR   (3244, $3.95)
by Joan Overfield

Justin Stockman thought he was doing the Laurence family a favor by marrying the docile sister and helping the family reverse their financial straits. The first thing he would do after the marriage was to marry off his independent and infuriating sister-in-law Amanda.

Amanda was intent on setting the arrogant Justin straight on a few matters, and the cozy holiday backdrop—from the intimate dinners to the spectacular Frost Fair—would be the perfect opportunities to let him know what life would be like with her as a sister-in-law. She would give a Merry Christmas indeed!

A CHRISTMAS HOLIDAY   (3245, $3.95)

A charming collection of Christmas short stories by Zebra's best Regency Romance writers. *The Holly Brooch, The Christmas Bride, The Glastonbury Thorn, The Yule Log, A Mistletoe Christmas,* and *Sheer Sorcery* will give you the warmth of the Holiday Season all year long.

Available wherever paperbacks are sold, or order direct from the Publisher. Send cover price plus 50¢ per copy for mailing and handling to Zebra Books, Dept. 3582, 475 Park Avenue South, New York, N.Y. 10016. Residents of New York, New Jersey and Pennsylvania must include sales tax. DO NOT SEND CASH.

A Christmas Charade

Karla Hocker

ZEBRA BOOKS
KENSINGTON PUBLISHING CORP.

To Nick and Jasmin, with love

ZEBRA BOOKS

are published by

Kensington Publishing Corp.
475 Park Avenue South
New York, NY 10016

Third printing: September, 1992

Printed in the United States of America

Prologue

She stood at one of the window slits in the southwest tower, which, like the other three towers, was built to protrude defensively from the castle walls. She was a wraith of a girl in a full skirt of striped cotton, an overdress of some dark blue material, and a frilled mobcap so voluminous it threatened to swallow her face.

In the pale light of a quarter moon, she watched the shadowy figures hurrying to and fro between the old landing stage and the cliffs below the castle. Let them hustle and grunt and heave, those "gentleman" traders. Let them drag their precious goods, the casks and oil-cloth-wrapped bales, into the safety of the hidden cave. Soon, lest they wanted to court danger and discovery, they must wait for the dark, moonless nights to carry out their trade. After forty-one years, Stenton Castle was about to open its gates once more.

Bold, defiant, invincible, the medieval stronghold of the Rowlands rose high above the chalk cliffs of Beachy Head. None of the family had set foot inside the thick walls since the tragedy. No carriage had approached the

Great North Gate on the road winding through the easternmost tip of the South Downs. No visitor had moored his yacht in the estuary where the Cuckmere River empties into the Channel at the foot of the steep cliff path leading to the castle's western gate.

But soon she would see the change, she would witness life again at the castle.

A bitter wind howled through the narrow apertures, which, in the olden days, had served the defenders of Stenton to rain arrows, rocks, and hot tar on marauders. The wind did not bother Annie, but habit made her hold on to her mobcap while she watched the freetraders. After a moment she turned away. She left the tower and slipped into the south wing—the wing that had been responsible for the desertion of the castle and now was the cornerstone of her hopes and dreams.

When craftsmen from Eastbourne and Brighton, laborers from Seaford, West Dean, and East Dean invaded the castle in October and transformed the charred remains of the south wing into chambers and suites more elegant than they had been before the tragedy, she had cautioned herself not to get her hopes up. But when the women of East Dean arrived during the height of the November gales to scrub and polish, to sweep and dust the whole castle, it became increasingly difficult to stay calm. All this activity must mean something!

When every bit of Holland covering was stored in the attics, when every room smelled of beeswax and potpourri, Annie had stood in the oriel window on the landing high above the front door and witnessed the opening of the main gate, the Great North Gate. It was a gratifying sight, awakening memories of the brief

6

time she had known the castle overflowing with family and visitors, with laughter and happiness—before the tragedy.

Four lads, two on each side, had pulled and heaved on the monstrous iron-studded gate wings until they could be secured against the gatehouse walls. Several wagons loaded with foodstuffs rumbled into the rain-slick cobbled yard, but what pleased Annie most was the fact that the gate had not been closed again. Surely, that meant more coaches were expected.

She was not disappointed. A butler, a housekeeper, a chef, and their minions moved into the servants' quarters in the north wing. A sennight later, two valets, several grooms leading a string of horses, and even a gardener arrived at the castle. Though what a gardener would do in December was more than she could say.

Hope and excitement soaring, she flitted from room to room and listened to the staff as they talked in awed tones about the castle's grandeur and whispered about the tragedy. The maids wondered if the south wing might be haunted and shivered when one of them said it surely must be. How could the poor duchess rest when she had so horribly burned to death with her children? Or the eight servants who had died trying to save their mistress and the little ones? It could not be wondered at if the poor souls walked at night in the south wing. No doubt, her grace would be heard keening and moaning in despair by those who'd occupy the rooms near the former nursery.

Annie could have reassured the maids that the duchess was very much at peace. And even if she weren't, her grace had not been the type of lady to keen or moan. But Annie glided away, quite impatient with silly girls who ought to know better. What were they thinking? That a ghost, a restless soul, had nothing better to do with her time than waste it on a lot of useless spooking or haunting?

Disgruntled, she went after the butler and the housekeeper, whose conversation she preferred in any case. From them she could hear about Stenton House in Grosvenor Square; about the London markets, where rich and poor alike shopped for fish, fruit, and vegetables; about the parks where, during a free hour on a Sunday afternoon, a girl could walk with her beau; about *everything* in London. Annie could not hear enough. The mere thought of London made her shiver with pleasure.

She was born and bred in London and had never intended to leave. But when her cousin Maude brought the news that a junior nursery maid was wanted for Stenton at thrice the wages Annie earned as a seamstress, there had truly been no choice. Annie Tuck had gone to the castle on the Sussex coast — and had been homesick every day of the forty-one years spent away from that bustling city she called home.

London. Someday, she would return. She must.

From Mr. Symes, the majestic butler, and Mrs. Rodwell, the always breathless housekeeper, Annie heard about Clive Rowland, Fifth Duke of Stenton, who had ordered the restoration of the south wing and the opening of the castle for a Christmas party. Mr. Reed, his grace's valet, who had been sent ahead, confirmed that the invitations had gone out and, as far as he knew, had been accepted.

Annie had not known there was a fifth duke. The only Duke of Stenton she had ever seen was Edward

Rowland, the fourth duke, who lost his wife and three children in the fire that gutted the south wing. But it did not matter which of the Rowlands planned to reopen the castle, as long as it *would* be inhabited once more.

Annie had waited forty-one years. A long time — even for a ghost.

Chapter One

One of the invitations sent out by Clive Rowland, Fifth Duke of Stenton, was delivered at an elegant manor house near Hitchin in Hertfordshire. The butler placed it beside Lady Astley's plate, then handed the rest of the post and two papers to Sir John Astley.

Miss Elizabeth Gore-Langton was in the breakfast room with Sir John. She hardly ever received a letter, but no one who saw her stare at the folded vellum beside Lady Astley's plate could suspect her of envy. The butler certainly did not. He rather thought Miss Gore-Langton looked flustered at the sight of the letter, her color fluctuating from pale to rosy pink and back to pale.

Sir John, shuffling through his own considerable stack of post, glanced up briefly. "Is that the Stenton frank on Louisa's letter?"

"Yes." Elizabeth's voice was flat. "Yes, it is."

"Good. Louisa will be pleased."

"Pleased, Sir John?" Elizabeth removed her gaze from the ducal frank in the corner of the letter and looked at

11

her employer's husband. "An understatement if ever I heard one."

He chuckled. "Aye, she'll be in alt."

Elizabeth stirred cream and sugar into her tea. Yes, Lady Astley would be ecstatic. Sir John did not hide his pleasure either. If the letter contained the expected invitation, they would soon be seeing their son Stewart, who had returned from the Peninsula almost three weeks ago.

Juliette, the Astley's daughter-in-law, had written that Stewart's left arm had to be amputated just above the elbow. Although he was doing fine physically, he was in low spirits and did not wish to drive to Hertfordshire or have his parents come to London.

But, Juliette added, she knew how much they must wish to see their son. They must not worry; she would arrange everything. Her cousin, the Duke of Stenton, was planning a Christmas party at Stenton Castle. He had asked Juliette and Stewart to join him, and Juliette would see to it that the Astleys received an invitation. Then they could all be together at Christmas.

"I only hope Louisa will be strong enough for such a long journey," said Sir John, whose thoughts had run along similar channels as Elizabeth's. "But between you and me, we'll make her as comfortable as possible. Won't we, m'dear?"

"Of course we shall."

Elizabeth knew she must go to Stenton with Lady Astley — if the duke had indeed issued the invitation. She had been engaged to make things as easy and comfortable as possible for the squire's wife, who suffered from a weak heart. It would be the shabbiest thing if she were to ask for a holiday now, merely because she did not wish to see the Duke of Stenton.

The breakfast room door opened to admit Lady Astley, a frail-looking woman in her early fifties. Her delicate features had a pinched look, as though she had suffered a restless night. But her eyes lit up at the sight of the letter by her plate.

"From Stenton!" Bestowing smiles on her husband and her companion, she broke the seal and scanned the sheet of paper covered in a bold scrawl.

Elizabeth watched the glow deepen on Lady Astley's face, and her heart sank. If she had harbored some slight hopes that the letter contained a polite excuse, that his grace could *not* have Sir John and Lady Astley stay at the castle for Christmas, these were now dashed. There was no doubt that the expected invitation had arrived.

"We are going to Stenton Castle!" Lady Astley exclaimed unnecessarily. "Elizabeth dear, we shall have to get busy packing!"

Elizabeth smiled. She could not possibly match Lady Astley's enthusiasm — not if she must face the man with whom she had believed herself head over heels in love eleven years ago, but who had never noticed her beside her friend Rosalind.

Of course, she knew now that it hadn't been love. Merely infatuation. She was no longer a green girl, a shy seventeen-year-old miss making her first curtsy to society. She was a staid, twenty-eight-year-old lady's companion. She had acquired dignity and composure. And pride would see her through any embarrassment she might suffer when a gleam of recognition lit his dark eyes.

Tuesday, the eighteenth of December, 1810, was a clear, crisp day. A hint of snow hung in the air when Clive Rowland, Fifth Duke of Stenton, and his friend Lord Nicholas Mackay left London early in the morning. Snug in heavy, caped driving coats, Russian fur caps covering their heads, the gentlemen were undismayed by a snowflake or two, or by a blast of winter air. At five-and-thirty they might not be striplings, but neither had they reached the state of decrepitude that demanded a closed carriage, numerous rugs, and hot bricks.

The farther south the two gentlemen traveled, the less they thought about the weather and merely congratulated themselves that they had sent their luggage and valets ahead and, against the advice of well-meaning acquaintances, had chosen the duke's racing curricle as their mode of travel. The lightness of the vehicle had twice saved them from getting mired, and the duke's matched team of grays carried them swiftly over the first half of their journey.

After an early but substantial luncheon at the King's Head in Rotherfield they continued with a hired team that might not be as good as the duke's own but was by no means made up of laggards. By afternoon, they had penetrated the elevations of the South Downs and were bowling through the village of West Dean — five miles north of Stenton Castle as the crow flies, but twice the distance by road.

For the first time since he had agreed to reopen the castle, Clive felt a stirring of curiosity and excitement. Stenton, on the promontory of Beachy Head, had since medieval times been the Rowlands' main seat, yet he had never seen it. What he knew of the castle's history, he had learned from his uncle, Lord Decimus Rowland; for Clive's father, the fourth duke, had spoken of Stenton as little as possible.

Clive flicked the whip over the leaders' ears. "Less than an hour, Nick, and we'll be there."

Lord Nicholas, a sporting gentleman, cast his eye over the deep ruts, the sharp curves and steadily increasing steepness of the road. He also took into consideration that his friend had never before traveled to Stenton.

"An hour," he said. "I'll wager a monkey you won't do it in under an hour."

"Done."

Nicholas pulled a watch from the pocket of his waistcoat. "It lacks ten minutes till three o'clock. Good luck, old boy."

For almost a mile they drove in silence. Despite a sudden rush of impatience, Clive had no intention of pressing the horses and settled them at a pace he could easily control even on this abominable road that, from the looks of it, hadn't seen repairs since his father abandoned Stenton forty-one years ago.

He cast Nicholas a sidelong look. "Think I don't know you've been burning to ask questions about this Christmas gathering at the castle? Might as well come out with them, since I don't plan to spend the rest of the trip in silence."

"Hmm," Nicholas said lazily. "I *could* say I didn't want to distract you, but I know that won't go over."

"No, it won't. The man—or woman for that matter—who can make me drop the reins or do something equally foolish has yet to be born."

Digging his chin into the fur collar of his driving coat, Nicholas stretched his legs as much as was possible in the curricle. "Truth is, old boy, you closed up like an oyster when I asked a question or two in London. I got the notion I was sticking my nose into matters that don't concern me."

"I apologize. I did not mean to snub you." Clive negotiated a hairpin turn around a rare stand of trees, then settled back against the squabs. "Unfortunately, I did not get word until this morning that it's all right to take you into my confidence."

"You sound like a dashed government official."

"Not an *official,* Nick." Clive gave the fur cap a nudge that put it at a rakish angle on his dark hair. "A government *secret agent.*"

The news would have startled anyone but Lord Nicholas, who was well known for his unflappable calm and his indolence.

"Suspected as much," Nicholas said. "Matter of fact, it wouldn't surprise me to learn you've been an agent for the past ten years."

"The deuce!" Clive gave a bark of laughter. "Damn it, Nick, you have a nasty habit of taking the fun out of every bit of news I want to spring on you."

"Gammon! May say I wouldn't be surprised, but — Dash it, Clive!" Betraying a more than perfunctory interest by the removal of his chin from the warmth of the collar, Nicholas looked straight at Clive. "You admit it, then?"

"Yes, I admit it. I went to Whitehall after Rosalind's death. Volunteered my services. Of course, what I really wanted was a commission, but, as my father pointed out, Harry was already in the army."

"Aye. Was in Holland at the time, wasn't he? Then came home on furlough and got buckled. And lost no time putting Lady Harry in the family way."

Clive nodded, but absently. His mind was on the six brief months of his own marriage. Rosalind had contracted the smallpox—the dickens knew how or where! And two days before his twenty-fifth birthday, he had been a widower. With a slight shock, Clive realized that in January it would be eleven years since Rosalind's death. No wonder his memories of her were blurred.

But, eleven years or not, he remembered the pain, the rage when she died, the desire to destroy something—someone. He had targeted those violent emotions on France, on the upstart Napoléon Bonaparte, whose armies had overrun Holland, Belgium, Germany, Italy. When he approached his father, however, the fourth duke had blanched and begged him in an unsteady voice to reconsider.

The duke was a strong, powerful man who usually looked and acted as though he were fifty years old rather than seventy. His distress had brought Clive to his senses. He had remembered that he, his younger brother Harry, and their sister Fanny were the fourth duke's second family. The only close family. Clive's mother, the duke's second wife, died in childbirth when Clive was eleven, Harry seven, and Fanny barely two years old. It was inconceivable that the duke, at age seventy, could remarry and start a third family should both his sons be killed in the war against France.

Quietly, Clive had given up his dream of joining the army and vanquishing Bonaparte. Then Harry had married Margaret Standish, and before he returned to his regiment the news was out that Lady Harry was *en-*

ceinte. Clive did not doubt that his brother had sired a son—an heir, should something happen to both Clive and Harry.

Without telling his father, Clive went to the Secretary for War and volunteered his services. For six years he led a dangerous double life that, until Margaret's confinement, cost him a pang of conscience each time he faced his father. He was Clive Rowland, Marquis Sandown, the son and heir of the Duke of Stenton; and he was the daring spy, using a number of different names to travel in France, Italy, and the Netherlands. Only during the brief Peace of Amiens did he visit Paris as the Marquis Sandown.

Clive was at home when the news arrived at Stenton House in Grosvenor Square that Harry was killed in a battle near Maida in Italy, but there was nothing he could do to soften the blow for his father. The fourth duke was seventy-six years old. He suffered a stroke from which he did not recover, and on the thirteenth of August, 1806, Clive was the Fifth duke of Stenton.

Nicholas, as though he had followed Clive's thoughts, said, "I wager those cloth-heads in Whitehall made you resign when Harry and your father died."

"They did, even though I pointed out that Harry left a son."

"And a daughter," Nicholas said wryly. "Had the pleasure of meeting them both. Twins. That must have been a surprise."

"It was, although Margaret says it shouldn't have been. Apparently, they've had twins in the family for generations."

"Nothing has changed since Harry and your father died," Nicholas pointed out. *"You* haven't married and

18

filled your nursery. So why the sudden change of mind at the War Office?"

"This past year, several important documents were lost or went astray at the Horse Guards."

"The Horse Guards," Nick repeated softly. "That's where Wellington's dispatches come in, don't they?"

"Precisely. And Yorke of the Admiralty reported similar problems. Secret memoranda apparently lost for a day or so, then recovered in some file when they had no business being filed at all."

"And the war's been going badly for us." Nicholas's blond brows knitted. "A traitor . . . damn his guts! It fair makes my blood boil."

Clive briefly took his eyes off the road. "I didn't think there was anything at all that could ruffle your calm."

"Well, you're wrong. Got strong feelings about a lot of things. Just don't show it. But how do you figure in that mess?"

Noting a stretch of fairly straight road ahead, Clive flicked the reins. "There are reports of a smugglers' nest on the Sussex coast, where not only contraband is landed but also French agents. It is feared that copies of our most secret documents leave the country from—"

"Don't tell me," drawled Nicholas, reverting to his habitual languor. "This smugglers' nest is at Stenton."

"Unfortunately. Or, perhaps, I should say fortunately, since it was what rescued me from a life of boredom."

"Yes, I see now why you'd leave town during the uproar about the Regency Bill. 'Twas what puzzled me the most about this whole business. What with the Whigs already celebrating their victory and all."

"Let's hope there won't be a regency. The latest word

from Windsor was that the king is getting better."

Nicholas grimaced, whether at Clive's optimism or because the wheels had hit a rut was impossible to tell. "King's been ill since the Golden Jubilee in October. A bad attack. Doesn't even know Amelia died. His favorite daughter, poor man! Heard he dreams she's gone to Hanover."

"Dash it, Nick! The mere thought of a regency, and Prinny's Whig friends appointed to high posts, is more than flesh and blood can stand."

"Aye. Let's talk about your business in Sussex. Are you acting on Liverpool's orders, then?"

"Yes and no. The War Office certainly has a hand in this scheme, but so does the Admiralty and the Foreign Office."

"Smoky, if you ask me." Nicholas cocked a brow. "Or so damned important that for once they put duty before their departmental bickering?"

"It's important. And so secret that Liverpool, Yorke, and Wellesley did not even brief their aides. And neither would they risk sending me to a deserted castle. Someone might smell a bubble and start asking questions."

"Dragoons!" said Nicholas. "Lots of 'em on the coast. Why didn't —"

"Dragoons could clean out the smugglers' nest, but chances are they'd lose the French agent in the fracas."

"Aye, and it's the spy Whitehall is after. He's the one to point a finger at the traitor. Or traitors. And that's where you and your castle come in. But why the house party?"

Clive slowed the horses as he caught his first glimpse of Stenton Castle in the distance. High walls concealing most of the main structure, four crenellated round towers . . . nothing fanciful, yet, somehow, impressive.

"Clive?"

"Ah, yes. The Christmas gathering. It's my cover, Nick. If I had gone to Stenton on my own with nothing to do but patrol the beach, the smugglers might have smelled a rat and refused to land such a dangerous cargo as a spy. We'd have to waste time looking for the spy's new landing place."

"Quite. But I cannot help thinking that a houseful of guests will be a nuisance."

"On the contrary. I have chosen my guests with care. They'll be involved in solving their own problems, or feuding with each other. There won't be any interference or unpleasant surprises—like one of them deciding to hang on to my sleeve."

"That's all very well, but your duties as host . . . "

Clive removed his gaze from the gatehouse and the open gate, which were now clearly discernible. He chuckled. "That, my friend, is where you come in. You'll substitute for me when the occasion demands."

Nicholas sat bolt upright. "The devil you say! You don't think I'll be left behind while you go after smugglers and spies!"

"*What?*" Clive did not drop the reins or even slacken his grip, but he did not check his voice. "Dammit, Nick! This is not the time to try one of your jests on me."

"No jest. Want to have an adventure. And if that surprises you, it shouldn't. Remember how we used to chase pirates and smugglers on the pond at Belfort?"

Clive stared at the friend whose sudden hankering

21

for an adventure threatened to overset his carefully laid plans.

"That was when we were boys. Cut line, Nick! I know you're having me on. First thing you said when I asked you down to Stenton was that you don't like the coast. You don't like the water, the damp, the sand, the cliffs, the wind, or anything about the coast. I had to beg you to accompany me. And now you want to catch a French agent? Doing it much too brown, old boy. You don't catch a spy while drinking punch by the fireside."

Nick's cheerfulness had faded during the recital of discomforts that must be expected outside the snug castle walls, but he said obstinately, "I don't give a straw. I'll survive a night or two on the beach while we wait for the spy to land. Besides, main reason I didn't want to leave town had nothing to do with sand or water."

Clive cocked a knowing brow. "A new charmer?"

"Thought so, but in the end she preferred Sylvester Throckmorton. So you needn't think I'm pining to go back to town. And now, tell me who else will be gracing your Christmas party."

Knowing full well that Nick's indolence was surpassed only by his mulishness, Clive resigned himself to his fate. With a certain amount of relish, he informed his friend to definitely expect Lord Decimus Rowland, his uncle, whom Nick considered the greatest bore on earth. But Nicholas only nodded absently, his mind obviously on the spy he planned to catch.

Nettled by this lack of response — although that was just what he should have expected — Clive guided his team through the castle gate. "Check your watch, old boy. I think you owe me a monkey."

"Hmm." Nicholas cast a look at his timepiece. "Made it with ten minutes to spare," he confirmed, still with that air of absentmindedness about him. "Who else is coming?"

Clive's thoughts as he named the rest of the party were glum. He was damnably out of practice as a government agent, else he wouldn't have slipped up so badly when he chose Nick as his substitute host. But who would have thought his indolent friend hankered after an adventure? He could only hope none of the other guests had a surprise in store for him.

Chapter Two

The duke's sister and her husband arrived at Stenton the following afternoon. They had left their snug manor house near Chilham, Kent, at the crack of dawn to reach the Sussex coast before the early winter dusk would obscure Lady Fanny's first view of the castle.

Lady Fanny, dark-haired and gray-eyed like many of the Rowlands, was as vivacious as her spouse was quiet. She could not and would not hide her excitement at the prospect of spending the Christmas holidays at the place that might have been her childhood home.

"Just look at this, George!" she cried, stepping into the Great Hall, a vast chamber two stories high and topped by a domed roof, which, in the early eighteenth century, had been embellished with stained-glass panels. "It's even grander than Uncle Decimus described it." Lord Wilmott gave her a fond look. "Yes, my love. It is something quite out of the ordinary."

Then, while Lady Fanny volubly admired the two huge fireplaces, the collection of ancient arms and suits of armor, and the chandelier suspended from a thick chain in the center of the hall, Wilmott turned to the butler and inquired politely for his brother-in-law.

Symes bowed majestically. "I fear his grace has not yet returned, my lord. But you'll find Lord Nicholas in the Blue Salon."

"But where did my brother go?" demanded Lady Fanny, withdrawing her gaze from the large painting on the wall opposite the entrance. "He knew we'd be here! I wrote him."

"I daresay his grace went to the beach, my lady."

Fanny blinked. *"Clive?"* she said, incredulous. "Walking on the beach? In winter, in near dark?"

"I believe his grace has conceived a fondness for the sea, my lady. He ventured out immediately after his arrival yesterday, and again this morning and after luncheon."

"In that case," said Lord Wilmott, "you had better show us to our rooms first."

"I hope we are in a tower room," said Lady Fanny.

"I'm afraid that's not possible, my lady. The towers have no rooms. They were built purely for the defense of the castle."

The butler started for one of the many passageways leading off the Great Hall. "Mrs. Rodwell had the ducal suite in the south wing prepared for you. It is, if I may venture to say so, quite the most beautiful suite in the castle."

Fanny said no more until she and George were alone in a sitting room that opened onto a bedroom on either side.

"George, do you realize that these are the rooms my father and his first wife occupied at the time of the fire? Well, Father didn't," she amended. "He was a Gentle-

25

man of the Bedchamber and was at Windsor attending the king. And he never got over feeling guilty that he wasn't here to help."

Wilmott studied the wainscoting, obviously of a very recent vintage. "A tidy bit of restoration. I must ask Clive whom he employed to carve the frieze. I've long wanted to have that panel in the gallery restored."

"I am more curious about Clive's reason for opening Stenton. He always said it would be far too costly to maintain, and now he even had the south wing restored. It must have cost a fortune!"

"No doubt he had his reasons," Wilmott said mildly. "My love, your hat is quite crooked. Do take it off."

Absently, she tugged at the ribbons tied beneath her chin. "And to open the place at Christmas, with most of the family invited! Even Flora and Amelia, when he knows Uncle Decimus cannot abide Flora. George, it's my belief there's more to this gathering than meets the eye."

"If so, we'll no doubt find out."

"Yes, but when? Clive can be so dashed close-mouthed." She dropped the hat onto a chair. "I wonder if he found the treasure?"

Wilmott had been about to go into his bedroom but turned back. "My love, you are a constant delight. I never know what surprise you'll spring at me when you open your mouth. Now what is this about a treasure?"

But Fanny's quicksilver mind had already moved on. "Or, perhaps, he finally decided to remarry. Do you think he asked us here to meet his intended bride, George?"

"No," Wilmott said uncompromisingly.

She did not meet his eye. "But he should marry. He needs a son. An heir."

He went to her, drawing her into his arms.

"An heir is not everything," he said quietly.

Her eyes were bright and glittering when she did look at him. In anyone but the vivacious Lady Fanny one would have suspected imminent tears.

"There are always cousins and nephews who may inherit," said Wilmott.

She smiled, if a little tremulously. "I know you think I should not meddle in Clive's affairs. But don't you see, dearest George? His case is not at all like yours . . . ours. If he doesn't marry, how will he ever know whether he might have had an heir?"

"Fanny, your brother will turn six-and-thirty next month. He does not need a sister, ten years his junior, to tell him how to conduct his life."

She was quick to catch the note of severity in his voice. She snuggled against him, secure in the knowledge that she knew just how to deal with her dear George.

"Oh, very well," she murmured, all outward compliance. "But I confess, I'm quite out of patience with Clive."

A tiny, satisfied smile curved her mouth. This time, Clive could not escape her when she approached him on the subject of his marriage. He could not pack up and leave, as he did when she invited him to her house. This time, he was the host and would just have to bear with her.

The following day, Thursday, the twentieth of December, four coaches rumbled through the hamlet of West Dean at intervals ranging from a few minutes to three hours.

The older inhabitants of West Dean, who had observed the two coaches carrying Lady Fanny and Lord Wilmott and their baggage the previous day, remembered the busy traffic before the tragedy and watched the progress of these new arrivals with pride and gratification.

Pride, because Stenton, although not nearly as magnificent as Arundel, was a grand castle as castles go. It was *their* castle, and it was finally coming to life again. Gratification, because the reopening of Stenton meant increased prosperity for the village. For as long as the old-timers could remember, the lads and maidens of West Dean and East Dean had been hired as undergrooms and under housemaids when the family was in residence.

The younger generation, including the lads and maidens who might expect employment at the castle, goggled at the splendid coaches. Except for the gig driven by Dr. Wimple from Seaford, they had scarcely seen a carriage at all.

The first conveyance, a cumbersome traveling chaise, carried the duke's uncle and his valet toward Stenton. Lord Decimus Rowland, who disliked travel as much as he disliked managing females, had started in a foul humor from his chambers in St. James's on the previous day and had broken the journey at the King's Head in Rotherfield, where Clive and Nicholas enjoyed their luncheon.

Unlike the two younger gentlemen, Lord Decimus had bespoken a room at the inn. When he had recouped his strength by partaking lavishly of a steak and kidney pie, a leg of lamb served with spinach, and a wedge of Stilton, he whiled away the hours by sampling some very fine sherry and, after an excellent dinner, a cognac as smooth as he could wish.

A night's repose and the quality of liquid refreshments at the inn had mellowed his mood. When he entered his chaise the following morning, he was beginning to look forward to his stay at the castle. In fact, it might not have been a bad thing at all that an extremely unlucky week at the gaming tables left him with his pockets to let so that he'd been obliged to accept his nephew's invitation for Christmas.

A beatific smile on his round cherub face crowned by a wreath of wispy gray hair, Lord Decimus settled into a corner of the chaise. Supplied by his valet with cushions and rugs, three hot bricks, and a flask of the inn's best cognac, he was prepared to suffer the discomforts of the narrow, winding road he remembered well from his younger days.

If the King's Head, many miles inland, could boast such a cognac, wouldn't Stenton, so much closer to the source, have an even more promising cellar? At least, Decimus hoped the smugglers who had supplied the fourth duke's household — or, rather, the sons and grandsons of those smugglers — would resume the delivery of tea and French wines when they learned of Clive's presence at the castle. But, then, why shouldn't they? The "gentleman" traders had always been generous with payment for the occasional use of the hidden cave below the castle's west wall.

The next carriage passing through West Dean conveyed the duke's widowed sister-in-law Margaret, Lady Harry, who was accompanied by her children, the nine-year-old twins Grace and Adam. They were closely followed by a second coach, carrying Lady Harry's maid, the children's nurse, the governess, and the tutor. Tempers in these two conveyances, especially the first, were frayed. But that was, perhaps, not surprising after the strenuous two-day-long drive from Bath.

Margaret, Lady Harry, was a pretty if slightly care-worn young woman with fine ash blond hair painstakingly curled and arranged in becoming ringlets every morning by her maid. She was the most loving of mothers and quite devoted to her children. If she had a fault, it was a tendency to overprotect Grace and Adam.

But who could blame her? She had married at eighteen. Harry had been twenty-one. She had scarcely had time to be a wife before Harry returned to his regiment and she became a mother. Harry had come home on leave once, when the twins were two years old. They did not remember the occasion, poor babies, and were fatherless shortly after celebrating their fifth birthday.

However, even a doting mother could not deny that nine-year-old twins were not ideal travel companions. With a sinking heart, Margaret noted that Adam was looking rather green around the gills. He was not a good traveler under the best of circumstances, poor boy, and the road through the downs was abominable. And Grace, who hated above all having to sit still, was bouncing on the seat again, which, inevitably, made Adam feel worse.

For one treacherous moment, as they neared Stenton Castle, Margaret wondered if Clive had not been right when he wrote she needed a rest. He had wanted her to

30

take the children to her parents and come alone to Stenton.

Unthinkable! She could not possibly enjoy herself or rest if Grace and Adam were separated from their mama at Christmas. Besides, Adam was Clive's heir. It was her duty to bring her son to the castle his father had never seen. Naturally, she had not mentioned this in her letter of acceptance to Clive, but, surely, her brother-in-law would be pleased to see his niece and nephew.

The fourth carriage also came from London. Major and Mrs. Stewart Astley had completed the journey in almost total silence.

Which was nothing new, thought Juliette. She did not usually allow pessimism to sink her spirits, but it could not be denied that Stewart had exchanged no more than a dozen words a day with her since his return from the Peninsula.

Except, of course, that first day — almost three weeks ago it was — when he had walked into her sitting room as though he had just returned from a stroll along Bond Street rather than a two-year tour of duty with the Light Dragoons. If she were of a nervous disposition, she'd have had a spasm or swooned from delirious happiness, for she had received no warning that he was to be restored to her.

Or that he was injured. His haggard appearance had shocked her. She had ached with compassion and love when she saw his thin frame, the deep grooves of pain and weariness etched into his dear face. But he was alive, thank God.

How Stewart had talked that first afternoon! Almost feverishly fast. He had spoken of the friends he had to leave behind in Portugal, of the advance into Spain he would miss. He had spoken of his love for her and of the times when only the memory of their four glorious honeymoon days had carried him through tough and dangerous missions.

Of course he resented his injury, for now he'd have to sell out. But she had not thought him despairing. She had been sure that her love would help him overcome the dark moments when his spirits were low. But the following morning he had risen, the grim and silent stranger who now sat opposite her in the carriage, his knees turned toward the left-hand door so they would not touch hers.

And, although he had not yet resigned from his commission, he no longer wore uniform. It was very disquieting, for pride in his regiment had equaled — perhaps even surpassed — his love for her.

Stewart's eyes were closed, but Juliette did not think he was asleep. She studied his pale face, the taut line of his mouth. No, not asleep but probably in pain. And he wouldn't thank her for noticing.

Her gaze was drawn to the empty sleeve pinned to the left coat pocket. How could the loss of one miserable arm — half an arm — wreak such havoc? They were married four days when Stewart had to return to his regiment. She had known this would happen and had borne the separation bravely — because he left, promising love and happiness on his return.

And now he had returned, but he had taken the crazy notion into his head to —

Juliette's hands clenched into tight fists inside her

32

muff. No, no, and no! She would not even think it! She was a Rowland. And the Rowlands were fighters, Cousin Edward, the fourth duke, had told her sternly. That was seven years ago, when he brought her, a sobbing bundle of thirteen-year-old misery, to Stenton House the day her parents sailed for Calcutta. But it applied today.

She had fought pain and self-pity then; she would fight them again. And she would fight for her marriage. For her love. Clive would help her. He had stood in her father's stead at the wedding two years ago and had given her away. He wouldn't want to see her marriage in ruins.

After one more glance at her husband's grim face, Juliette turned to the window to catch the first glimpse of Stenton Castle, where her fate and her future would be decided. By Christmas.

Did miracles still happen?

Chapter Three

"What a hobble!" Clive took a long draft of the punch Nicholas had ladled into crystal cups. "I've a mind to send Margaret and her entourage back to Bath first thing in the morning. What on earth possessed her to bring not only the twins but a governess, a tutor, *and* a nurse? They'll be forever underfoot."

"Aye." Nicholas stretched his legs toward the bricked fireplace in the library where they had retired when the rest of the company dispersed to the various bedchambers. "A right fine mull you made of it, old boy. Carefully selected guests, forsooth! Should have known Margaret wouldn't leave the brats behind."

"She might have warned me."

"Females. They never do. Besides, it's Christmas. *You* may not set much store by it, but I'll wager a monkey Grace and Adam do."

"What the devil do you mean, *I* don't set much store by Christmas?"

Nicholas raised a lazy brow. "When was the last time

you spent Christmas in the bosom of your family?"

"Blast you, Nick." Clive spoke without rancor, but he was aware of a pinprick of annoyance. Or was it a guilty conscience?

The punch bowl sat conveniently close on a table between them. Sparring for wind, Clive made quite a ceremony of refilling his cup.

The last Christmas spent with the family . . . it was the year he had married . . . the year Rosalind showed the symptoms of illness on Christmas Eve morning. . . .

After her death, he had made it a habit to invite Nicholas and other bachelor friends to his hunting box in Leicestershire or to the snug little property near Hobkirk, just inside the Scottish border. Or, while he worked for the government, he had arranged to be abroad in December and January. Running away from painful memories, he admitted. At least, that was the case the first three or four years. But he had continued to avoid the family at Christmas even after the pain was gone and the sense of loss had dimmed.

"You're right, Nick. It's been a long time since I had a family Christmas. But it was habit rather than a dislike of family gatherings and celebrations that kept me away. It's quite lowering to realize how easily a man can fall into a rut and not be aware of it."

"Thought that was it." Nicholas nodded. "Thought you couldn't have turned into a curmudgeon. Not truly going to give Margaret her marching orders, are you? What I mean is, the twins seemed dashed glad to see you."

Clive choked on a sip of punch. "A curmudgeon! Devil a bit, Nick! Would serve you right if I gave *you*

35

your marching orders. Of course Margaret and the children will stay. Mind you, I don't like the surprise she sprang on me, but I can deal with it."

"Housekeeper will, if you don't," Nicholas said encouragingly. "Just tell her to engage another maid to wait on the nursery party.

Clive had already spoken with Mrs. Rodwell, but he could not resist saying, "Do you think that's necessary? I thought the children might take their meals with us. After all, they're on holiday."

This made Nicholas sit up. After a sharp, searching look at Clive he relaxed again.

"Gammon! Next you'll say you want that nurse to join us at the table. Strange woman. Heard her mutter about hidden evil in old castles. And when you took Margaret and the children to the south wing, she crossed herself!"

Clive drained his second cup of punch. He grinned at his friend. "Muttered about curses, too. And about spooks that creep around a place where a violent death occurred."

"Foreigners! German, ain't she? No doubt that explains it."

"German or not, Nurse Gertrud is a force to be reckoned with. She was Margaret's nurse and her brothers' and sisters' before that. You saw how Margaret buckled under when the old woman insisted they must all be moved from the south wing to the west wing."

"Now *that* I cannot find fault with. I'd rather not have Nurse Gertrud anywhere near me."

"But now we have Decimus next to us. I cannot say I like that any better."

Nicholas frowned into his punch cup. "I say, Clive!

36

D'you think I should have squeezed another orange? This punch isn't what it ought to be."

For some minutes the two gentlemen were absorbed in the task of judging the steaming brew. Finally, they agreed that a few drops of orange juice could only improve the aroma, but that the addition of a generous shot of arrack was an absolute must.

Nicholas resumed his negligent pose in the stuffed chair by the fire. He looked at Clive through half-closed eyes.

" 'Twasn't just the unexpected addition of the twins and their mentors to the gathering that made you uneasy, was it? Watched you at dinner and, dammit, if you didn't remind me of a cat on a hot bake-stone. What is it, Clive? Second thoughts about this mission of yours?"

"No. I'll get my man. I've no doubts about that."

"If it's not that, what *is* it that's making you uneasy?"

Casting a cursory look at the shelves filled with leather-bound books, Clive took a turn about the room. "I'll be damned if I know. Nothing I can put a finger on."

Nicholas raised a quizzing brow. "Can you not, old boy? That's not like you at all."

"It's little things like Juliette pressing me for a private interview. My sister pestering me with questions as to *why* I've opened the castle, *why* I didn't accept her invitation last month to spend a weekend at her house when she particularly wanted me to meet a special friend of hers."

"Matchmaking again, is she?" Nicholas grinned. "I doubt Fanny will ever give up."

"She may try, but she won't succeed. I'm too set in

my ways now to try matrimony again. Unless . . . unless I met a truly exceptional lady. But the thing is, between them, Fanny and Juliette will have cut up my peace before Christmas Day. On the other hand . . ."

Clive shrugged, feeling like a damned fool. He'd had uneasy moments *before* Margaret, Juliette, and Fanny arrived, the kind of disquiet he had experienced during his spying years, when he suspected he was followed by an enemy agent. But here at Stenton it was not so much a sense of being followed as of being *accompanied* while he explored the castle. In fact, he had an uneasy feeling right now, the same feeling he'd had earlier in the dining room—a suspicion that someone was listening to the conversation.

But it was nonsense, of course. Since no one but Yorke, Liverpool, Wellesley—and now Nick—knew his purpose here at Stenton, it was impossible that a French agent had gotten wind of the operation and installed himself in the castle. Besides, there was Chamberlain in the gardener's cottage. No one at all knew about Chamberlain, and he could trust the fellow with his life. Had, in fact, done so more than once in past years. Chamberlain had been at Stenton close to a sennight; he'd have noticed if there were something amiss.

"On the other hand?" prompted Nicholas. "What is it you were going to say, Clive?"

He shrugged again. The strange feeling was gone. Besides, it wouldn't do to admit his fancies to Nick. And fancies they were, for he had already, after Nicholas had gone to bed the previous night, sounded the paneling around the library fireplace and examined the shelves for a hidden door. There was none.

"As I said, Nick. It's nothing I can lay a finger on."

38

"Know what it is?" Nicholas gently stirred the punch before filling his glass. "It's your Uncle Decimus prosing on about Prinny and his ramshackle set. Always said Decimus is a bore. Damned thick skinned, too! Stayed deaf to every hint that he ought to take himself off to bed before midnight."

"Yes," said Clive. "I was afraid Uncle Decimus might prove a stumbling block when we want to start watching for the smugglers. That's why I wasn't particularly pleased when he picked a chamber here in the south wing. A pox on Nurse Gertrud and her superstitions! Surely she doesn't expect another fire?"

"Don't know what's on her mind, old boy. What's more, I don't give a damn," Nicholas said with unusual heat. "But I'm devilish glad she decided the south wing don't suit her and her charges."

Clive grinned. "I believe you're afraid of the nurse."

"Devil a bit! Not afraid of anyone, least of all a cross old woman. Only saying the nipperkins might have been more of a handicap than your uncle will be."

Clive twitched aside one of the heavy brocade curtains that draped the library window and studied the faint silver glow of the moon on the dark Channel waters.

"Conditions should be right fairly soon," said Nicholas. "Moon's almost gone."

"Sunday, I think. It should be dark enough then."

Clive let the curtain drop. A gleam of laughter in his eye, he faced Nicholas. "I'm almost certain I solved the problem of my uncle's late-night habits. Did you notice how fast he trotted off when I mentioned the cognac I sent to his room?"

"Aye, which reminds me — did you hear him ask your

butler whether a shipment of wine has arrived yet?"

"What?" Clive drew his chair closer to the fire and sat down. "Decimus sending his own wine from town? You must have misheard, Nick."

"That's what I thought at first. But he was quite insistent. Told Symes to let him know the moment the delivery was made."

Clive did not argue, but he was convinced there had been some misunderstanding. His uncle might sport his blunt quite freely and in a lavish style that was way beyond his means, but he would consider it a waste to spend as little as a farthing on the shipment of his own store of wines when he could avail himself of someone else's cellars. He might not manage his income as wisely as he should, but he was *not*, as Decimus had assured his nephew more than once, a wastrel and a spendthrift.

Settling down with another cup of punch, Clive enjoyed the warmth and the mellowing effect of rum and arrack. For a few moments, he forgot uneasiness, even the purpose of his visit to Stenton.

As he stared into the dancing flames, he thought about the approaching yuletide. It'd be a novelty—and not unwelcome—to celebrate with family and friends. They ought to decorate the Great Hall . . . and get a yule log. Adam and Grace would goggle . . . the two fireplaces in the Great Hall were wide enough to accommodate a whole tree trunk each.

"You planning to explore once more tomorrow morning?" asked Nicholas.

Clive drained his cup. "Yes. I want to know every inch of the cliff path, every rock, every dip and rise of the beach, and every patch of bog along the estuary be-

40

fore Sunday night. Nor have I given up yet on finding a cave."

"To tell the truth, old boy, I don't quite understand why you're so sure there must be a cave somewhere in the cliffs."

"Stands to reason, doesn't it? The same moonless nights that are ideal for landing a cargo undetected by excisemen are devilish inconvenient for overland travel. Thus, the smugglers have to store the goods until they can be transported. Also, if they have taken to carrying passengers, the Frenchman will need a place to hide until the free-traders are ready to sail."

"Dammit, Clive, if you aren't a knowing one!" A gleam lit Nicholas's eye. "But, then, I shouldn't wonder if you've hidden in caves waiting for smugglers or rebels to carry you wherever Whitehall wanted you to go."

Clive chuckled. "A government agent tells no tales, my friend. Are you going with me in the morning?"

"Count me out tomorrow. Crawled around the beach and cliffs all day yesterday and this morning. Devilish windy and damp. Got my boots scratched, too." Nicholas yawned. "Go with you Saturday, though. And then, of course, Sunday night."

Clive suppressed a grin. He was more than half convinced that by Sunday Nick would lose interest in the French agent who might or might not land on the beach below Stenton Castle. There was nothing like the painstaking examination, the charting of every minute detail of the estuary and the beach to cool an amateur's desire for an adventure.

"Very well." He set the empty cup on the bricked hearth and rose. "But if you don't care to accompany me, you'll have to play host tomorrow morning."

Nicholas yawned again. "Stewart said something about taking out one of your hacks. Thought I'd ride with him."

Clive was not deceived by his friend's sleepy look and casual tone. Nick was as worried as he was about Major Stewart Astley.

"Excellent. Try to have him back by luncheon, though. Sir John and Lady Astley should be here by then."

"Have they seen him since he returned?"

"No. Stewart and Juliette meant to visit them in Hertfordshire, but for some reason or other nothing came of it. I think it was Stewart who balked at the last moment, and that's why Juliette asked me to invite his parents to join us here at Stenton."

"It's a damned shame about his arm. But I never thought he'd take it so devilish hard."

"Stewart's a proud man. Try to imagine yourself without an arm."

"By Jove!" exclaimed Nicholas, much struck. "I'd have to let Treadwell tie my cravats!"

"And someone would have to cut up your meat." Clive's mouth tightened as he remembered dinner. He had wanted to shake Juliette for performing the service for Stewart. Much better to have let a footman do it. But he also had to admire her calm acceptance of the situation.

"Adjustment will take awhile. But I doubt not that Stewart *will* adjust." He turned to the door. "I'll bid you good night. I want to be up and gone before my guests arise."

"No need to worry about the ladies. I'll swallow my quizzing glass if one of them is down before ten. But Wilmott, I believe, is an early riser."

"I trust you to do your duty by him."

Clive lit one of the bedroom candles a footman had set out on the piecrust table just inside the door and left Nicholas to the pleasures of the punch bowl.

The library as well as his chambers were located on the first floor of the south wing, but at opposite ends. Leaving the library, he must walk past the billiard room, various estate offices, the muniment room, and the so-called ducal suite, all facing the Channel. The passage then turned sharply right into the former nurseries, which had been converted into bedchambers, some of them with an adjacent sitting room. These chambers all boasted a splendid view of the estuary.

The candles in the wall sconces had long been extinguished, and the light from Clive's bedroom candle hardly served to let him see two or three feet ahead. The gloomy darkness was a nuisance, but quite his own fault. He should have personally overseen the renovations of the south wing and ordered the wall sconces replaced by oil lamps.

His footsteps echoed dully on the parquet floor. Once again uneasiness stole over him. Was he imagining the second set of footsteps? Soft, whispered steps. Yet there was no stealth in them.

Shielding the candle flame with his hand, he swung around. He saw nothing but the closed door of the muniment room, the steep darkness of the corridor, and his shadow on the wall paneling. But wait! Wasn't there a second shadow, much paler than his own?

Slowly he turned. As he completed the circle, he stepped closer to the wall where he had seen the shadows—and gave a snort of disgust. Only the thought of his sister Fanny and her husband asleep behind the next set of doors kept him from laughing aloud at his own foolishness. Of course there had not been two shadows. The paler image he had seen was a tapestry showing the white-capped waters of the Channel with Stenton Castle atop the chalk cliffs in the background.

And of course there was no second set of footsteps. Just his own as he walked on and rounded the corner. He had become a doddering fool during the four years of retirement. To be imagining spies and agents at every corner! Fie! And he did not even have the excuse of being foxed. Now, if he'd had more than three or four cups of punch . . . but he hadn't, and he was neither on the go nor even a little above par.

Still, he could not shake the strange sensation that he had a companion in that long, dark corridor leading past several unoccupied bedchambers, past his uncle's and Nick's chambers, and toward his own rooms. As soon as he stepped into his bedroom, however, and shut the door, the sensation was gone.

"And I dashed well hope it stays away," he said to no one in particular, for he never asked of his valet to sit up and wait upon him after midnight. "Who knows but that I would fire my pistol at some imagined intruder and wake up the whole damned castle."

Annie Tuck gave a little sniff and glided away. His grace had nothing to fear. She knew quite well that it would be highly improper if she were to go into his chamber while he got ready for bed.

She was about to slip through the thick door that separated the servants' wing from the rest of the castle when she stopped abruptly. And just *how* did she know that his grace referred to her presence when he spoke of some imagined intruder? How did she know that he was aware of her escort in the corridor?

"Gorblimey," she said reverently, "I can read a human's mind." She did a little skip as excitement bubbled over. "And won't *that* come in right handy!"

Chapter Four

It started to rain on Friday when Sir John Astley's traveling coach swung into the last curve before the mile-long straight approach to Stenton Castle.

"Just what you can expect on the coast, eh, Louisa?" Sir John said with the forced cheerfulness he had employed throughout the drive. Not for anything would he let his dear wife know that the most dreadful apprehension befell him whenever he thought about Stewart, or that he feared Louisa's frail constitution might not be up to the rigors of the long drive. "None of the snow we left behind, but buckets of water pouring down on us."

Lady Astley knew him too well to be totally deceived. "If you're worried that the damp will affect my health, pray don't be. As you see, I've stood the journey better than you or Dr. Ashe expected. And it was quite damp everywhere."

"You've borne up beautifully, my dear."

She gave him a loving smile. "Once I'm installed by a warm fire at Stenton, I shan't mind if it rains every day.

As long as I may see Stewart and dear Juliette. Oh, John! I think this will be a wonderful Christmas."

"Aye." He gave her hand a little squeeze. "We've missed him, haven't we?"

While Sir John and Lady Astley fell into reminiscences, Elizabeth Gore-Langton kept one cheek pressed to the coach window and her gaze fixed on the towers and the part of the castle wall that had come into view a few moments earlier.

Elizabeth *did* mind the rain. It obstructed her view of the castle, but she voiced no complaint. She also doubted that this would be a wonderful Christmas. At least for her, depending on the circumstances, the next ten days could be fraught with embarrassment.

While Lady Astley had become more animated with every mile that took them away from the manor house in Hertfordshire and closer to Stenton Castle on the Sussex coast, Elizabeth had become quieter. They had traveled in easy stages, taking four days for a journey that might have been accomplished in half that time. Now, with their destination looming ahead, Elizabeth sat tense and apprehensive in her corner.

She gave silent thanks to Sir John for offering her the seat beside his wife on this last stretch of the journey. The forward position gave her the excuse to turn her face to the window and pretend an absorption in the view of the castle. Although, in truth, her absorption was not totally pretense. She was quite curious about Stenton. More curious still about Clive Rowland, Fifth Duke of Stenton, whom she had known eleven years ago as the Marquis Sandown.

Would he recognize her? There was a vast difference between a girl of barely seventeen and a woman approaching her twenty-ninth year. Her mother had considered her too young to be launched into the *ton*, but Elizabeth had begged and pleaded to be presented with Rosalind, her friend, her idol, who was already nineteen and as beautiful as a fairy-tale princess.

Elizabeth's hands clenched inside her muff. She did not know what would be worse — to have Clive Rowland recognize her or *not* to be recognized.

He had no notion that she was coming to Stenton. The letter apprising his grace of Miss Gore-Langton's inclusion in the Astley party had never been posted.

Deliberately, she relaxed her hands. Thank goodness, Sir John and Lady Astley were preoccupied, else they would have noticed her apprehension and inquired about the cause.

The carriage slowed as it passed through the castle's outer gate, a gatehouse and a watchtower on either side. It presently picked up speed again, and the wheels rattled noisily across the cobbled inner yard. Elizabeth craned her neck to get a look at the castle's main front, but a gust of rain all but obliterated the view of a wide sweep of steps leading up to the portico and the imposing entrance.

One wing of the huge door opened as the coach rolled to a stop. Two footmen and a butler, each carrying a large black umbrella, descended to the carriageway. One of the footmen opened the carriage door and let down the steps.

"Lady Astley. Sir John." The butler bowed, his expression just the correct mixture of deference and stiffness, his bearing majestic despite the awkwardness attached to wielding an open umbrella.

Deftly assisting Lady Astley from the coach, he said,

"I am Symes, my lady. Permit me to welcome you and Sir John to Stenton Castle."

As Symes returned his attention to the coach, his gaze fell on the third occupant, a young lady, though not, he observed, in the first blush of youth. She was enveloped in a cloak of leaf green wool. A fur cap— Symes recognized common rabbit as quickly as any fashion-conscious lady would—sat atop thick brown hair severely brushed back and caught in a knot at the nape of her neck.

Not a lady of fashion. But of one thing Symes was certain. Whatever her position in the Astley household, she was clearly a lady of quality and could not be assigned a room in the servants' quarters.

He directed an inquiring look at Sir John, but the baronet, forgetting manners in the fervent desire to be reunited with his son, availed himself of the second footman's umbrella and followed his wife into the castle without a backward glance.

Symes bent a stern look on the young woman. This was not the way things were done, but, perhaps, an anxious father must be forgiven a lapse in civility.

"Miss?"

If Elizabeth hadn't been aware of it already, the butler's tone and look would have alerted her that she was *not* expected. Gathering her dignity, Lady Astley's reticule, shawl, and muff, as well as her own belongings, she prepared to descend from the coach.

She smiled at the butler. "I am Miss Gore-Langton. Lady Astley's companion."

With not so much as the flicker of an eyelid did he betray that it was beneath his dignity to assist a mere companion. He bowed and shielded her against the rain as solicitously as if she were a duchess. When they reached the top steps, sheltered by the portico, Symes closed the umbrella.

Elizabeth shook the moisture from her cloak. "Does it often pour like this?"

"Having been here only a fortnight, I couldn't say with certainty, Miss Gore-Langton. But during that time we've had no less than eight rainstorms."

"That is discouraging news."

She was about to step into the shelter of the entrance hall when she heard a resounding crash inside. At the same time, the butler, looking toward the courtyard, exclaimed, "Your grace!"

The crash forgotten, Elizabeth swung around. She saw a man, tall and broad shouldered, approach the steps with long strides. His boots were muddied, and the rain had molded coat and breeches to his muscular frame.

She thought she must have recognized him anywhere. He had not changed, and yet he was different. The shoulders were, perhaps, wider than they had been when he was four-and-twenty. He was hatless, and she could see the dark hair curling damply around his head. But she also saw a fine streak of white running from the left temple to the crown of his hair.

And then he stood before her. The face she had known eleven years ago had matured. The mouth was firmer, the chin more jutting, and the angles of his cheekbones were more harshly sculpted. But the dark gray eyes had not changed. They were still mysterious, spellbinding. They came to rest on her, devoid of the slightest spark of recognition.

Her hands started to tremble and she closed them

tightly on the reticules and muffs in her arms. This re-action to Clive Rowland might be relief, but she rather feared it was chagrin. She had been of two minds as to whether she wanted him to recognize her, but now that he had *not,* she felt quite humiliated.

"Your grace." The butler bowed deeply. "This is Miss Gore-Langton, Lady Astley's companion."

"Pleasure, Miss Gore-Langton. I trust you had a comfortable journey?"

His voice had not changed either. Deep and reso-nant, it caressed the listener. *Caressed!* She was too fan-ciful by half. He was merely being gracious. She remembered that he had always been polite and had addressed her, Rosalind's friend, with meticulous civil-ity. But he had never truly noticed her — or any other young lady for that matter. He'd had eyes for Rosalind alone.

"Was it too abominable for words?"

She blinked, confused by his quizzing look. "I beg your pardon?"

"Your journey, ma'am."

"Oh! No, not at all."

If she were a swearing woman, she'd roundly damn the weakness that once more assailed her limbs, her wits, and even her voice, which sounded in her own ears like a feeble croak. She raised her chin, hoping the gesture would make up for the lamentable lack of pluck she was showing.

He looked into the upturned face and wondered why she scraped her beautiful hair back in such an unbe-coming fashion. It was thick and glossy with just a hint of chestnut here and there in the deep brown. She'd never be called pretty, but with a little effort she'd be a striking woman. One, moreover, who wouldn't lose her looks with age.

Those wide, brilliant green eyes were quite arresting, and there was beauty in the high cheekbones, the somewhat masterful little nose, the firm chin. The mouth, too, looked like it could be firm on occasion; only at present it trembled quite disconcertingly.

In fact, Miss Gore-Langton was trembling all over. And he was a graceless oaf, keeping her standing outside in the cold. Even if she was an unexpected arrival.

"Allow me." Without ceremony, Clive took the muffs from her shaking hands and tucked them under one arm.

Clasping her elbow, he propelled her into the Great Hall. Here, in front of the wide fireplace to his left, he found not only Sir John and Lady Astley, Stewart and Juliette assembled, but also Margaret and the twins and most of the staff a little farther down the hall.

While he stopped to survey the scene, Miss Gore-Langton lost no time in removing her elbow from his clasp. In fact, she tugged so sharply that he looked at her in some astonishment.

A trace of color mounted in her face, but she offered no explanation or apology.

"You had better come to the fire, ma'am. It may be a minute or two before my housekeeper has sorted out the room arrangements."

Now her cheeks were quite pink. Becomingly so, he thought, but he was at a loss as to why she should be embarrassed or meet his gaze with a defiant glare.

"Lady Astley wrote, informing you that I would accompany her," she said, the tone of her voice as defiant as her look. "Unfortunately the letter slipped beneath

52

the blotter and was not discovered until we were about to leave."

"And you believed your unexpected arrival would set the household at sixes and sevens?" He smiled. "Miss Gore-Langton, did you *look* at the place when you drove up? The castle is large enough to accommodate three dozen unexpected visitors."

She unbent slightly, though not enough to return his smile. "Even three score, I'd say. Thank you, your grace. You are very kind."

"Don't mention it. But come along now. I rather suspect that *something* has indeed occurred to put my staff in a flutter."

Without a backward glance to see if Lady Astley's shy companion followed, he strode across the expanse of tiled floor toward the fireplace. Since he could not believe that his sister-in-law would be so gauche as to intrude upon the first greeting of the junior and the senior Astleys, he must assume that Margaret's presence, and that of the staff, had to do with his enterprising niece and nephew. Indeed, one glance at Grace and Adam, huddled together and looking too innocent by far, confirmed his suspicion. They had been up to their tricks — again!

Only a few hours earlier, he had hauled the twins off the top of the southwest tower, where they'd been hanging over the low parapet to wave and shout to him down on the beach. He had deposited them with the tutor and the governess, who were turning the west wing upside down in a desperate search for their missing charges, then had ordered all accesses to the towers locked.

But the twins, and whatever dangerous mischief they

had perpetrated now, would have to wait. He must welcome Sir John and his lady, whom he had not seen in a while.

They had aged, but that was to be expected. What was unexpected and rather disturbing, was that his parents' arrival had not erased the grim look on Stewart's face. He stood ramrod stiff, his left hand clenched at his side. Juliette's smile was brittle. Only Sir John and his wife looked pleased.

Noting the lines of fatigue in Lady Astley's thin face, Clive suggested she might wish to retire to her room until luncheon, which would be served at one o'clock.

"That leaves you an hour, ma'am, to rest and visit with Stewart and Juliette in private."

Lady Astley gave him a grateful look. "Thank you, Clive, but perhaps you shouldn't count on John and me for luncheon. You see, our luggage, John's valet, and my maid haven't arrived yet and I wouldn't want to sit at the table in traveling dress."

"A worn trace," said Sir John. "Shouldn't have taken long to fix. I don't doubt they'll be here at any moment."

Juliette placed a solicitous arm around her mother-in-law. "And if not, I'll bring you a tray. Come, ma'am, I'll show you to the east wing. Your rooms are close to Stewart's and mine."

The two ladies, followed by their husbands, started to move off. After a few steps Lady Astley turned, searching the Great Hall anxiously until her eyes lit on her companion.

"Elizabeth, dear!" she said, conscience-stricken. "Come and let me introduce you to our host."

"Not at all necessary," Clive assured her immediately.

"Miss Gore-Langton and I are already acquainted."

"Yes, indeed," that young lady said tonelessly.

Now, what had he said to make her quiver and blanch? Indeed, she was a most disconcerting female, this Elizabeth Gore-Langton.

Elizabeth Gore-Langton . . . the name struck a faint chord. Elizabeth . . .

Nonsense. Giving himself a mental shake, he said, "Don't worry about the young lady, dear ma'am. I'll see that a room is prepared without delay."

"Dear Clive. So thoughtful," said Lady Astley.

Juliette waved, and the smile she directed at her mother-in-law's companion held none of the brittle quality Clive had noticed earlier.

"Elizabeth! Lovely to see you! Make yourself comfortable. I shall come for you in a little while."

Clive turned to the back of the hall, where he had seen the staff, Margaret, and the twins upon his entrance. Most of the servants had slipped away while he was engaged with his newly arrived guests. But his sister-in-law was still there, a child clasped protectively in each arm. And the butler and housekeeper had stood their ground.

His gaze fell upon a suit of armor which had previously been hidden from his view by footmen and maids. When last he passed through the Great Hall, the suit had stood upright. Now, it reposed on the ground, the helmet, gorget, and shoulder pieces lying at some distance from the rest of the armor. He had no need to ask how that came about.

"Mrs. Rodwell, pray see to it that a chamber is readied for Miss Gore-Langton. Close to Lady Astley's room, if possible."

The housekeeper curtsied and hurried off.

Clive met the butler's questioning eye. "Yes, Symes, you may have the armor re-erected. But first, please, ask Reed to have my bath ready in fifteen minutes."

He faced Margaret and the children. Margaret had the look of a tigress worn out by her cubs' antics yet ready to defend them to the death.

Suddenly, he felt tired. He had risen early, scrambled down the cliff path to the estuary, raced up the murderous path again when he saw his niece and nephew atop the tower, had climbed some hundred-odd narrow steps in great haste to snatch the imps from certain death, then had spent several hours walking the beach and the estuary bank below the castle.

"Margaret," he said, fixing his silent sister-in-law with a dark look. "Don't you dare say a word. I shan't beat those imps of Satan — this time. But if you, a governess, a tutor, and a nurse cannot control them, I *will* have something to say about discipline and punishment."

She uttered a protest, but he cut in ruthlessly. "Recollect, Margaret, that Harry appointed me their guardian."

"But, Uncle Clive!" said Grace, turning dark gray Rowland eyes on him. "We only wanted to see how a knight could walk in a suit of armor."

Adam manfully withdrew from his mother's protective hold. "Sir, I told her that knights didn't walk. They rode. But she wouldn't believe me."

Miss Gore-Langton spoke up from the settle in front of the cavernous fireplace. "True. Knights rode. But they did have to walk from their horses to their tents,

56

which proved so much trouble that in the end they decided armor was a nuisance."

"Doesn't surprise me," said Grace. Casting off her mother's arm, she raised her frilled skirts. "Look, Uncle Clive. I fell with the armor. Tore my stocking and scraped my knee."

"It's no more than you deserve," he said unfeelingly. "Now go back to your rooms. No doubt Miss Whitlock and Mr. Ponsonby are looking for you."

"But I haven't had my turn yet." Adam, who had inherited his mother's light blue eyes, gave his uncle a pleading look. "Grace always wants to go first on account of being half an inch taller than me."

"I'm also older!" Grace tossed her head. "Almost ten minutes!"

Clive fixed his nephew with a stern look. "There are some things, my boy, a gentleman will *not* allow a lady to do first. And if a young lady proposes something foolhardy, like climbing to the top of a tower and hanging over the parapet, a gentleman *stops* her. Now, both of you, scoot!"

They did, without a word. Margaret gave him a reproachful look before hurrying after her beloved children, and he knew that only the presence of Lady Astley's companion had saved him from a homily on his harshness toward his niece and nephew. Burgeoning gratitude was snuffed, however, by the lady's cynical exclamation.

"Oh, well done, your grace!"

He swung around to face Miss Gore-Langton. She had removed the fur cap, and the fire's glow lit a dazzling quantity of chestnut highlights in her brown hair.

"If you believe the little boy heard more than the first

part of your strictures, you're quite mistaken. Now you'll have him fighting his sister about who goes first, but he'll never stop her more headlong starts."

He strode toward her. "I daresay you speak from experience?"

"If you mean, did I have brothers I wanted to outshine, then no. I have no brothers. Or sisters. But if you refer to experience with human nature, then yes. I have quite a bit of that."

Coming to a stop in front of her, he measured her trim shape, the creamy complexion. His ill humor vanished. "Indeed! Stricken in years as you are. You must be all of four-and-twenty."

"I am eight-and-twenty," she said quietly.

"In fact, an ancient." His mouth twisted in a lopsided grin. "Come now, Miss Gore-Langton. Let us not be pulling caps."

"No," she said. "That would be putting you at a disadvantage, wouldn't it? Pulling caps is another thing a *gentleman* would not do."

He looked into the most brilliantly green eyes he had seen. Again a chord struck somewhere in the deepest recess of his memory.

"Miss Gore-Langton, forgive me. But have we met before?"

All color drained from her face.

"No," she said, and it was such a blatant lie that he felt as though she had deliberately slapped him. "No, your grace, we have not."

Chapter Five

Now, why had she done that? Almost before the words of denial left her mouth, Elizabeth knew she had blundered.

Something had obviously stirred his memory. If she had kept her composure and said that they had been introduced over a decade ago, his grace would have apologized for his forgetfulness, and that would have been the end of it.

As it was, she had roused curiosity — and pique. She saw it in the narrowed eyes, and she could only be grateful that the housekeeper came bustling into the hall before he had time to formulate another question.

"Miss Gore-Langton," said the housekeeper, gasping for breath. "If you please . . . I'll show you to your room."

"Thank you."

Elizabeth rose. She gathered her fur cap, Lady Astley's shawl, and the two reticules in one hand and held out the other. "May I relieve you of the muffs, your grace?"

He had been so busy welcoming the Astleys and scolding his niece and nephew that the two muffs under his arm had quite slipped his mind. He was surprised into a bark of laughter. What an odd picture he must have presented, especially to the twins. Lucky for them that they hadn't remarked on it.

"By all means, Miss Gore-Langton. Relieve me of the blasted things. I wouldn't know what to do with them."

He threaded one onto the arm stretched toward him and held the second muff until she grasped it securely. But even then he did not let go immediately. He might have forgotten the muffs, but he had *not* forgotten the lady's denial that they had met before this day.

"My dear Miss Gore-Langton," he said softly, so his voice would not carry to Mrs. Rodwell. "You're an abominable little liar. We *have* met. I'm convinced of it, and I shan't rest until I recall when and where."

Here was an opening to set the record straight. Not often does one get a second chance; Elizabeth was well aware of it. Yet, perversely, she did not avail herself of the proffered opportunity.

An abominable little liar, was she? Well, she'd be dashed if she reminded him of the many times they had met! Let him cudgel his memory. The exercise, no doubt, would do him good.

She smiled at him, but at odds with the smile was the angry spark in her eyes.

"I'm afraid you mistake me for another, your grace. Will you excuse me? I'm sure your housekeeper has much to do besides waiting to show me to my room."

He received the snub with equanimity. "Of course,

Miss Gore-Langton. Go with Mrs. Rodwell now. I shall see you at luncheon."

"But I shan't . . ." Her voice trailed off, for he had turned and was striding toward one of the passages leading from the Great Hall at what she judged to be the south or southwest end.

Unconsciously squaring her shoulders, Elizabeth approached the housekeeper, who stood patiently awaiting her pleasure.

"If you'll be so kind as to point me in the right direction, Mrs. Rodwell, I daresay I'll be able to find the room quite easily."

"Oh, no, miss!" Looking scandalized, Mrs. Rodwell set her ample form in motion. She ushered Elizabeth into the passage the Astleys had taken earlier. "I'll show you the way. A nice to-do it'd be if guests were made to fend for themselves! And when you're ready, miss, you have but to ring and a maid will fetch you to the dining room."

Elizabeth was silenced. She had started to utter a protest when Clive Rowland said he'd see her at luncheon. Now, the housekeeper, too, assumed she'd be taking her meals with the family.

Of course, she always did so at the Astleys' home, but Elizabeth knew herself to be privileged. More often than not a companion, like a governess, found herself relegated into that limbo between lady of quality and upper servant and was condemned to lonely meals eaten off a tray in her room. Elizabeth certainly had not expected privileged treatment in the ducal household.

"Here, miss." Slowing at the foot of a wide stairway with intricately carved balusters, the housekeeper held out an imperative hand. "Best let me take the shawl. You're trailing it, and before you know it, you'll trip and hurt yourself."

The housekeeper's tone strongly reminded Elizabeth of her old nurse, a forceful woman addicted to issuing orders — and having them obeyed. Meekly, she handed the article over.

"All around the Great Hall on the ground floor you'll find the state rooms, the salons, drawing rooms, dining rooms, breakfast parlor, and the like," said Mrs. Rodwell. "The bedchambers and a number of sitting rooms are on the first floor. There *is* a second story, but it needs refurbishing before any of the rooms are fit to be occupied."

They had reached the top of the stairs and stood in a wide corridor branching to the right and to the left. The housekeeper was wheezing from the exertion of the climb, but, with barely a check, she turned down the right arm of the hallway.

"This is the east wing, miss, where you'll find some of the most beautiful chambers. Aside from the south wing, of course, which was just restored." Mrs. Rodwell paused to catch her breath. "The windows here face the gardens mostly. Not that there's much to see at this time of year, but I always say it's a better view than all that water on the south and west side of the castle."

Elizabeth would rather have had the view of the Channel. She had grown up on the edge of Romney Marsh, and her favorite ride had been into Lydd. There she could sit on the seawall and breathe the tangy air and gaze her fill of the Channel's rolling waves.

"Are all the guests put up in this wing, Mrs. Rodwell?"

"Oh, dear me, no! Just the Astleys — Sir John and his lady — and the major and his wife. And you."

So Juliette would be close by. . . . Hard upon the thought, a door opened and Mrs. Stewart Astley peeked out.

"I thought I heard voices," said Juliette, stepping into the corridor. "Mrs. Rodwell, where have you put Miss Gore-Langton? I shall accompany her."

"It's the room after yours, Mrs. Astley. Just around the corner. And if you'll be so kind . . ." Mrs. Rodwell handed the shawl to Juliette. "I'm much obliged. What with inexperienced village girls to help out in the kitchens and in the house, there's almost more work than a body can do."

With a swish of stiff bombazine skirts, the housekeeper hurried off.

Juliette tucked a hand into Elizabeth's arm. "I am *so* glad my mama-in-law brought you along. Come to your room, where we can be comfortable."

"The chamber you just left, I suppose it is Lady Astley's? Should I check on her before you take me to my room?"

"Oh, no." Juliette's firm little hand propelled Elizabeth on. "She's resting, and . . . and Stewart is with her."

Elizabeth heard the tremor in the younger woman's voice and gave her a searching look, noting the drooping mouth, the dark shadows beneath lackluster eyes. She had expected to see Juliette glowing with happiness. After all, for two years the young lady had prayed to be reunited with her beloved Stewart, her husband of four short days.

"This is Stewart's room. And that, mine." Juliette indicated the last two doors before the right-angled turn of the hallway, then opened the first door past the corner. "And this, I suppose, must be yours."

"How beautiful."

Elizabeth's feet sank into soft Turkey rugs as she walked toward the object of her admiration, a fourposter bed with gilded posts, the canopy and sides draped with ivory velvet. Heavy gold velvet and clouds of white gauze curtained three mullioned windows and made a stunning contrast to the dark wainscoting and the gleaming mahogany furniture.

"Do you like it?" Juliette stepped up to a window and raised the gauze curtain. "All the rooms I've seen are beautiful. It rather astonished me, since it is such an old castle and no one has lived in it for ages. Oh, look! You can see the Channel from here. I cannot from my window."

Elizabeth let the reticules drop where she stood, flung the muffs onto the bed, and hurriedly joined Juliette.

"Are you certain? Mrs. Rodwell said—" She gave a sigh of satisfaction.

True, the prospect from the window was mostly of a stretch of muddy garden, crisscrossed by flagged paths and the bare skeletons of some shrubbery. On the left, the stark wall of the southeast tower protruded boldly and cut off her view. But to her right the ground dropped off sharply and beyond the drop lay the Channel, the waters dark gray in the rain, and just a few whitecaps showing here and there.

She could not see a beach, but she knew there must

be one, if only a narrow strip, at the foot of the chalk cliffs. Nothing, not rain, not wind or cold, would stop her from exploring. She turned to ask Juliette for the best approach to the beach below the castle, but the look of misery in the young lady's eyes gave her pause.

"Juliette. Whatever is the matter, my dear?" She held out a hand.

Juliette clasped it tightly. During the two years of her marriage, while Stewart was off fighting that horrid Bonaparte who seemed determined to conquer all of the Continent, she had spent much time at the Astley home in Hertfordshire. Despite a disparity in age — she was only twenty, a mere girl to Elizabeth's twenty-eight years — she and her mother-in-law's companion had become friends. And it was Elizabeth's friendship and support she stood in need of now.

She could not stop her mouth from trembling, but her voice was firm enough. "It's Stewart. He . . . he wants to have our marriage annulled."

Shock rendered Elizabeth speechless. Her mind reeled. *Why?*

She had witnessed a part of Stewart's whirlwind courtship of Miss Juliette Rowland while he was home on leave. No one could have doubted that he was head over heels in love. No one could have mistaken the glow of adoration in Juliette's eyes. Due to a feverish cold, Elizabeth had not been able to attend the wedding, but she had seen the young couple after their four-day honeymoon. Despite their sorrow at having to part within hours, they had radiated love and happiness.

She looked at Juliette's tragic face. "Nonsense," she said bracingly. "He cannot have the marriage annulled. It was consummated, wasn't it?"

Juliette turned pink. "It was."

"Well, then?"

"Something happened . . . something went wrong that first night after his return . ." Juliette stammered, then finished in a rush, "and he hasn't come near me since."

"Are you saying that since his return, Stewart has not claimed his conjugal rights?"

The incredulous note in Elizabeth's voice made Juliette blush more fiercely. Pressing her hands to her flaming cheeks, she fled to the settee by the fireplace. For an instant, after blurting out the crazy notion Stewart had taken into his head, she had felt . . . perhaps not relieved but as if sharing her great fear had reduced it to bearable proportions.

Now she was aware of disappointment and, unreasonably, crossness. In retrospect, it seemed foolish that she had expected Elizabeth to understand or to know what to do. Elizabeth wasn't married. In fact, she shouldn't have talked to her at all. It was improper to mention the subject of marital relations to an unmarried lady.

But she simply *had* to talk to *somebody*. In the three weeks since Stewart's return she had suffered bewilderment, hurt, guilt. She was not aware of wrongdoing but felt vaguely that *somehow* she was to blame for Stewart's coldness.

She had planned to speak to Clive, had even asked him for a private interview, then had changed her mind. It would be so very awkward talking to a man. There was Fanny, of course. But Juliette was not on intimate terms with the young matron, who had married and removed from Stenton

House scarcely a month after Juliette moved in.

And it was, of course, unthinkable to approach Stewart's mama, even though Lady Astley was a perfect dear and closer to her—in spirit and in geography—than her own mother, who still resided at Government House in Calcutta and was giving dinners and card parties for the English officers and their wives and the more important officials of East India Company.

But even if by some miracle her mother had suddenly appeared in London, it was doubtful Juliette would have confided in her. In the seven years since her parents left, she had seen them twice. They had come to England for a six-month visit the year before her marriage and prior to that, they had arrived for a whirlwind stay of three weeks when they received the notice of the fourth duke's death.

There had been some vague talk at the time of removing Juliette from Stenton House. The fifth duke—Clive was one-and-thirty then—was too young to have the guardianship of a sixteen-year-old girl, her papa had said. But it all came to nothing, because her mama felt that Juliette would be better off in London, where she could make friends with the girls who would be brought out the same year Juliette would make her curtsy to society. And it was unthinkable that Juliette should not have a Season in London, said Mrs. Rowland. For how else was she to meet eligible young men? The only young men in Calcutta were officers, and they, as everyone knew, were mostly younger sons and a rakish lot at that. No, Mrs. Rowland did not particularly want to see her daughter wed to an officer who'd be here today, there tomorrow, fighting some war or other.

Thus, Mr. and Mrs. Rowland had sailed back to India, and their daughter remained at Stenton House. At the right time, Juliette was dutifully brought out by some distant but well-connected Rowland cousin and promptly fell in love with Lieutenant Stewart Astley, home from service in India to recuperate from a lingering fever before he would join Sir John Moore in Portugal. And if that wasn't ironic, what was? Except that Stewart was not a younger son, of course. He was an only child.

"Juliette!" Elizabeth spoke rather sharply. The girl sat motionless, sunk in gloom. This would not do at all!

She went to her young friend. "You must have misunderstood about the annulment. I do not see how it can be done. Or does Stewart plan to apply for a divorce by Act of Parliament?"

"No, he doesn't." Hope flared in Juliette's eyes, then died. "But I did not misunderstand. Stewart is certain the marriage can be voided. It seems there is some old church law about . . . incapacity."

Elizabeth blinked in astonishment. Stewart had lost an *arm,* not one of his nether parts!

"What shall I do?" Juliette asked desperately.

Elizabeth pulled herself together. "Talk to Stewart," she urged. "Ask him what is wrong."

"No!" Juliette sat up with a violent start. "I drove him from the house with questions! He spent the days and evenings at his club and only came home when he was certain I must have gone to bed. No, Elizabeth, I cannot ask him again. If I did, he would pack up and leave Stenton immediately."

So emphatic was Juliette that, for a moment, Elizabeth was at her wit's end. There seemed to be nothing else to say.

But it was not without reason that she was considered a sensible and levelheaded young woman by those who knew her well. Common sense and composure might have temporarily deserted her while she faced his grace, the Duke of Stenton, but Clive Rowland was not present to disconcert and confuse her now.

"Do you know, Juliette," she said, "I cannot help but think that you're wrong. I don't doubt that Stewart might *wish* to leave in order to avoid questions, but he would not *do* it. Just think! How would he explain a sudden departure to his parents? Or to his host?"

Juliette was about to reply when, her eyes widening, she swung around on the settee and stared toward the dressing table.

"Did you hear that, Elizabeth?"

Elizabeth also stared at the dressing table. There wasn't a sound in the room, not the whisper of a noise, save for their breathing.

She regained composure first. "Gracious! What the atmosphere of an old house can do to one! For a moment there, I was convinced someone applauded."

"Yes, but it was nothing, was it?"

"Not quite nothing, perhaps," said Elizabeth. "I'm sure we heard *something*, but most likely it was something to do with the old timber. Do you realize how ancient this castle is?"

"Wood beetles?" Juliette said doubtfully. With one last, lingering look at the dressing table, she rose.

She took a tentative step toward the door. "But I tell you this, Elizabeth. If we weren't dealing with Stewart, I daresay your good sense would merit applause."

"Stewart isn't any better or worse than other men," Elizabeth said reasonably. "He would not want to hurt his parents' feelings, and neither would he want to cause talk. Or are you saying that Stewart is too thick-headed to realize that his leaving would give rise to speculation?"

"He wouldn't give a straw. He did not care when he spent the days and evenings at the clubs instead of getting reacquainted with his wife. Or do you believe the gentlemen who saw him at White's or at Boodle's and Brooks's did not speculate?"

Reluctantly, Elizabeth admitted defeat. "No, I do not believe that."

She was not given to sighing, but, indisputably, her words were followed by a sigh of disappointment. It startled her, for she wasn't aware of having indulged in the habit she had always denounced as lachrymose. Undoubtedly, though, that was something else the atmosphere of an old house or, rather, an old castle did to one.

Juliette continued toward the door. This time, she did not stop until she reached it.

Pulling it open, she said in a carefully controlled voice, "Stewart informed me this morning that he doesn't want me to go back to London with him after Christmas. Until matters are settled, he wants me to stay in Hertfordshire."

"And you? Will you do as he bids?"

Juliette, her back to Elizabeth, stood quite still. "I don't know—I don't have a choice, do I? A wife must obey."

Elizabeth knew that was so. Still, she could not believe that Juliette would be so poor spirited as to give in

70

without a fight. She was about to rally her young friend, when she saw Juliette's shoulders straighten.

"I may have to obey in the end," said Juliette. A martial light kindling in her eye, she looked over her shoulder at Elizabeth. "But there's no law that says a wife mustn't try to change her husband's mind, is there?"

Annie Tuck, perched on a corner of the dressing table, was torn between applauding once more and heaving an even deeper sigh than had slipped out earlier. But she didn't make a sound.

She dared not make a sound. When the two young ladies had turned to the dressing table after Annie clapped her hands, she had been quite as startled as Miss Juliette and Miss Elizabeth. She had not known that anyone could hear her.

This was a fine kettle of fish! She had believed herself beyond detection by human eye or ear, yet there was no doubt that her clapping had been heard, if faintly. Wood beetles, indeed!

But, at least, she was invisible. With a challenging look at Miss Elizabeth, who had closed the door behind her friend and approached the dressing table where Annie perched, she kicked up her full skirt and frilled petticoats and crossed her legs. She wouldn't have dared cross her legs while Old Nurse still reigned over the Stenton nurseries. But those days were gone. Annie could do as she liked.

Miss Elizabeth sat down in front of the dressing table. She removed the pins from her hair and as she reached for a comb, her hand brushed Annie's gown. Miss Elizabeth gave no sign of having noticed any-

71

thing. Still, to be on the safe side, Annie switched to the opposite end of the dressing table.

Poor Juliette, thought Elizabeth, absently dragging the comb through her long hair.

Aye. Poor Miss Juliette, Annie echoed silently. The young lady's problem wasn't as simple as she had at first supposed.

Annie had never been married—she was thirteen when she was apprenticed to a milliner, and a sewing girl didn't have much of an opportunity to find herself a beau. She did harbor expectations when she left London for Stenton Castle. But, alas! Again, there had been no opportunity. Annie remembered, however, that every spat between her mum and her da had been happily resolved on the rustling straw pallet behind the curtain in the corner of the family bedroom.

But Major Astley wasn't at all like her da. And neither was Miss Juliette like Annie's mum. Annie's mother had been a knowing one. If she had told a friend of her troubles, she wouldn't have blushed and stammered. In fact, she wouldn't have needed to ask for advice; she would have known what to do if her goodman hadn't faithfully shared the marriage bed every night.

For Miss Juliette and Major Astley, however, trouble lay ahead. And that was a pity—and a nuisance. The Astleys had seemed the perfect solution to Annie's problem. But it wouldn't do at all if the major planned to return to London alone. No, not at all.

Disgruntled, Annie slid off the dressing table. No doubt Miss Elizabeth, who considered herself a sensible, levelheaded woman, would do what she could to help Miss Juliette. But when Annie thought of Miss

Elizabeth's encounter with his grace, she wondered about the young lady's ability to keep a cool head.

And besides, what *could* she do? Miss Elizabeth was a spinster — and a lady of quality. In Annie's experience, a spinster *lady,* no matter what age, no matter how sensible and wise, knew less about life than a newborn babe — or a blushing bride.

Indeed, it would be better if Annie herself took a hand. There wasn't much time. Christmas was just a few days off, and everyone would be ready to depart the day after New Year.

And what could *she* do? A ghost, invisible but not, if she wished, inaudible? Annie had ever been an optimist. Her spirits soared. There must be a great many things she could do now that she knew she could be heard.

Chapter Six

Elizabeth did not take luncheon in the dining room after all. The second coach carrying the luggage, Sir John's valet, and Lady Astley's maid had still not arrived when a footman sounded the gong in the Great Hall. Lady Astley, determined not to appear at table in her traveling dress, invited Elizabeth and Juliette to share the meal in her chamber.

Elizabeth had mixed feelings about a postponement of her next meeting with the Duke of Stenton. She admitted to chagrin that he did not remember her, but was by no means certain that a belated recognition would soothe the blow to her pride. She had wanted him to cudgel his brains over her identity, but it was one thing to wish so in a fit of pique and quite another to have to face the possible results of his mind-searching.

If he remembered Rosalind's friend . . . And he should! He had seen her often enough, for Rosalind would never have been permitted to ride or drive with him unless Elizabeth and one or two other young people joined in the excursions.

Truly, there should be no harm in his remembering Rosalind's friend. Unless . . . unless he had been aware of that foolish friend's infatuation with him.

Elizabeth's face flamed at the mere thought, but she consoled herself that *his* embarrassment when he finally remembered her from that long ago season of '99 would be no less than hers. He would be ashamed to realize that he had forgotten a young lady with whom he had stood up at every ball, a young lady who had been the first guest in the house he bought for Rosalind when they returned from their honeymoon.

Still, she could not deny that she would anticipate the approaching holidays with a great deal more pleasure if she weren't obliged to spend them at Stenton — or if her host were someone other than Clive Rowland.

Since those were impossibilities, she must either brazen out the charade she had so foolishly begun and hope that the moment of recognition would never come, or she must take the bull by its horns and confess.

For a dignified lady of her age and position it should not be a difficult decision to make. But Elizabeth learned to her dismay that dignity, wisdom, and whatever other benefits she expected to have gained with advanced age, deserted her at the prospect of facing Stenton with a confession. The trouble was, she realized, she did not know how he would react. And neither did she know how she *wanted* him to react.

Calling herself a coward of no mean order, she ac-

75

cepted Lady Astley's invitation to luncheon and stayed with her employer long after Juliette left. She had always enjoyed reading to Lady Astley, but this afternoon not even the antics of Tom Jones in Henry Fielding's novel could distract her. She was feeling properly blue-deviled, and all because of the man who had not recognized her when she wasn't even certain that she *wanted* to be recognized. Dash it! It was quite insupportable.

The arrival of the truant coach and the luggage provided an excuse to spend an hour or two in her chamber. When every one of her few gowns had been shaken and smoothed at least a half-dozen times, when the last handkerchief was neatly placed in a drawer, Elizabeth cast an imploring look at the rivulets of water running down the window panes. If only it would stop raining, she could go for a walk. Bracing sea air would lift her spirits in no time at all.

But the rain did not stop, and by the time Juliette knocked on the door and offered to take Elizabeth to the Crimson Drawing Room where the company would assemble before dinner, she was still of two minds whether she wanted to confront his grace or wait cowardly until he recognized her. She could not even decide whether to take Juliette into her confidence.

This last decision at least was taken out of her hands when they entered the Great Hall. The candles in the huge chandelier had not been lit, but the glow from several wall sconces and the two fireplaces was sufficient to show the look of surprise on the face of the gentleman entering the hall from another passage.

Lord Nicholas raised a quizzing glass to his eye,

but let it drop again immediately. "Elizabeth — Miss Gore-Langton! Where did you spring from?"

"Good evening, Lord Nicholas. I arrived this morning with Sir John and Lady Astley."

She smiled as she shook hands, though inside she quaked with dismay. Lord Nicholas Mackay had been there eleven years ago when she and Rosalind were presented to the *ton*.

"Thought I was seeing a ghost when I first clapped eyes on you." Lord Nicholas once more raised his glass and surveyed her carefully. "You haven't changed since I last saw you. When was it? Five, six years ago? Lud! You were with old Lady Henley then."

"Yes. But Lady Henley died shortly afterward and I had to find a new position."

"Why, this is famous!" Juliette broke in. "You know each other! And I was afraid poor Elizabeth would feel lost among so many strangers."

"Devil a bit, no such thing!" exclaimed Nicholas, grinning cheerfully. "I've known Miss Gore-Langton since she made her first curtsy to society. And so has Clive. Just wait till he claps eyes on her!"

"He saw her this morning." A puzzled note crept into Juliette's voice. "To be sure, I don't perfectly remember in the excitement of greeting Stewart's parents, but I did not have the impression that Clive knew Elizabeth."

Keeping her smile firmly in place, Elizabeth said, "And your impression was quite correct, Juliette. His grace did not recognize me."

Lord Nicholas merely raised a brow, but Juliette, after the tiniest of incredulous silences, clapped her hands. "Oh, how I shall tease him about this! Clive always accuses *me* of having the most shocking memory."

"Please don't," said Elizabeth, experiencing once again that detestable quake of dismay. "I mean—" She broke off, shrugging.

"You didn't set him straight," Nicholas said drily. He narrowed his eyes. "He didn't recognize you at all? I find that hard to believe."

"He suspects he met me somewhere," she admitted.

"But you denied it," said Juliette with unexpected shrewdness. She gave Elizabeth a speculative look. "I daresay I would have done the same, because now he's forced to rack his brains to remember where and when he met you."

An involuntary chuckle escaped Elizabeth. "That's indeed what I intended. I thought it would serve him right for being so forgetful. But I shouldn't have done it."

"Why ever not?" asked Nicholas.

Under his quizzical gaze, warmth stole into her face. Did Nicholas remember that he had found her crying at Clive and Rosalind's wedding? She'd had herself well in control while the vows were spoken, but after the wedding breakfast, when the young couple departed on their honeymoon, she could no longer stop the tears. An elderly lady had patted her back and told her to go ahead and have a good cry; it's what a bridesmaid is supposed to do at her best friend's wedding.

But Nicholas, when he found her in one of the anterooms at Stenton House, had handed her his handkerchief and, in an awkward attempt to comfort, had assured her that she'd get over it. Clive was not the only man on earth. Without a doubt, she'd fall in love again before the year was out.

She had been so horrified, her tears had dried on the instant. How had she given herself away? She had been so very careful to conceal her feelings, for there was nothing more detestable than a lady wearing her heart upon her sleeve.

She had immediately, haughtily, informed Lord Nicholas that he had quite misunderstood. She was crying because she knew how much she'd miss Rosalind. And for no other reason! Nicholas had nodded, looking grave but, unfortunately, unconvinced.

It was then that a most horrid suspicion had crept into her mind and left her paralyzed with embarrassment — the suspicion that she had, unwittingly, betrayed her feelings to others as well. To Rosalind, perhaps. Worse, to Clive Rowland himself.

Elizabeth shook off the memory and stole a look at Nicholas's face. She saw mischief in the blue eyes but not, as she had feared, pity.

"Give you ten to one," he said, "that Clive will remember who you are before Christmas. He's got a restless mind. Won't give him any peace till he's figured out where he met you before."

"I dearly love a wager," Juliette cut in. "I'll take you on if Elizabeth won't."

"Done." Nicholas shook hands with Juliette, then turned to Elizabeth. "And you? Will you place your bet, Miss Gore-Langton?"

"You're out of your mind!" she said indignantly. "Both of you."

"Pooh!" Juliette gave her a sidelong look. "Don't be so stodgy, Elizabeth. This is the most diverting thing that's happened since I arrived at Stenton. *I* shall not back down from the wager, and if you won't join in—"

"I will tell Stenton myself who I am before I enter into such a harebrained wager."

Juliette gasped, but Nicholas shook his head and grinned.

"No, you won't. Because it would spoil my wager with Juliette, and I remember the occasion when you very kindly explained to me that a wager once made cannot be undone."

"That was different!" she protested. "You and I had agreed to race."

"And I offered you a bet that your mare could not beat my mount. You agreed and lost. And when I did not want to claim my prize—those striking peacock feathers off your hat—you reminded me that our wager was as valid as if it had been entered in the betting book at White's. Now don't tell me you've forgotten that you rode home with a sadly denuded hat."

"I haven't forgotten, but—"

"But nothing. Juliette and I have shaken hands on a bet. You must realize that you cannot spoil sport now."

Elizabeth protested no more. Everything her father had ever told her about the strict code governing bets bore out what Lord Nicholas had said.

Juliette tugged at Nicholas's sleeve. "We must set the time limit. Shall we say Christmas Eve, midnight?"

"Christmas Eve, midnight, it is. Three days from now." His eyes laughed at Elizabeth. "Sure you won't change your mind?"

Elizabeth threw her hands up in disgust. "You're

impossible! I wish there were a way to make you both lose."

But, strangely, as reprehensible as she considered the wager, she no longer suffered from the blue devils. She was in no mood, however, to discover why.

Her heart beat a little faster than usual when she entered the Crimson Drawing Room with Juliette and Nicholas. It had nothing to do with the Duke of Stenton, who saw them and immediately crossed the room to greet them. No, she blamed the erratic beat on the overwhelming splendor of the vast chamber.

Crimson velvet covered chairs and couches and draped the row of windows along one wall, bright splashes of color against champagne-colored carpets. Four gold-and-crystal chandeliers ablaze with light hung from the ceiling, where nymphs and satyrs chased each other in a sea of bluebells, and the wall opposite the windows was hung with paintings, one of which Elizabeth believed to be a Raphael.

She had no time to fully appreciate the magnificence of the chamber before Stenton addressed her.

"Miss Gore-Langton, allow me to introduce you to my other guests. My friend Lord Nicholas Mackay, I take it, has already made himself known to you?"

Again, her heartbeat quickened. Carefully avoiding Nicholas's and Juliette's eye, she said, "We met in the hall, your grace."

Nicholas grinned widely. "Indeed. You'd be wasting your breath on a formal introduction, Clive, old boy."

Clive looked from one to the other. Miss Gore-Langton looked as shy and confused as she had this morning. But Nicholas—dash it! He was too familiar with Nick's grin not to recognize that some mischief was afoot. But what mischief? It was more than he could tell.

He bore Miss Gore-Langton off to meet the rest of the company. As they crossed the room to a group of chairs and couches near the fireplace, it occurred to him that he might have made her acquaintance at one of the many parties his sister had arranged to introduce him to eligible young ladies.

But neither his sister nor his brother-in-law gave any sign of having met Miss Gore-Langton before. Of course, George might have forgotten a previous meeting, since Fanny's friends were legion. But Fanny was no dissembler, and Clive could tell from the speculative light in her eyes as she greeted Miss Gore-Langton that this was the first time she saw Lady Astley's companion.

He could not like that speculative look, but even less did he like the hard stare Margaret directed at Elizabeth. It was always the same when he was obliged to introduce a young lady to them. In Fanny an introduction raised instant hope that he had finally decided to forgo widowerhood; in Margaret it raised immediate enmity toward the lady in question.

When they approached his uncle, who was sitting with Stewart and Sir John and Lady Astley, Clive thought Miss Gore-Langton's step dragged a bit. But he must have been mistaken, for she showed no hesitancy in conversing with Decimus when his uncle said he had known her father.

"I am sure you did, sir," she said with a smile. "He used to be a friend of the Prince of Wales as, I believe, you are."

"Demmed shame he died so young. A hunting accident, wasn't it? Must've been hard for you and your mother."

"My mother died two months earlier, sir."

Decimus looked startled. "She did, did she? Pray accept my condolences."

"Thank you, sir. But it all happened a decade ago."

Before Decimus could say anything else, Fanny joined them.

"Clive, I was telling Margaret about the treasure, and she suggested we hold a treasure hunt tomorrow. I think it's a splendid notion. What do you say?"

"I cannot imagine what you're talking about. What treasure?"

"Have you forgotten? Uncle Decimus told us all about it!"

"The jewels!" exclaimed Decimus. "By jove, if I didn't forget about them myself!"

Clive gave his uncle a hard stare. "The jewels of the *first* fourth duchess? Devil a bit, Decimus! I was sure you told the tale merely to satisfy our childish craving for romance and excitement."

"No such thing, my boy! Edward's first wife brought into the marriage jewelry worth a king's ransom. The baubles were kept—"

"In a small marquetry chest!" interjected Clive and Fanny simultaneously.

Fanny added, "And since the fire, no one has seen either the chest or the jewels."

"How exciting!" said Elizabeth. "A treasure hunt would be just the thing to keep those delightful children I met this morning out of trouble."

Fanny beamed. "My niece and nephew. And Clive's, of course. They *are* delightful, aren't they? So bright and lively. Of course they must join us. *Everyone* must join in."

"Count me out," said Clive. "I have business to attend."

Decimus looked shocked. "My boy, you've got your priorities mixed up. If you find the jewels, you won't *need* to attend to business of any kind."

"If you find anything, I trust you to hand it over to the rightful heir." Clive grinned. "But, frankly, Decimus, I doubt there is a treasure. I grant you that Father shied away from Stenton, but he'd never have left a fortune to molder when he could have used it on the Shropshire farms."

"Edward did look for the jewels," Decimus admitted. "Drove down here about six or seven months after the tragedy. But he found nothing. Told me he believed some servant made off with the chest."

"There you are, then."

Fanny encompassed both men in an indignant look. "Well, I think there *is* a treasure."

"Go hunt for it," said Clive. "I've no objections."

"After you've taken all the fun out of it?" Fanny shook her head. "I think not. But I tell you something, Clive! If you don't watch out, you'll turn into a regular dry old stick. A killjoy. A crepehanger!"

Chuckling, Clive drew Elizabeth away. "What do you think, Miss Gore-Langton? Are the jewels hidden somewhere in the castle or have they been carried off?"

"My opinion is of no importance, your grace. But allow me to point out that a treasure hidden somewhere in the castle might serve its purpose if the weather continues rainy."

84

He gave her a sidelong look. How prim she was.

A crooked grin twisted his mouth. "I'm much obliged to you, Miss Gore-Langton. But I'd be even more obliged if you would stop calling me your grace and admit that we have met before."

This time, she could not attribute the flutter of her heart to the splendor of her surroundings.

She forced herself to meet his gaze. "How can I admit to something neither one of us remembers?"

"You still are an abominable little liar," he said softly. "But I'll remember before long. Lay you odds I'll—"

"Don't tempt me!"

Surely one wager on the outcome of this foolish charade was more than enough! She was still annoyed with Nicholas and Juliette for forcing her hand. If they hadn't entered upon the bet with such unseemly haste, she could have—

"Afraid to lose, Miss Gore-Langton?"

"No." She collected her wits. "To win."

He raised a skeptical brow, but was prevented from pursuing the matter by the entrance of Miss Whitlock and Mr. Ponsonby. He introduced Grace and Adam's mentors to Elizabeth, then offered to fetch a glass of sherry for her and ratafia for Miss Whitlock.

Elizabeth's gaze rested on the broad-shouldered back as he strode off, but she turned when she heard Juliette laugh. She realized this was the first time she had heard that bright sound. Earlier, when they talked about Stewart, Juliette had looked as though she'd never laugh again.

She was standing with Nicholas in front of the fireplace and when she met Elizabeth's eye, she winked.

It was not difficult to guess that Juliette and Nicholas had been talking about their wager.

So be it! If a silly bet could give Juliette's mind a different direction, it must be a good thing after all.

Her gaze fell on Stewart, seated beside his father. Stewart, too, had turned at the sound of Juliette's laugh and was watching her. His face was grim, but Elizabeth was close enough to see the pain and longing in his eyes. He did not look like a man who wanted to divorce his wife.

Chapter Seven

By Saturday morning the rain had stopped. Dressed in buckskins, boots, and a heavy corduroy coat, Clive left his bedchamber at eight o'clock. He knocked on Nicholas's door and, when no reply was forthcoming, shrugged and continued along the corridor to the stairwell.

It didn't surprise him at all that Nicholas was not ready to accompany him on another exploration of the beach and cliffs. For one thing, Nick had dipped rather deeply into the punch bowl the previous night—not that he was cast-away, merely a trifle up in the world.

Mainly, though, Nick considered a further search for a cave or some other hiding place a waste of time. "Scrambled all over those damned chalk rocks twice," he had said, pausing with the ladle halfway between punch bowl and cup. A corner of his mouth turned down. "And what did we find, my friend? A crumbling bird nest!"

Which was only too true. But Clive was of a pertinacious nature and could not easily be swayed from a purpose. He was prepared to examine the ragged cliffs once more.

The great door in the hall was still bolted. Rather than upsetting the butler's routine by unbolting the door himself, Clive crossed to the north wing, which housed the pantries, the sculleries and kitchens on the ground floor, the servants' hall and chambers for the male house staff on the first floor, and ample accommodations for a score of maids and the housekeeper on the second floor.

While the rest of the castle was quite open — east wing running into south wing, and south wing leading into west wing — sturdy walls and doors closed off the north wing built around the northeast tower. At ground level, several doors opened onto the kitchen gardens and into the courtyard. Beneath the kitchens, the north wing boasted cellars dug into the chalk cliffs.

This early in the morning, Clive had no interest in the cellars, which housed the wines he had sent down from London. But he was partial to coffee and knew that a cup of the Turkish brew would be available in the kitchen, for it was also a favorite beverage of Monsieur Maurice, a Swiss with the temperament and the culinary artistry of a true French chef.

Before Clive had ventured more than a few steps along the kitchen passage, a tantalizing aroma of fruit and spices teased his nose. It was a scent that brought to mind the days when he and Harry sneaked into the kitchens of Rowland Manor in Shropshire during the Christmas holidays to sample the mince meat slowly simmering on the stove and to take a turn at stirring the Christmas pudding.

Clive checked his step in the arched doorway of the secondary kitchen. There, at one end of the kitchen table, sat his niece and nephew, regaling themselves with thick slices of bread still warm from the oven and mugs of sweet hot chocolate liberally laced with milk. At the other end Monsieur Maurice was ensconced with Nurse Gertrud. The Swiss, a linguist as well as a cook, was talking volubly in German. The only word Clive understood was *Weihnachten*, Christmas.

Grace caught sight of her uncle, dropped her slice of bread and butter, and hurtled toward him to be caught in a hug.

"Uncle Clive!" She immediately squirmed out of his arms again. "You have no Christmas trees at Stenton. We must go back to Bath and fetch one!"

Clive knew, but had forgotten, that his sister-in-law put up a decorated fir tree for the twins every Christmas Eve, a German custom Nurse Gertrud had introduced to Margaret's family three decades ago. He did not suggest to Adam and Grace that they might just for once do without a Christmas tree, but cast about in his mind where they would find the required fir.

Shaking hands with Adam and ruffling the boy's hair, he said, "I hope we won't have to travel all the way to Bath for a Christmas tree."

"No, sir." Adam gave him a troubled look. "But, Uncle Clive, I didn't see any fir trees close to Stenton when we drove up."

"In fact, you didn't see very many trees at all. However, I am sure we'll find something suitable around West Dean."

Grace did a little skip. "Will you take us, Uncle Clive? Now? Just to make *sure?*"

"I will not, you little imp. I happen to know that your governess and tutor expect you for lessons at half-past eight."

"It's not fair!" his niece protested. "Mama promised us a holiday."

"I'd say two hours of lessons *is* a holiday. You have all afternoon to play."

"But, Uncle Clive!" Her gray Rowland eyes widened. "Just think how horrid it would be if we drove to West Dean on Christmas Eve, only to find out that there is *no* Christmas tree!"

"Yes," said Adam, fixing blue eyes on his uncle. "Properly floored we'd be."

"Miss Grace! Master Adam!" Nurse Gertrud's accent was unmistakably German. She and Monsieur Maurice had risen as soon as they became aware of Clive's presence, and she now drew herself up to her full height of five-foot-one. "Will you stop pestering your uncle! He'll think you no better than a pair of *Strassenkinder.*"

The children—unlike Lord Nicholas Mackay when he set eyes on the nurse—were not at all intimidated by the sharp voice and the snapping dark eyes. If the nurse called them "street urchins," one of her most favored German expressions, they knew her reprimand was a mere formality. They flew to her side, Grace hugging the old woman's waist, and Adam, as always a little behind, catching one of her hands.

"Darling Nurse Trudy," Grace said coaxingly, "tell Uncle Clive that we cannot take a chance with the Christmas tree."

"Or with the yule log." Adam looked at his uncle, and his voice held as much conviction as it held persuasion when he said, "I know you wouldn't want to be without a yule log for the Great Hall, Uncle Clive."

"No, indeed." Clive made a show of looking like a man who had been dealt a blow. "The Great Hall without a yule log is unthinkable!"

"You *must* take us to look for a tree and for a yule log, Uncle Clive," said Grace. "We brought all the decorations and even holly and ivy and stuff, 'cause Mama said we couldn't be sure what we'd find here. But if we don't have a tree. . . !"

Clive had been prepared to tease the children a bit longer, but Grace's unhappy face changed his mind. "I will send one of the grooms to scout the area around West Dean. And if he doesn't find your tree or a yule log, he'll have to search farther north, in the Weald."

Their eyes glowed, and if they were disappointed that they would not be a part of the scouting expedition, they did not say so.

Adam only said gravely, "A groom may not know the kind of tree we need. Perhaps, sir, you wouldn't mind sending the gardener?"

Clive did not think that the many talents of Chamberlain, his man in the gardener's cottage, encompassed a knowledge of trees. But that was hardly something he could admit to his nephew. On the other hand, Chamberlain might do no worse than a groom.

"The gardener it is," he told Adam.

Grace tugged at his sleeve. "Can he look for two trees, Uncle Clive? One for the Great Hall and one for the servants' hall? Monsieur Maurice used to have a Christmas tree when he was a boy in Switzerland. I'm sure he'd like one now."

"Ah, yes!" A sigh swelled the chef's massive chest.

91

"Always we had the prettiest little fir tree, hung with tiny carved toys. And when we lit the candles, it was *magnifique!*"

Clive raised his hands in resignation. "By all means, let's have two trees. And now, before you take it into your heads that we shall need a Christmas tree atop each tower and one in each wing, off you go! I want to drink a cup of coffee without a couple of magpies chattering in my ear."

Laughing, the children departed with Nurse Gertrud. However, before Clive had taken his first sip, Grace was back.

She slipped a hand in his. "Uncle Clive? You'll take us on Christmas Eve, won't you? To fetch the yule log and to cut the trees?"

He looked into the expectant little face and was glad that Margaret had brought the children.

"Certainly." He gently pinched her chin. "You and Adam must be there. After all, they are *your* Christmas trees."

When Clive finally left the kitchens, it was considerably later than he had planned. True to his word, he stopped at the gardener's cottage built in the shelter of the east wall. Chamberlain, a tall, lean man a few years older than Clive, received him with a raised brow. They had agreed that the less contact they had with each other, the better it would be for the success of Clive's mission.

When Chamberlain heard his assignment, however, he chuckled. "Aye, your grace. One fir, not less than fifteen feet tall, and one a bit shorter. And two ash logs. Seems to me, these orders will be easier to fulfill than the ones you gave me in London."

"For your sake, I hope so." Clive lowered his voice. "You saw nothing last night?"

"Nothing. But, then we didn't expect anything, did we?"

"No." Clive glanced at the gray sky. "Clouds are as bad as a full moon. Even an experienced free-trader will need to see a star or two to navigate by."

"Talk in East Dean is that the clouds will be clearing by tomorrow."

Clive nodded. "Any other talk in the village?"

"A number of the men I approached about coming to the castle to prune those scraggly shrubs in your garden and to repair the flagways said they won't be able to start work until Friday or Saturday next week."

"A long Christmas holiday?" A gleam entered Clive's eye. "In view of that bit of news, I daresay the flagways can wait. But watch how you talk about those shrubs, my friend. You're supposed to be a gardener."

Chamberlain grinned. "Aye, but I've been careful to spread the word that I've always been and always will be an insubordinate dog. It's my expertise laying out gardens that got me this post, not obsequiousness. In fact, I'm considered another 'Capability Brown,' and you're not likely to dismiss me until I've finished my work here."

" 'Capability Brown'!" Clive gave a snort. "I'll eat my boots if you know a rose from a lily. Not that I care, my friend. But you had better know a fir tree from an oak!"

Whistling softly, Clive strode off. What Chamberlain had learned in the village told its own tale. It did not surprise him that East Dean, so close to the coast, was involved in the smuggling activities. And, undoubtedly, West Dean and Seaford were in it as well.

But he had supposed the men were helping only to land the cargo, and that was clearly not the case. If some of the men could not work at the castle until the end of the following week, it indicated that they expected to be gone for several days. The question was, would they be carrying a French agent back to France when they sailed, or would they bring an agent across on their return?

Lost in thought, Clive crossed the wide courtyard and approached the west wall, against which a coach house, the stables, and two barns were built. The large gate set in the wall between the coach house and the stables stood open, but he passed it by without a second glance.

His response to stable lads muttering a greeting was polite if distracted. He was bent on reaching the small, arched doorway beyond the last barn, the postern gate that opened onto the cliff path. But when his head groom came out of the stables and hurried toward him, he felt obliged to stop.

"Your grace!" Sam Nutley's weatherbeaten face was set in grim, rigid lines. "If ye're headed for the beach, ye might want to look out for the young lady as went down there. Against my advice, I might add."

Clive narrowed his eyes. There was only one young female whose name Sam might not yet know. The young lady who had arrived the previous day and pretended she hadn't met the Duke of Stenton before.

"Devil a bit! What is Miss Gore-Langton doing on the beach? In winter!"

"Just what I asked her. And I told her I don't hold with young ladies scrambling down steep, slippery cliffs. Told her she'd end up breaking a leg, or worse, her neck. And how did she expect us to bring her up on a hurdle on that path?"

"And still she left?" Clive raised a quizzing brow. "You surprise me, Sam. When you disapprove of something, your scowl intimidates even me."

"Which is just as it should be," Sam Nutley said repressively. He had taught his grace to ride his first pony thirty years ago, and he could still teach him a trick or two.

Recalling the matter at hand, Sam scowled. "The young lady wouldn't listen to no remonstrations. Only smiled and said thank you. Ever so polite she was, telling me not to worry."

"Don't, then. I'll keep an eye out for her."

Clive turned to leave, but the head groom fell into step beside him.

"Said she was familiar with chalk cliffs, and off she goes, cool as a cucumber, out the small gate."

Clive could not like it either that Miss Gore-Langton had ventured down the cliff path, yet he could not quite suppress a grin. If Sam Nutley disliked something, it was having his warnings and prophecies disregarded, and Miss Gore-Langton had properly set up the groom's back.

Come to think of it, he wouldn't have expected her to show pluck. Nothing in her demeanor, either yesterday morning when he encountered her on his doorstep or last night in the drawing room, had led him to

believe that she might be strong willed and coura-
geous. And it did take courage to venture down the
cliff path. It seemed that Lady Astley's shy companion
was made of sterner stuff than he had supposed.

"Said she wouldn't be gone above an hour." Sam
gave him a look that showed exasperation as much as
concern. "But it's going on nine o'clock, and she left
not much after seven."

"Seven!" This bit of news brought Clive up sharply.
"It was barely light then."

Without giving Sam a chance to say anything else,
he strode off, leaving the groom behind. In a few moments, he had rounded the last barn and lifted the
latch of the postern gate. He ducked his head as he
passed through the opening. Bitter experience had
taught him that the gate had not been built for a man
topping six feet.

He stood atop the mighty chalk cliffs that supported
Stenton Castle close to one hundred feet above the
Channel. To his right, rocky ground stretched as far
as the eye could see. Barely discernible were wheel
tracks made by carts and carriages that, in the past,
were sent on a roundabout way to fetch visitors who
arrived by yacht and anchored in the estuary. To his
left, a scarce fifteen feet away, began the steep drop to
the beach.

By now, Clive was familiar with every inch of the
narrow path. He knew where the rock was crumbly
and might start to slide under a careless step; he knew
the handholds on a particularly steep stretch.

As always when he went down the path, the
strength of the wind surprised him. It was by no
means calm at the higher elevation around the castle,

but the lower he climbed the sharper the gusts blowing off the Channel tugged at his coat and tried to press him against the rock.

Every now and then, he stopped to scan the stretch of beach visible below on his left. It was a fairly wide stretch at present, for the tide was only beginning to come in. But there was no sign of a solitary figure walking, or gathering shells, or whatever it was that Miss Gore-Langton had planned to do.

Thus, he did not waste time pacing the beach but turned right, where the shoreline made a sharp jog inland and formed the east side of the estuary where the Cuckmere River emptied into the Channel.

Here the sandy beach soon changed to marshy ground. Even in December, reeds and some spiky shrub made walking difficult, but if one followed the estuary northward, one met up eventually with the carriage track leading to the castle.

And this, Clive thought, was exactly what Miss Gore-Langton must have done. Having climbed down the slippery cliff path, she had shied away from returning by the same difficult route and had decided to follow the river inland, then turn east toward the castle where the approach would be less steep.

Still, he could not deny concern for the young lady. He called out her name every twenty paces or so even though he realized that he must see her if she were in the vicinity, since none of the plant growth was tall enough to obscure his view.

He had walked about five hundred feet and had reached the place where, on his first day's exploration, he discovered the old private harbor for Stenton Castle. Some of the piling was still intact, as was a landing stage raised on thick posts where the ground sloped downward near the water.

"Miss Gore-Langton!" he shouted again, then, growing tired of the long name, "Elizabeth!"

Only a sea gull answered his call.

He looked at the castle, perched high above him on his right. He was about even with the northeast tower, and if Miss Gore-Langton had come this way — and if she had any sense at all — she would have walked on a few paces and seen the carriage track winding its gradual way up to Stenton.

He took a step or two toward the track, then turned back and followed the well-trodden path to the landing stage. He didn't think he'd find Miss Gore-Langton there — unless she had fallen asleep among the reeds — but the path, so well defined among the growth, fascinated him. He was prepared to wager a plum that the smugglers used the old landing stage for their own sinister purposes.

Although the planks looked solid enough — too solid for wood that must have been laid down more than forty years ago — he stepped warily.

Later, he was to thank the stars that he had been cautious. Otherwise, he surely would have toppled into the estuary when he reached the end of the landing stage and saw on his left, among the reeds, the leaf green cloak worn the day before by Miss Gore-Langton. A second look disclosed a pair of dainty brown boots poking out from beneath the cloak.

Chapter Eight

Stifling an oath, Clive lowered himself onto the marshy ground. Immediately, his boots were covered by an inch of soft mud. And no wonder; the area around the landing stage stood under water at high tide.

It was only a few steps to the still form in the green cloak, but those steps were not easy to accomplish and only the excellent fit of his boots saved him from a walk in stockinged feet.

"Miss Gore-Langton! Elizabeth!"

As he reached her side, he finally saw her face and drew in his breath sharply. She was pale, her lips bloodless.

Abandoning all caution, he dropped to his knees beside her. He saw a dab of blood matting the dark brown hair above her right ear, and, incongruously, her head rested on a folded panel of oilcloth. Probing the bloodied area on her head, he discovered a lump the size of a guinea piece.

He clasped one of her hands, chafing it gently. It was cold and muddied. Lud! How long had she been lying here? Her cloak was soaked through; the only dry part of her seemed to be her hair, protected from the wet marsh by the piece of oilcloth.

He could not feel a pulse in her wrist and she had not moved, yet he did not doubt that she was alive. If he could not rouse her, he'd have to carry her to the landing stage—a difficult feat over boggy ground, but not impossible.

He chafed and kneaded her hand more vigorously. "Elizabeth!" he said sharply, trying to penetrate her unconsciousness. "Wake up! We must get you home. Do you hear me, Elizabeth? Wake up."

She gave a soft moan and thrust about with her free hand as if to hit him. He caught it, holding it tightly.

"Elizabeth, it's Stenton. Wake up! I want to take you home."

To his relief, her eyes opened. Again he was struck by their unusual color, an emerald green, darkened now in confusion and fear. She started to struggle.

He spoke soothingly. "You're safe, Elizabeth. Don't fight. You know me. I'm Stenton. You're staying in my house, remember?"

She lay still, looking at him rather hazily. After a moment, her gaze cleared and she nodded.

"Yes, I know you." Incredibly, a mischievous smile flickered across the pale features. "Indeed, I know you very well."

"Indeed."

The casual tone of his voice hid a sudden alertness, a sense of unease. Perhaps she was still confused and did not know what she was saying. But there had been that flicker of a smile. What could she be playing at, this young woman who denied having met him before and who had gotten into trouble in a spot that was obviously a smugglers' haven?

He said, "You'll have to explain that cryptic remark. But not now. My first objective is to get you home."

A frown gathered in her eyes as she glanced about her. "What happened?"

"I hoped *you* would be able to tell me." He eased one knee out of the bog. "Your head appears to have sustained some slight injury. Are you hurt anywhere else, or do you think you can get up if I help you?"

"I can get up."

She winced when she raised her head. Cautiously, she put a hand on the bloodied spot, feeling the lump.

"Now I remember." Indignation drove color into her cheeks. "I was hit!"

"You shall tell me all about it presently. But first let me get you to your feet and out of this morass."

Crouching behind her, he anchored his hands beneath her arms and helped her into a sitting position.

"Make sure your boots are not entangled in your cloak," he ordered.

She felt a bit dizzy, but his voice, clear and crisp, had a bracing effect. Without ceremony, she drew cloak and gown up to her calves.

"We had better hurry, your grace. With my weight

centered on a certain part of my anatomy, I can feel myself sinking. In a few more minutes, you'll need a dozen men to pull me out."

He was startled into a crack of laughter. "I cannot believe you're the same young lady I met yesterday."

She could not blame him. Yesterday, she had blushed and stammered in his presence. But she would have cut off her tongue rather than confess that their encounter had rendered her as shy and insecure as the seventeen-year-old Elizabeth had been when they were introduced over a decade ago. A night's repose and a stern talk she'd had with herself during the solitary walk along the beach had quite restored her natural ebullience. She had never been a coward and would not be one now.

Elizabeth started to rise, and he quickly and deftly assisted her. She stood for a moment, swaying a little, grateful that the strong hands under her arms were not immediately withdrawn.

"I'm sorry." The rock-solid body behind her gave her strength. "It's my head and, I think, the ground, which seems to shift beneath my feet. I don't know how I came to be here. I remember being hit, but that was on the landing stage."

"We'll talk about it later. Let me help you remove your cloak. It must weigh a ton with all that water it soaked up."

She had felt the cold when he roused her, but when the heavy, wet cloak came off her shoulders, the wind bit through the soft wool of her gown and chilled her to the bone. She started to shake.

"Here, take this."

Planting his feet apart for better balance, he shrugged out of his coat, helped her into the sleeves, then, with an arm wound firmly around her waist, propelled her toward the landing stage.

His body heat stored in the garment revived her, but it seemed an eternity before they reached the wooden platform. Each time she pulled a foot out of the bog and moved it a step forward, a stab of pain shot through her head. And when they finally reached their goal, she could only stare helplessly at the raised planks. They were no more than waist high, but she did not have the strength to draw herself up.

"Turn around," said Clive and, when she did so, he lifted her and set her down on the landing stage, then swung himself up beside her.

"This was the easy part." He gave her a searching look. "How do you feel?"

"Well enough to go on. So don't even think of leaving me here while you get help."

A corner of his mouth twitched upward, and she thought that he had not changed very much. He still had that lopsided grin that could make a female heart flutter alarmingly.

Of course, *she* did not have to worry about a flutter of the heart. She had just recovered from a hit on the head, then had to trudge through a quagmire. Any irregularity of heartbeat must be directly attributed to her travail.

He pulled her to her feet. "We had better go, then, before my groom sends his men with *two* hurdles."

Standing made her feel dizzy again, even a little sick in the stomach. But she forced herself to smile. "He told you he tried to stop me? Then, I suppose, you came looking for me."

"I did." Again he caught her around the waist. "But, to tell the truth, I didn't expect to find you. I believed you must have returned to the castle by way of the carriage track."

"That's what I meant to do."

She cast a look around, at the spot where she had lain unconscious, and which suddenly seemed much closer to the water than she remembered it; at the abandoned cloak, brand new but now beyond salvation; at the surging water beyond the landing stage.

And she realized that two things had changed since she first stepped onto the landing stage and was knocked senseless. The tide was coming in. Fast. And the boat was gone."

She felt the pressure of his arm against her back, heard his voice urging her on.

She looked up at him. "A boat—I took it for a revenue cutter—it was anchored here when I arrived. It's gone!

"The devil you say!"

He steered her off the landing stage and toward the carriage track. His eyes swept the estuary as far as he could see, but there was nothing. No revenue cutter. No boat at all. But, then, he had not expected to see anything.

After a moment, she said, "It was very strange, I realize now. There was no one aboard, and I should think that at least one preventive officer would have been left to guard the boat. And besides, a preventive officer would hardly hit me over the head, would he?"

Clive had a fairly good notion that the boat in question was a smuggling vessel and Miss Gore-Langton's attacker a free-trader.

Anger boiled in him that they had dared lay a hand on her, but he said, "One never knows what the excisemen might or might not do. I'll come back later and have a look around."

"Oh, no! I don't think—"

He felt her sway and, fearing she was about to swoon, caught her up in his arms and carried her. She murmured some unintelligible protest, which he ignored, and after a while she subsided. She was not unconscious but looked up at him with a troubled frown.

"Don't go back," she said. "It's dangerous."

"Hush, Elizabeth! No more talk. Must save my breath for the climb."

The carriage track was not steep, but it was very rough, and even though his fair burden was slight, he was beginning to feel a little breathless. He was damnably out of shape!

About halfway up the track, Elizabeth insisted that she walk again. Since she was shivering, despite the coat, he did not try to dissuade her. The cloak had not completely saved her gown from getting damp. Walking might exhaust her, but at least it would get her warm.

When the western gate came in sight, he picked her up again and thus entered the castle yard with

Elizabeth in his arms—a mistake, he found, for Sam Nutley was waiting to tell him I told you so.

"Hold your tongue, Sam!" he said before the head groom could open his mouth. "Have one of the local lads ride for a physician. And saddle Rambunctious."

At this last order, Miss Gore-Langton again muttered something about "dangerous" and "don't go!" But since her teeth were chattering and she was shaking all over, he did not bother to reply but made all haste to the castle.

He lowered his burden onto a settle by the fire in the Great Hall, sent one footman running for the housekeeper, and told another to take hot water to Miss Gore-Langton's room. By the time Mrs. Rodwell arrived breathlessly in the hall and exclaimed over Miss Gore-Langton's disheveled state, the young lady had recovered sufficiently to beg Clive once more not to return to the estuary.

She was so persistent, that he wondered if she was withholding information from him.

He asked, "Why? What do you think will happen to me if I look around on my own property?"

"The same fate that befell me," she said, shivering.

Mrs. Rodwell instantly pounced on her. "That's enough talk, my dear. You come with me, and don't you worry none about his grace. He's well able to take care of himself. And any questions he may have, he can ask *after* Dr. Wimple has seen you." She shot a look at Clive. "The physician has been sent for, I hope?"

"Yes, ma'am," he said meekly.

Miss Gore-Langton rose from the settle. She gave

a weak chuckle. "I did not think *you'd* stand in awe of Mrs. Rodwell."

"Oh, I do. She was my nurse, and I still quake at the prospect of a tongue lashing."

Miss Gore-Langton slipped her arms out of his coat and handed it to him. "Thank you. I believe you saved my life."

"Nonsense. You would not have stayed unconscious very long once the tidewater started nipping at your feet."

"The temperature in December not being conducive to sea bathing?" Again she chuckled.

It was a rich, surprisingly deep sound he found delightful. And he could not help but admire her pluck. When another woman would have been in hysterics, or at least tearful, she could still see a certain humor in a potentially dangerous situation.

"Hush, now!" Mrs. Rodwell clasped Elizabeth's elbow. "I don't know what happened to put you in this state, my dear. And I don't want to know! Not until I've seen you into bed with hot bricks and a nice tisane."

He watched until they disappeared in the passage leading to the east wing. He saw Elizabeth sway once and started after her, but the housekeeper had already placed a plump arm around her waist. There was no need to be concerned. He was certain Elizabeth was not seriously hurt, and Mrs. Rodwell was more than able to deal with her.

Pulling on his coat, Clive strode toward the front door. Before he was halfway there, he was hailed by his uncle, emerging from the south wing passage.

"Clive, my boy!" Huffing a little, Lord Decimus trundled toward his nephew. "A word with you, if you please."

Instinct urged Clive to hurry back to the landing stage immediately. Manners dictated that he stay and greet his elderly relative, who usually did not leave his room before noon.

"Good morning, Decimus. I trust you slept well? Or is your early appearance due to a lumpy mattress?"

"No, no, my boy. The mattress is fine. In fact, the whole chamber is what you young people call bang up to the knocker."

Clive did not think of himself as "young people"; neither did he indulge in such flash terms as "bang up to the knocker."

Curbing his impatience, he said, "Thank you. How can I be of service?"

Decimus's cherubic face puckered into a frown. "I'm not sure, though, that restoring the south wing wasn't a foolish waste. Must have cost a pretty penny, and there are plenty of rooms without the south wing and the second story—if you want to live here, that is—which, I confess, has me in a puzzle. Why would you want to be at Stenton when you have a perfectly comfortable house in London?"

"I hadn't planned on staying permanently. But, pardon me, Decimus. I'm in a bit of a rush. Why—"

"Not planned on it!" Decimus sputtered. He peered shortsightedly into his nephew's face. "Dash it, Clive! Have you gone mad? Why waste your blunt on Stenton if you don't mean to live here? If you have money to burn, you might make me another loan!"

Clive could not help but grin. Making Decimus a loan was indeed burning money. His uncle kept strict tally of the amounts borrowed from Clive, even calculated the interest. But whether he'd ever be able to repay the loans was another matter.

"Under the hatches again, Decimus? Is that why you wanted to speak to me?"

"Of course I'm under the hatches. What else would bring me to this forsaken place?"

Clive raised a quizzing brow. "Family?"

"No," Decimus replied without a moment's hesitation. "Shouldn't think so at all. And neither is family or the south wing what I wanted to talk to you about."

He drew himself up, a move that gave him the looks of a plump pouter pigeon. "It's that butler of yours!"

The accusatory note in Decimus's voice fairly took Clive aback. "Lud! You knew Symes when he was a footman at Stenton House. What the deuce did he do to make you call him *that butler?*"

"Don't know that he did anything." Decimus narrowed his eyes. "But if you ask me, I think it's damned fishy that every time I inquire about the delivery, he says it has not yet been made. Stap me! That's impossible!"

Clive remembered that Nicholas had said something about Decimus questioning the butler regarding a shipment of wine.

"Are you talking about a wine delivery, Decimus? I cannot believe you sent some of your own store. After you've assured me over and over again that my cellars are as well stocked as my father's were?"

But Decimus wasn't listening. "Symes won't convince me that *nothing* has arrived," he said indignantly. "Why, you've been here since Tuesday. Today is Saturday. Symes himself has been here a fortnight or more. No, no, my boy! The 'gentlemen' are never backward. And never stingy. They pay immediately and generously."

Excitement made Decimus breathless. He could only wave pudgy hands, but it was quite unnecessary for him to say anything else.

"Great Scot, sir! You're talking about smuggled wine! Delivered by free-traders."

"They prefer to be called 'gentleman' traders. You had better remember that, my boy, when you speak of them hereabout."

Clive stared at his uncle, who had taken an enameled snuffbox from his coat pocket, flicked open the lid, and delicately inhaled a pinch of snuff. *Decimus and the free-traders!* He had not counted on that complication.

Or was it a complication? Like Elizabeth earlier, Clive began to see some humor in the situation.

"Tell me, Decimus. When and how did you get in touch with the smug—the 'gentleman' traders?"

Having sneezed twice, Decimus once more peered shortsightedly at his nephew. "So you don't know about the arrangement, eh?"

"What arrangement?"

110

"Didn't I mention it when you and Harry were nippers and pestered me to tell you about Stenton?"

"You said nothing about smugglers."

Decimus shrugged. "In any case, your father should've told you."

"Please get to the point. What should I have been told?"

"That we Rowlands have always closed our eyes and ears when the 'gentlemen' land in the estuary and store their goods in the cave. It's for a short while only, until the moon is bright enough so the casks can be carried overland. And for the use of the landing stage and the cave, the 'gentlemen' leave a keg of wine or cognac at the kitchen door, sometimes tea or a dress length of silk as well."

Clive took a deep breath.

"What cave, Decimus?" he asked quietly.

"The hidden cave below the west wall, Clive, my boy. Where your father and I used to play at pirates and smugglers."

"How appropriate," said Clive, still very quietly. "The west wall is long. Can you be more specific?"

"I'd show you if it weren't for my gouty foot." Decimus tried to peer at his foot over the expanse of his stomach but gave it up as futile.

He directed an amiable smile at Clive. "The cave is in the cliffs below the western gate and the southwest tower. Rather more toward the tower than the gate, I think. Or is it the other way around? But you'll find it, my boy. Unlike me, you have a pair of devilish sharp eyes in your head."

"Thank you," Clive said dryly.

He caught sight of his brother-in-law and Nicholas entering the Great Hall.

Recalling the morning he and Nick had scrambled over rocks and boulders all along the south side of the castle in search of just such a cave as Decimus knew on the west side, recalling Nick's grumbling about the wind, the cold, the damp, the scratched boots, Clive started to laugh. The irony of the situation was even more exquisite than he had at first perceived.

But he must count himself fortunate that the Home Office did not have a say in this tangle of a mission he had agreed to undertake. The Home Secretary would most certainly have ordered him to put a stop to the smuggling. And then where would he be? He, a Rowland bound by tradition to turn a blind eye on the illegal traffic in the estuary.

The recollection of his mission sobered Clive, but a glint of laughter still lurked in his eyes as he hailed the two men. There was no point in trying to keep George Wilmott or any of the guests in ignorance of the smugglers' activities. Not when Decimus knew.

And not—his look grew steely—when Miss Gore-Langton lay upstairs with a bump on her head. He could ignore smuggling but not an attack on one of his guests.

"Nick! George! Come and let Decimus tell you about the smugglers who pay in wine and cognac for the use of my landing stage and a cave in the cliffs."

The gentlemen obligingly veered from the direct path to the breakfast parlor.

"A smugglers' cave." Even at a distance, indignation but also a hint of concern were clearly discernible on Nicholas's face. "And Lord Decimus knew. Fancy that! Before long, everyone will know."

"Indeed," said Decimus. "It's too good a story to keep to myself. I must tell Sir John. They don't have smugglers in Hertfordshire."

Clive met and held Nicholas's eye. "The sooner the story is told the better. And I doubt it'll evoke the interest you seem to fear, Nick. Only the children—"

"What the deuce?" Nicholas raised a quizzing glass to his eye and stared at Clive's muddied boots and buckskins. He shuddered. "I was about to apologize for oversleeping, but I can see I wouldn't have liked it at all if I had accompanied you this morning."

Lord Wilmott, always good-natured, said, "If you're planning on breaking your fast, Clive, may I suggest a change of raiment? Fanny is already down, and she'll rake you over the coals and say you need a wife to keep you in order if you show yourself in the breakfast parlor looking like that."

"What's amiss?" asked Decimus, but no one paid him any heed.

Clive grinned at his brother-in-law. "Don't worry, George. I'll change—just as soon as I return."

"Return from where?" Decimus had followed Nicholas's example and put a glass to his eye, through which he examined his nephew's nether garments. "Clive, my boy, I don't know where you mean to go, but you cannot go out looking like a mudlark!"

"Can I not?" Clive's smile turned grim. "But I'm

going to the landing stage, where I muddied my boots in the first place."

"Ah!" Decimus nodded wisely. "The boards have rotted and you fell into the bog."

"Not at all, sir. The planks, apparently, have been kept in good repair by the smugglers. I had to wade through the bog to rescue Miss Gore-Langton, who was knocked senseless and dumped among the reeds by your friends, the 'gentlemen.' "

Leaving Nicholas and George openmouthed and his uncle protesting that he had never claimed friendship with the "gentlemen," Clive strode off to the stables.

Chapter Nine

Lying in bed, warm flannel-wrapped bricks all around her, Elizabeth called herself all kinds of fool. Clive—

Now, when had she started thinking of him as Clive? *Stenton* had said he'd go back to the estuary to take a look around. And like a ninny, she had done no more than beg him not to go. As if that would stop him!

On the other hand, telling him of her suspicion that the boat was a smuggling vessel would undoubtedly have sent him off in an even greater hurry.

So what should she have done? Turning onto her side, Elizabeth pulled a rueful face. Ten years as a companion to elderly ladies had left her woefully inexperienced in the management of a gentleman. Especially if that gentleman was as strong willed and forceful as she remembered Clive Rowland to be. And that he hadn't changed was obvious from the way he had scooped her up and carried her, despite her protest.

She remembered the feel of his arms around her. Since he had given her his coat, he wore only a lawn shirt. But he was warm . . . and strong. . . .

Her musings were interrupted by a knock. One of the maids, Mary, who had earlier assisted her with a bath, announced the arrival of Dr. Wimple, the physician from Seaford.

Dr. Wimple was a dour-faced small man with gentle hands who examined the bump on her head and made her swallow an evil-smelling concoction. He grumbled about visitors who didn't know better than to go walking on the beach in winter or poking around places where they had no business being in the first place—which made her wonder what he had been told about her.

Then Dr. Wimple patted her shoulder and assured her she'd be shipshape by morning. "That's supposing, of course, you didn't contract an inflammation of the lungs and start running a fever."

Elizabeth liked his brusque manner and smiled at him. "I'm not at all susceptible to chills and fevers, Dr. Wimple."

"Hmph!" He closed his bag with a snap. "At least you don't have a concussion. I should know. I've seen more head injuries than I ever hoped to see." He gave her a stern look. "All contracted by fools climbing the cliffs or walking the beach at the wrong time."

"I'll choose a better time when I go again," she promised.

"Go again?" His shrewd eyes rested on her for a moment. He shook his head in resignation and stalked off. At the door he stopped.

"Mary," he said to the maid who had accompanied him to Elizabeth's chamber, "see to it that the young lady stays in bed today. Let her sleep as much as she cares to. And if you have any sense at all, you'll explain to her when is *not* a good time to go walking along the estuary."

Without waiting for a reply, he addressed Elizabeth again. "Not that I think it'll do any good. I suspect you already know what goes on. But Mary is from East Dean. Has lived here all her life. You could do worse than listen to her."

"Dr. Wimple, believe me, I have no intention of interfering with free-traders," said Elizabeth. "I grew up near Lydd. I know how excitable and dangerous the 'gentlemen' are."

"Do you now?" Dr. Wimple gave a snort. "In that case, I'd have expected you to know better than to visit the beach early in the morning."

"I know better *now,* and next time, I promise you, I'll go in the afternoon. But I very much fear that his grace does not understand the ways of our men on the Channel coast, and he, I am told, is very much addicted to walking on the beach and along the estuary in the early morning hours and late at night."

"So I have been given to understand. In fact, I planned to drop a word of warning in his ear."

"Thank you, Dr. Wimple. That is exactly what I hoped—"

"Well, I cannot do that. Saw him ride off as I drove up. And come to think on it, *you* are in a

117

much better position to tell him to stay off the beach."

"*I?*" Elizabeth shot up so fast that her head started to throb again. "I have no authority, no right to tell him anything."

The physician's dour expression lightened. A generous-minded person might have considered the slight stretch of his mouth a smile. Elizabeth did not feel generous.

"My dear young lady," he said, "you've as much as told me that the lump on your head won't keep you from visiting the beach or the estuary again. You are a stubborn lady, and I have no doubt whatsoever that, authority or not, you'll know exactly how to put the situation to his grace."

And, to clinch the matter, Dr. Wimple whisked himself out of the room and shut the door.

Elizabeth sank back against the pillows. A sound, half moan, half chuckle, escaped her. Authority or not, she'd know exactly how to put the matter to his grace? Lud! Even if she was stubborn, that didn't make her a managing, interfering female. What made the good doctor jump to that conclusion?

She became aware of Mary looking at her rather uncertainly.

"Would you bring me the hand mirror please, Mary? It should be on the dressing table. And if you don't mind, let's talk about the beach and smuggling and things some other time. I am a little tired."

"Yes, ma'am." Mary handed her the mirror. "I doubt not you'll sleep for hours, ma'am. I know that

118

bottle Dr. Wimple measured from. That syrup will put a horse to sleep."

"Syrup of poppies. But it's mixed with something else." Elizabeth yawned. "Thank you, Mary. Perhaps you'll be kind enough to wake me in time to dress for dinner?"

The little maid said doubtfully, "Yes, ma'am. If it's all right with Mrs. Rodwell, ma'am."

Curtsying several times, Mary backed out of the room leaving Elizabeth to stare into her mirror.

Ma'am! When had she ceased to be *miss?* A sixteen-year-old village girl might justifiably consider a woman a dozen years her senior as old. But even Stenton had called her ma'am during their first encounter. And Dr. Wimple might address her as *young lady*, yet he believed her capable of stopping the Duke of Stenton from walking on his own beach.

Even after an extended scrutiny of her face, Elizabeth could see no signs of a shrewish temperament that might have misled the physician and, with a little sniff of disgust at her vanity, set the mirror on the bedside table.

Yawning, she slid lower in the bed and pulled the cover up around her chin. She'd do all she could to convince Stenton that the beach and the estuary were best left alone . . . after she had slept a little.

Unbidden, the thought crept into her mind that, if she wanted to avoid being called an abominable little liar, she should keep away from the Duke of Stenton. It was a prospect she could not like at all, and she promptly dismissed the notion of avoiding his company.

Closing her eyes, Elizabeth yawned again. Suddenly, she tensed. She opened one eye, then quickly closed it again. Surely she could not be hearing someone softly clapping in applause? Not again!

Climbing the carriage track while supporting or carrying Elizabeth had taken half an hour or longer. On horseback, it was a matter of minutes before Clive reached the estuary bank.

At the landing stage, he dismounted. He had no qualms about leaving the roan untethered. Rambunctious was well trained; he would not startle and run at the screech of a seabird, nor would he wander off without his rider.

As soon as Clive set foot on the wooden planks, he knew that he had returned too late to retrieve the piece of oilcloth. Not only had the water risen sufficiently to cover the spot where Elizabeth had lain unconscious, but the leaf green cloak, which had been left behind in the bog, now hung over one of the posts of the landing stage.

His mouth tightened in irritation. Damn! If Decimus hadn't stopped him —

No, he was being unfair. Even if Decimus had not delayed him, he would have been gone from the landing stage close to three-quarters of an hour. More than enough time for someone to collect the oilcloth or, if no one had come to retrieve it, for the tide to wash it away. But someone had been here. The tide had not draped the cloak over that post.

He picked up the cloak. It smelled marshy, but

most of the mud stains were gone and the fabric was dripping as if it had been rinsed in the rolling, lapping waters of the estuary. He did not know whether a woolen garment would retain the smell of mud and rotting vegetation, and if it had been his own, he would have left it. But he had seen Elizabeth glance back at the cloak and wondered if she had regretted having to leave it behind.

With barely a moment's hesitation, he took it with him. It had once been a good, serviceable piece of clothing, not as brilliant in color as Elizabeth's eyes, but near enough to be called a match. No doubt, she had paid a handsome price for it and would not easily be able to purchase another.

Rambunctious snorted in disgust when Clive slung the soggy garment over the saddle and rivulets of water rolled down the horse's smooth coat.

"Sorry, old boy." Clasping the rein, Clive started to lead the roan. "I'm afraid you'll have to suffer awhile. If I cannot have the oilcloth, I want at least to take a look at Decimus's cave."

Slowly, he made his way southward, the swollen estuary on his right, the castle atop the chalk cliffs on his left. Every now and again, he looked up, and when he judged he was about even with the big gate in the west wall, he once more left the roan to its own devices.

Clive patted the horse's neck before leaving and ran a hand through the stiff mane. "Like Nick, you wouldn't appreciate the rocks and loose stones where I'm going."

It was indeed rough walking directly at the foot of

the cliffs where giant fingers of chalk rock jutted from the ground. Undeterred by cuts and scrapes to his boots, by stubbed toes, by sharp stones that hurt the soles of his feet, Clive pressed on. He meant to find the cave.

Here, unlike on the Channel side, the cliffs presented a smooth, wall-like appearance, which was why he had not previously searched this area for a cave that could be used as a storage place by the smugglers. Or as a hiding place by French agents. But appearances could be deceiving. There might be an unsuspected crevice in the cliff wall, a narrow slit hidden by a boulder and widening into a cave deep inside the chalk rock.

So absorbed was he in the study of the cliff wall that he lost his footing and stumbled when he was addressed in a creaky, rusty old voice.

"Mornin', yer grace."

Regaining his balance, Clive faced an old man perched on a hunk of chalk rock less than five feet distant. The ancient's head was covered with a knitted cap, bony shoulders supported a patched greatcoat that had been tailored for a much larger man, and on his feet he wore a pair of very muddy ankle boots.

"Good morning," said Clive, his frame stiffening despite the old man's harmless looks. "I'm afraid you have the advantage of me."

The gaffer mulled over Clive's words, then widened his mouth in a smile that revealed a gap where his front teeth should have been.

"Fancy talk," he said. "Us folks hereabouts ain't

used to it no more since his grace, yer sainted pa, left. But I'm Will from East Dean, if that's what ye was wishful of knowing. Used to work up at Stenton. Second undergardener I was."

"My gardener is looking for help. You can apply to him if you'd like to work at Stenton again."

"Ain't no use." Old Will stretched out hands covered by mittens, showing fingers as gnarled and twisted as the branches of an ancient apple tree. "Yer gardener says I'm too old."

"I'll speak to him."

Saluting the ancient, Clive walked on. He would have passed the man, but Will tottered to his feet to stand squarely in his path.

"Ye'd best not go on, yer grace. Ain't safe hereabouts, and Jed Beamish of the Crown an' Anchor sent me to make sure no one comes to no harm. Jed says yer grace canna be 'xpected to know what's safe and what ain't."

Clive could have brushed Will aside, but it went against the pluck to raise even a finger against a man so much older and weaker than he. Clive was also curious.

"The innkeeper sent you?" Now this was a bit of news to pass on to Chamberlain. "What is Jed Beamish's interest in the estuary?"

Like Decimus, Will apparently heard only what he wanted to hear. At least, he answered only Clive's first question.

"Aye, yer grace. Jed Beamish, he be the innkeeper *and* the mayor *and* the constable. Sent me and Ole Fergus to watch that no one from the castle comes to harm. Ole Fergus, he be sittin' down at the mouth o' the estuary."

Thus cutting off the approach to the estuary from the cliff path.

"The devil you say! And undoubtedly Fergus is as young as you are."

Will snickered. "I can give him a year or two."

"Congratulations."

Again, Clive dismissed the notion of overpowering the old man. All guards must change at some time. And if not this night, then the following night when the moon was dark and the clouds had disappeared, the village ancients would be replaced by sturdy men. Clive would have no compunction in knocking some burly lads' hard heads together.

He scowled at Will. "If you were sent to watch over my safety and that of my guests, I wish you had been here earlier this morning. A young lady from the castle was knocked unconscious by one of your smug—" Recalling Decimus's strictures, Clive corrected himself. "By one of your 'gentlemen.' "

"We was here, yer grace." The wrinkles in Will's face deepened in distress. "We couldn't do nothing. But I swear on me mother's grave it weren't one of our lads as hit the young lady. We don't hold with no vi'lence, nor with no drownings."

"That, I suppose," Clive said cuttingly, "is why she was left on the estuary bank with the tide coming in?"

"We wouldn't have let her drown, yer grace. But we couldn't carry her, Fergus and me. That's why we tried to make her head comf'table when she wouldn't wake up. And when we heard ye come down the cliff path, we hid so *you* could find her."

"Well, I'll be—" Clive narrowed his eyes. "Then *who*, if it wasn't one of the 'gentleman' traders, hit the young lady?"

Chapter Ten

But Will had suddenly turned quite deaf. "Go on home, yer grace," he urged. "And keep away from the beach and the estuary the next five, six days."

Clive thought he saw a flicker of fear in the old man's eyes and nodded. "Don't fret," he said curtly. "*You* won't see me again. But I do want to know who attacked the young lady."

There was no doubt that Will was afraid. His weathered face had a pinched look, and the gnarled hands trembled.

"Don't ask no more questions, yer grace," he said hoarsely. "Not if ye value yer life. And mine."

"Gammon! You sound like a character in a melodrama. But I'm not falling for it, Will. Not after you assured me that the free-traders don't like violence."

"Aye, and I stand by my word, yer grace." The ancient cast surreptitious looks around him. "But this got nothing to do with the 'gentlemen.'"

Irritation boiled in Clive. "Just give me the word with no bark on it, Will! Who hit the young lady?"

126

The gaffer shook his head.

"If it wasn't one of the local men," pressed Clive, "was it a Frenchman?"

His mouth tightening obstinately, Will stared at his muddy footgear.

Clive's hands clenched when he realized he wouldn't get another word out of the old man, and for a moment he was too angry to speak.

But there was one other he could question.

"Count yourself lucky that the young lady is not badly hurt," he said. "Else I'd wring your neck — venerable old age or not! And if you want a bit of advice, go home and sit by your fire. You're too old for the dangerous game you're dabbling in."

"I *would* go home," Will said quietly. "But a man's got to make a living. Any way he can."

Their eyes locked. Clive saw no reproach or blame in the man's gaze. Yet he understood that it had been his father's desertion and neglect of Stenton that had caused Will's straightened circumstances. How many more had depended on Stenton for their livelihood?

Not all the blame rested with Edward Rowland, the fourth duke. Clive had now owned Stenton for four years. But not once had he driven down to look over the property.

Mayhap it was not too late to do something. . . . But whatever he'd come up with, it would have to wait until he had completed his mission.

Clive turned on his heel and retraced his steps to Rambunctious, who stood precisely where he had left him, head drooping and his whole posture proclaiming abject misery.

He rubbed the roan's nose before shifting the dripping cloak. "Forget it, old boy. You're not half as miserable as I'll be, sitting in a wet saddle."

Back at the castle, he entered through one of the kitchen doors. The housekeeper was there, and after some fussing and clucking said, she'd be able to clean and dry Miss Gore-Langton's cloak.

"And when can I speak with Miss Gore-Langton?" asked Clive.

"I shouldn't think you'll be seeing the poor young lady before morning, your grace. Oh, and before I forget, the children want to decorate the Great Hall. I told them I'd check with you."

"I have no objections," he said absently. *"Why* can I not see Miss Gore-Langton until tomorrow? What is wrong?"

"Dr. Wimple ordered her to stay in bed today."

"An excellent prescription, and I wouldn't dream of dragging Miss Gore-Langton from her couch. I will see her in her chamber."

Mrs. Rodwell clucked again. "Your grace, it's impossible —"

"Nonsense! You may chaperone us. Or Miss Juliette will. I understand she and Miss Gore-Langton are friends."

"Oh, it's not that, your grace! But, you see, Dr. Wimple saw fit to douse the young lady with laudanum."

"Why?" Concern made his voice harsh. "It's not concussion, is it? I was certain she wasn't badly hurt."

"And neither is she. Now don't you fret yourself, your grace. It's exposure to the elements that's left

128

her sadly pulled and the doctor wants her to sleep. She won't be in any shape to talk or," the housekeeper said, giving him a shrewd look, "to answer questions before Sunday morning."

"Thank you, Mrs. Rodwell." Clive nodded rather stiffly and turned to leave.

"And you need not fret either that the children will get into mischief, your grace. Lady Fanny said she'd help."

"The children?" He shot her a frowning look over his shoulder. "Ah, yes! The decorating of the hall. I wish Fanny joy of it. The brats have never yet managed to stay out of trouble."

Mrs. Rodwell chuckled, and he left quickly before she could think of some other matter she felt she ought to bring to his attention.

Clive was not a patient man. The delay in seeing Elizabeth chafed him. It had given him a nasty jolt when he heard that the physician found it necessary to administer a heavy dose of laudanum. But that inside-twisting moment when he feared she was suffering from a concussion or worse had been brief and was followed by an equally violent feeling of relief when Mrs. Rodwell assured him Elizabeth was all right.

Then the housekeeper had pointed out that Elizabeth wouldn't be able to answer questions until Sunday morning, and relief had turned into irritation. Since old Will had denied one of the free-traders hit Elizabeth, he wanted to know if she had seen her assailant or could describe the boat in detail. And he wanted to know it now.

More than that, he wanted to find out what had

drawn her to the beach at seven o'clock in the morning when patches of mist still obscured the cliff path and shrouded the shoreline. He wanted to ask what she meant with, "Indeed, I know you very well."

And, he acknowledged grudgingly, he wanted to see for himself if some bloom had returned to Miss Gore-Langton's blanched face. 'Twas only natural that he should. She was a guest in his house. He felt responsible.

And now she was asleep! Harboring strong feelings of ill usage, Clive opened the door which closed off the kitchen wing from the Great Hall.

A stepladder stood just outside the door with Margaret balancing precariously on one of the top rungs and Fanny clutching the frame in a futile attempt to keep the ladder from wobbling. Clive had no difficulty giving his irritation a new direction.

"Margaret!" he barked. "What the devil are you doing? Get down!"

His sister-in-law squealed and dropped the greens tied with a red bow she had been trying to tack to a wooden beam.

"Clive, are you mad?" Fanny shot him an indignant look. "You ought to know better than to shout at someone on a ladder."

It did not soothe his temper that Fanny was in the right. Grimly, he clasped the sides of the ladder. "Come down, Margaret. Now!"

Without a word, she complied. As soon as her feet touched the ground, however, she rounded on him, her eyes flashing with anger and her usually pale face flushed pink.

"How dare you use that tone with me! I am trying

130

to make this house party into what it is supposed to be — a *Christmas* gathering. And for my pains I am barked at and ordered about like a lackey!"

"I apologize," he said stiffly. "I was afraid you'd fall."

She was slightly mollified. "Oh, let's forget about it, shall we? But you must admit that you've been very remiss in your duties. We were all invited for Christmas, yet there isn't a bit of decoration anywhere. And when Grace and Adam said they had your permission to decorate, Fanny and I decided to get started."

"But I think it may be better to have one of the footmen work on the ladder," suggested Fanny.

"Much better," he said coldly. He turned to Margaret. "If the twins said they had my permission, they misled you. I heard only just now from —"

"My children don't lie!" Once again, Margaret turned pink with anger. "And surely you're not trying to tell me that you *don't* want them to have the fun of putting up Christmas decorations?"

"Of course not."

Fanny said soothingly, "They asked Mrs. Rodwell and she told them she'd check with you, Clive. To the children that's as good as having your permission. They know you won't say no, and I admit I encouraged them. *I* wanted to decorate, too."

He was tired of arguments and, in an effort to introduce a lighter note, said, "Where are they, by the way? I'd have expected to see them in the midst of all this."

With a sweep of his arm he indicated piles of fir and pine branches, ivy garlands, baskets filled with

131

holly, others with ribbons, littering the tiled floor of the Great Hall.

"They're fetching the kissing-bough frame from my room," said Margaret.

"The kissing bough," he muttered. And why the hell should that bring to mind a pair of green eyes and a mischievous smile?

He should be thinking of getting Miss Gore-Langton to talk rather than wonder if he'd catch her beneath the mistletoe for a kiss. He was the first to admit there was more to the young lady than met the eye, but he suspected he wouldn't like it at all when he discovered why she denied having met him before, or what she'd been doing on the beach to get herself knocked on the head.

Margaret, sounding defensive, said, "Don't look so grumpy, Clive! If I hadn't had the foresight to bring greens and ribbons for garlands, and the kissing bough, you'd find yourself at point non-plus."

But he hardly listened. Once they had taken hold of his mind, thoughts of Elizabeth and the kissing bough were not easily dislodged.

"What Clive needs," said Fanny, "is a wife to take charge of his establishments."

Margaret was quick to contradict. "Not at all. *I* for one will not push him into marriage. *I* can understand only too well that he wouldn't want to see Rosalind supplanted by another."

"Oh, fiddle! You just don't want Clive to set up his own nursery."

"If that's what he wanted, he would have remarried years ago."

Arms akimbo, Fanny faced her sister-in-law. "I tell

132

you this, Margaret! You're doing Adam a great disservice, raising him in the belief that he is Clive's heir. Clive is not in his dotage yet. He has years and years to fill his nursery. And as for not wanting to supplant Rosalind, why I've never heard such nauseating twaddle!"

"Fanny!" Clive spoke sharply. "You sound like a fishwife."

"I am correct, though!"

Clive turned and picked his way through evergreens and ribbons to the back of the Great Hall and the passage to the south wing. Of course Fanny was right. It was not at all desirable that Adam grew up believing himself heir to a dukedom.

Not that he wouldn't be quite satisfied to have the boy follow in his footsteps — if fate so decreed. But, as Fanny said, he was not in his dotage yet. He might meet another woman with whom he could contemplate sharing his life.

Again, he thought of the kissing bough. But the picture conjured this time was of Rosalind beneath the fragrant greens that long-ago Christmas Eve. He had caught her in his arms and kissed her soundly. And then she had swayed and complained of a headache. . . .

They had been married six months when she died. Eleven years ago. Rosalind was a memory, warm and pleasant, to be taken out and dusted off every once in a while. He would always think it was a damned shame she had to die so young, but never would he entertain a maudlin notion like Margaret's, that another woman would "supplant" Rosalind.

It would have served no purpose, however, to set

Margaret straight. Fanny would immediately have made plans to thrust yet another batch of very nice, very eligible, and very insipid young ladies his way.

Quick, light footsteps pursued him. "Oh, Clive!"

He did not stop but cast a wary glance over his shoulder. "What is it now, Fanny?"

"George said that Miss Gore-Langton met with an accident and that the physician has seen her. Is there any news?"

Irritation returned full strength. Irritation with the physician who doled out laudanum as if it were a treat, with sisters who meddled in his life, with females in general and one in particular.

"Yes, there's news. She is asleep!"

And with these bitter words, he retired to his chambers for a bath and a change of raiment.

Clad in champagne-colored pantaloons and a cambric shirt, he was brushing his damp hair when, after the most cursory of knocks, Lord Nicholas Mackay strode into the room. One glance at Nicholas's face sufficed to show Clive he was not the only one laboring under a sense of ill usage.

Perversely, his mood lightened at the sight of the thundercloud on Nicholas's brow. He put down the hairbrush and allowed his valet to help him into a coat of blue superfine.

"Thank you, Reed. That will be all."

The door had barely shut behind Reed, when Nicholas burst out, "Devil a bit, Clive! You toss the news at us that Miss Gore-Langton was knocked unconscious by a bunch of smugglers, then simply walk out the door. Unhandsome, I call it!"

"Quite outrageous," Clive said agreeably.

"And if your housekeeper hadn't assured me that Miss Gore-Langton is all right, I might have gone after you."

Clive grinned. "You would have risked your boots? Why? To catch the villain?"

"To draw your cork."

"To *try* to draw my cork," Clive corrected.

He stepped through the connecting door into his sitting room, where he knew a tray with decanters and glasses was set out on a console table. It was past eleven and he was sharp-set for the meats awaiting him in the breakfast parlor, but he could not ask Nicholas to contain his spleen and his curiosity another half-hour.

"A glass of claret, Nick?"

Taking a snort in the other room for assent, he poured two glasses.

Nicholas joined him. "Don't think you can weasel out of an explanation by plying me with wine."

"I have every intention of explaining the situation to you, my friend. But even though I may have to go hungry I see no reason to go thirsty as well."

"If by that you mean you cannot talk in front of the footmen and whichever of your guests may still linger in the breakfast parlor, your discretion comes a bit late, doesn't it?"

"I don't think so."

Clive chose a deep chair in front of the fireplace and stretched his legs toward the dancing flames. Damn, but he was out of shape! He ached all over.

Or was he getting old? He couldn't remember his feet feeling sore or his legs being tired when he trudged all over Italy in '05. Neither had his muscles ached from climbing a cliff path or carrying a load—be it a pack of clothing and rations or one slender female.

Disgusted with his body's show of weakness, he tossed off the glass of wine. The claret hit his empty stomach, then spread a welcome warmth. He was *not* getting old. Must have been Fanny's talk of marriage and nurseries that planted the notion of age in his mind.

Nicholas, contrary to his indolent nature, started to pace.

After a moment of heavy silence, Nicholas said grudgingly, "Very well. I admit it wasn't your fault that we looked for the cave in the wrong place. And since Decimus knew about the smugglers, I admit also that there was no point keeping it from George Wilmott or anyone else. I wonder, though, how your uncle knew."

"The smugglers were already plying their trade when he and my father grew up here at Stenton."

"The deuce!" Nicholas choked on a sip of wine. "I can understand that *you* didn't know, since your father never talked of Stenton. But Whitehall? Didn't Liverpool or Yorke look into the matter?"

"The way they talked, they were convinced the smugglers started using Stenton property this past summer. But I shouldn't have set too much store by their words. After all, they're interested only in the French agents. It was in July when one of Liverpool's men followed an agent as far as West Dean, then lost him. And in September, someone from the Admiralty traced his quarry to East Dean."

"And lost him." Never one to nurse a grudge, Nicholas refilled their glasses, then joined Clive by the fire.

"Dashed wily, those Frenchmen," he said, handing Clive his glass. "And," he added pensively, "so are Frenchwomen."

Clive cocked a brow. "You sound hipped. Was she French, then, the charmer who preferred Sylvester Throckmorton's bulging paunch and purse to your lean frame and—"

"And lean purse?" Nicholas cut in. He laughed. "Aye. She's of an *émigré* family. A diamond of the first water."

Clive knew of several diamonds among the young French ladies who preferred to be mistresses of wealthy Englishmen rather than wives of impoverished Frenchmen. And Sylvester Throckmorton was one of the warmest men in England. A true nabob. Against him, Lord Nicholas Mackay, the younger brother of the Marquis of Belfort, did not stand a chance.

"Tell me about Miss Gore-Langton," said Nicholas, lounging against the fireplace mantel. "How came she to be knocked down? Did you truly find her by the old landing stage?"

The tale was quickly told. Clive expected more questions from Nicholas, but he only said, "Miss Gore-Langton must have been overjoyed to see you. 'Twas a truly gallant rescue, Clive, old boy."

Clive gave him a hard look. There was something in the tone of Nick's voice and in his eyes . . . amusement? Speculation? What the dickens would Nick be amused about? Miss Gore-Langton? Or the rescue?

But the wine made Clive lazy. The questions did not seem worth pursuing. He moved his long legs. Having soaked up the fire's heat, they were beginning to feel better.

"Gallant?" he muttered.

He remembered the tiny, mischievous smile when she assured him that she knew him very well indeed. The smile more than her words had aroused curiosity and suspicion, but he had refrained from demanding an explanation.

"Aye, gallant I was even if my armor has turned a bit rusty."

Chapter Eleven

Major Stewart Astley softly closed the door to his mother's chamber. For a moment he stood motionless.

He had left his parents bewildered and more anxious than they had been when they first saw that matters between their son and daughter-in-law did not stand well at all. Stewart had meant to tell them straight off what he planned to do, had, in fact, made the attempt three times since their arrival the previous day, but in the end could never find the words. Neither had he been able to explain when they asked what was amiss.

Slowly, Stewart walked past the open door of a sitting room to his own bedchamber. John Piggott, his former batman, was already there, waiting to help him change. They were quite a pair, he and John. The one minus an arm; the other sporting a limp.

All in all, Stewart was glad he had kept John Piggott on. The short, bow-legged man was taciturn to the point of rudeness but knew exactly what to do for him and served him better than any high-nosed valet could. He had even stopped laying out the uniform his master no longer had the heart to wear.

But, dammit, it was galling to know that there was very little he could do without the assistance of a batman or a valet. Couldn't even take his damned boots off unless he wanted to ruin them with the use of a boot jack.

At first, it hadn't seemed to matter. Nothing much had mattered when he gained consciousness in the hospital tent and realized that many of his friends lay dead at Busaco while he had gotten away with a deep bayonet cut across his left forearm.

When the surgeon told him he could not save the arm, that too much muscle and bone had been severed, Stewart had not sunk into self-pity or despair like many others facing amputation. He had said grimly, "I'm alive, aren't I? Go ahead. Cut off a piece of me and bury it with my friends."

The knowledge that Juliette was waiting sped recovery after the amputation, and long before the date predicted by the sawbones, he had been able to sail for England.

Deliberately closing his mind to John Piggott's ministrations as pantaloons took the place of breeches, a coat of superfine that of the corduroy riding coat, Stewart recalled those first hours of the reunion with his wife. It seemed a long time ago. Yet only three weeks had passed.

Dear, sweet, beautiful Juliette. His Julie. She had laughed and cried at the same time. Called him her handsome hero and, in the same breath, a thin scarecrow whom she must coddle and pamper before he could be allowed to travel into Hertfordshire to see his parents.

She did not seem to mind about his injury—until that night. He had gone to her with all the pent-up ardor of two long years. And Julie, his wife, his beloved, had gasped at the sight of the ugly, scarred stump that was left of his arm. He could not miss the shudder that racked her slim body before she caught herself and, with tears streaming down her face, opened her arms to him.

Too late. During those few seconds while her flesh shivered, his ardor was doused and their lovemaking doomed to dismal failure.

It was agony facing her afterward. She did not understand, asked him what was wrong until he could bear it no longer. He took refuge at the clubs, in the company of men.

He still wanted her. Damn, he wanted her! But he would not make her face the ugly stump again. And neither could *he* face another failure.

Instinctively, his eyes sought the door connecting his and Juliette's bedchambers. He could hear her move about, her footsteps quick, impatient whispers on the carpet. She was coming toward his chamber, then stopped in front of the door he had shut when they arrived and had not opened since.

His breath caught. He strained to hear the knock demanding admittance. But all he heard was the swish of her skirts as she turned and walked away. He was glad, he told himself.

Juliette was young, her only experience of love the

141

four days after the wedding. She did not understand what she had done to him. He did not quite understand it himself. He loved her so, yet he knew he could never make love to her again.

But Juliette, his darling Julie, deserved to be loved. She was a scarce twenty years old and had already given him two years of her life, yet had received none of the happiness and pleasures a woman could expect from matrimony. Instead of enjoying the social whirl under the aegis of a devoted husband, she had spent those two long years with an ailing mother-in-law in Hertfordshire or with a staid, elderly cousin in the small house he had bought her on the fringe of Russell Square.

"Major!" John Piggott's raspy voice cut through the thick fog of his thoughts. "Lest ye want to go down in stockings, ye'd best sit and let me pull on yer Hessians."

Stewart sat down on the edge of the bed. "I shouldn't have come here, John."

He hardly noticed that he spoke his thoughts aloud. It was a habit acquired during his soldiering days, and John never made the mistake of thinking that a reply was expected. At times, Stewart wondered whether the batman even listened.

"I should've stayed in town," he muttered. "Alone."

Apparently, John did listen. He gave a grunt, but whether it denoted denial or agreement Stewart could not tell.

"Should've sent Juliette off by herself. *She* wants a family Christmas. *I* don't."

The batman flicked a cloth over the shining Hessian boots he had placed on the major's feet and rose.

"I have a mind to return to London, John. There's much that needs to be done. They expect me at the Horse Guards. I haven't resigned my commission yet."

John picked up the discarded breeches. "Time aplenty to resign *after* Christmas."

Since the batman spoke only when it was absolutely necessary, the sound of the raspy voice gave Stewart quite a jolt. But, perhaps, the response had taken him off stride because the Horse Guards had not been uppermost on his mind when he spoke of business in London.

He must file a petition to have his marriage voided, but he hadn't the vaguest notion how to go about it.

Stewart walked over to one of the mullioned windows. Frowning, he stared at the bleak view of denuded flowerbeds and scraggly, leafless hedges.

Must he see a bishop? An archbishop? He knew only that there was a canon law permitting an ecclesiastical court to void a marriage on the grounds of physical incapacity of either spouse.

To free Juliette from an obligation that had become distasteful to her, he was willing to plead incapacity. And he had better do it immediately, before he changed his mind.

He looked around for John Piggott to tell him to start packing, but the batman had left with the riding coat and breeches. Stewart's mouth thinned. There were times when John's taciturnity was a damned nuisance. A proper valet would at least have asked if there was anything else he could do before leaving his master.

Determined to see his gear packed by the time luncheon was over, Stewart strode to the bellpull dangling between the frame of the connecting door and a tall chest of drawers. He was about to clasp the silken tassel when it twitched out of his reach as if yanked by an unseen hand. Reflex made him lunge for it, but he missed and overbalanced, stumbling against the chest and toppling the heavy shaving mirror atop it.

Muttering an oath, Stewart pushed away from the piece of furniture. His eyes went to the bellpull on the wall. It hung perfectly still and straight.

He could not imagine what had happened, how the bellpull could have twitched aside of its own accord. Unless he had stumbled first, and as he fell his perception had altered? But he was certain — well, almost certain — that he had fallen only because he tried to catch the swinging bellpull.

"I'll be . . ." Stewart rubbed the back of his neck, as was his wont when he was puzzled.

He heard a chuckle, the merest breath of a sound, from the direction of the closed door, the door to Juliette's chamber. He heard, but he did not see Annie Tuck, hand clapped to her mouth to stifle the laughter bubbling in her, and mischief gleaming in her eye.

Annie knew she shouldn't be laughing, but she

couldn't help it. Not having encountered humans in forty-one years—save for an occasional glimpse of the smugglers far below the castle—she had not realized the power she held.

She hadn't known she could read minds until his grace arrived. She hadn't known she could be heard until Miss Juliette and Miss Elizabeth mistook her clapping for the tapping of wood beetles. And she hadn't known she could flip aside a bellpull since she had never tried to move a thing of substance. She had never even thought about substance; she simply passed through walls and closed doors. Stairs did not make her breathless. She simply floated upward.

But she had wanted to stop the major, and in that short, desperate moment she hadn't been able to think of anything more effective than snatching the tassel out of his reach. And it had worked.

Oh, it was hard not to laugh aloud, filled as she was with glee at the discovery of what she could do if she put her mind to it. But she mustn't. The major would hear her, and there was no telling what he'd do then. She had startled him enough with the bellpull and the chuckle.

Annie peeked into the next room. If only Miss Juliette would hurry! Miss Juliette wanted to knock on the door—Annie knew it as surely as if the wish were her own. But every time the young lady approached the door, courage fled, and she turned away again.

Pluck up, Miss Juliette!

It wouldn't do at all to employ the same trick again to stop the major from summoning his man.

145

* * *

Stewart listened tensely.

Was that another chuckle? Juliette, peeking through the keyhole? She must have seen his clumsiness as he overbalanced. Must have seen him miss the bellpull that could not possibly be missed.

Again he rubbed the back of his neck. And why shouldn't she be amused? For a moment, as he pictured Juliette, a hand pressed to her lips to stifle giggles, gray eyes alight with laughter, his mouth relaxed in a half-smile. If things were different, they would have laughed together.

But he did not want to think about laughs or joys they could be sharing. Besides, he had probably imagined the chuckle. Not a sound from the next room penetrated the door.

He was reaching for the bellpull again when, suddenly, he checked himself.

Annie Tuck held her breath as his hand, slowly at first, then in a desperate lunge, clasped the doorknob. Annie sighed in relief. Now, it was up to Miss Juliette. The young lady must do what she could with the proffered opportunity.

Pulling the door open, Stewart found himself face to face with Juliette.

"Oh!" She dropped the hand that had been raised, knuckles pointed toward the door. "I was about to knock. I . . . I need to beg a favor."

As always when he came upon her suddenly, his heartbeat quickened. She was so lovely, her golden curls becomingly disheveled, her cheeks a delicate pink that slowly deepened under his gaze.

"Stewart?" She cocked her head questioningly.

"A favor. Yes, of course." It was difficult to assume the distant manner he usually adopted toward her. He wanted to ask about the chuckle, wanted to . . .

Speaking more stiffly even than he had intended, he said, "What can I do, Julie?"

Juliette did not notice the tone of his voice. He had called her Julie, the affectionate name he had first used the day he proposed! There was hope, wasn't there? Perhaps miracles still happened after all.

But even a miracle might need a helping hand. She'd had a scheme in mind—a plan of attack— when they left London. His calling her Julie was the encouragement she needed to put the plan in motion.

"Stewart, will you please button my gown?"

She turned, revealing the back he had likened to that of the Venus de Milo during their honeymoon.

Watching him over her shoulder, she did not miss the flush that darkened his face. Did he, too, remember the four days he had delighted in acting her maid?

"I told you not to give your maid a holiday," he said grimly but stepped across the threshold into her chamber.

"So you did. But it's past mending now, and I'd appreciate your help."

She felt his fingers on her back. His touch against her bare skin—brief though it was before the fabric of her gown interfered—made her catch her breath.

"Stand up straight," he ordered. "And hold still."

She did, closing her eyes as she mentally followed his progress, button by button. He used to kiss the nape of her neck when he reached the top.

One of the tiny mother-of-pearl buttons proved recalcitrant. He glared at it, remembering the times he had *un*buttoned his wife's gowns.

"Dash it, Juliette! You should have rung for one of the Stenton maids."

"They are all village girls, as clumsy as can be," she said, ruthlessly maligning young Mary, who had assisted her very competently on several occasions.

It had not been a part of her plan to make use of the Stenton housemaids when she gave her own woman a holiday. Neither had she meant to wait this long before soliciting Stewart's assistance. But there had been that closed door. A most daunting sight.

However, now that Stewart had opened it once . . . A tiny crease appeared between her brows. Just why did he open the door?

His fingers brushed her neck as he worked the top button. Heart in her throat, she waited. Waited for the kiss on the nape of her neck.

The kiss that did not happen.

"There you are." His hand fell onto her shoulder. He gave her a little push. "Couldn't have done it faster had I two arms and hands."

Chapter Twelve

Juliette stood quite still. As always when she sensed Stewart's bitterness, she ached inside. If only she knew how to help.

Slowly she turned. "Stewart, I believe there is *nothing* you cannot do as well with one arm as other men accomplish with two. You are strong and brave. And I love—"

"Don't!"

His face twisted. She had been about to say I love you. But he wanted no merciful lies. Did she believe he'd forget the look on her face, the shudder that had convulsed her slim body when she saw the ugly, scarred stump of flesh and bone? She might lie to herself, feeling honor bound to abide by her marriage vows. But he could not and would not accept a sacrifice.

He spoke with stiff formality. "Juliette, I have decided to return to town. The sooner I get our marriage voided the better it'll be for both of us."

"No!"

She felt as if he had punched her, but there was no time to think about the pain inside her. He was turning away and she must not allow him to shut the door again. If she let him, she knew that everything would be lost.

"Stewart Astley, you are a selfish, inconsiderate beast!"

He stopped abruptly, just inside his chamber, his hand gripping the door as if he were about to slam it. He did not look at her.

The sight of his stiff back infuriated her. It was all she had seen of him these past three weeks, his back—poker straight, proud, rebuffing advances when he left the house to hide in his club. Deliberately fanning the flames of a healthy anger, she flung at him the arguments first raised by Elizabeth.

"How do you think your parents will feel when you tell them you won't spend Christmas with them? How do you think *I* will feel when you tell Clive you're leaving me behind?"

He spun. "Juliette, for goodness' sake!"

"For goodness' sake nothing! You don't care, do you? You didn't give a straw for my feelings when you showed your friends—and all of London!—that you cannot stand the sight of your wife!"

He was pale. His eyes flamed and the veins in his neck corded darkly. Juliette knew the satisfaction of having pierced the shield of coldness, but it was not enough.

"How can you stand there with your mouth folded, like some prim and disapproving parson!" She stamped a foot. "Dash it, Stewart! You want to discard me like—like an old cloak! You don't have the decency or the courage to say why, but you expect me to accept your decision without demur. Well, I shan't!"

"Juliette—"

"If you put in motion the divorce or annulment or whatever it is, I shall fight you. *You* may think nothing of our marriage vows, but *I* respect them. And I shall *not* agree to a divorce!"

Stewart's hand clenched. The marriage vows. Just as he suspected, her sense of honor would not permit her to admit that the vow to love and cherish could not be forced.

"Juliette," he said stiffly, "my mind is made up, and I'm afraid there is nothing you can do. I hope that someday you will recognize I'm doing this as much for your sake as for mine."

"For *my* sake?" Arms akimbo, eyes sparking in anger, she closed the short distance separating them. "In that case, my husband, I demand to know how *I* shall benefit by a divorce!"

He gripped her shoulder, turning her and propelling her with ease back into her own room.

"You can marry again, Juliette. And be happy."

He started to close the door in her outraged face. "And I would appreciate it if next time you would contain your laughter at my clumsiness until I am out of earshot."

She had never laughed at him, clumsy or not. The unjust accusation was the last straw.

"I shall laugh if and when I please! And I forbid you to leave Stenton and upset your parents and the

151

Christmas party. If you want to ruin my life, you can dashed well wait until after the holidays!"

"As you wish."

"Gorblimey!" Annie had meant to be as quiet as a mouse but was unable to stop herself. "What a set of gudgeons!"

"What did you say?" Stewart and Juliette demanded of each other simultaneously.

Juliette glared at him. "*I* said nothing!"

Tight-lipped, he bowed and shut the door.

Tears sprang to Juliette's eyes. She was in no shape to judge whether she had won the round or lost it.

She trembled all over, but with a final spurt of fury, she shouted, "And don't think you can hide from me behind a closed door!"

In reply, the key grated in the lock.

Shaking her head at the folly of humans, Annie watched Miss Juliette wipe her eyes and blow her nose before snatching up a comb. The young lady attacked her tangled curls with a vigor that boded ill for the shining golden tresses.

Noiselessly, Annie flitted off. If Miss Juliette wanted to appear bald at the luncheon table, that was *her* affair. Annie wouldn't stop her. She had done what she could for now. And see where it had gotten them! The major and Miss Juliette were in worse trouble than ever.

"Gudgeons!" she said once more, with feeling.

This so startled a footman coming out of the library, where he had replenished the firewood supply and filled the wine decanters, that he dropped the wood basket and an empty sherry bottle.

"And you're a gudgeon, too, my fine fellow," Annie said scornfully and passed right through him. "And a noddicock if you think I'm talking to you!"

The footman pressed a shaking hand to his forehead. Never, ever again would he touch a drop of his grace's wine! Cross his heart and hope to die.

Annie's full skirts swished as she whisked into the south wing. She skimmed past the library, the billiard room, the offices, the muniment room, past Lady Fanny and Lord Wilmott's chambers, and rounded the corner into the former nursery wing. Although she could not quite approve of the changed appearance, this was still her favorite part of the castle.

True, it was here in the nurseries that the fire had started. It was here that tragedy had touched the Rowlands and those in the family's employ. But whatever was in the past held no horror for Annie. It was the future that made her restless.

She stopped at the door of the former day nursery, now Lord Decimus's chamber. She heard the clink of glass, the softly gurgling sound of wine pouring from a decanter. Undecided, she hovered outside the door.

Annie had been strictly reared. She knew it wasn't seemly to enter a gentleman's chamber, and she had ventured into Major Astley's room only because the case had been desperate. Lord Decimus was a different kettle of fish. He was a bachelor, and he wasn't in any kind of trouble requiring Annie's assistance.

But Lord Decimus lived in London where Annie wanted to go. And if Miss Juliette did not make up with her major and ended up going to Hertfordshire, Lord Decimus must be Annie's next choice of travel companion. She wouldn't dream of driving with Major Astley or Lord Nicholas or the duke. They were what her mum used to call handsome young blades, to be avoided like the plague lest a girl wanted to be thought fast.

At least, Lord Decimus was old. Surely it wouldn't hurt just to make his acquaintance? Resolute, Annie slipped inside and sank into a chair opposite Lord Decimus.

She tilted her head, subjecting the rotund gentleman, whose face looked like that of an elderly angel, to a judicious scrutiny. Whether he had not been at the castle or whether he'd simply had no interest in the nurseries forty-one years ago, Annie did not know. But she thanked her lucky star that she had not made his acquaintance then. He was just the kind of gentleman a young girl in service should avoid, a charming rake, one who would easily sweet-talk a girl into a heap of trouble.

Well, he was no danger to her now. At his time of life, he was nothing but a harmless if amusing old rattle. And he looked lonely the way he sat there, contemplating the contents of his wine glass.

An impish smile lifted the corners of her mouth. Perhaps a bit of conversation would cheer him.

Hands folded primly in her lap, her feet in their buckled shoes placed neatly side by side, she said softly, "Good afternoon, my lord. You look out of sorts. Is the wine not to your liking?"

"Eh?" Lord Decimus appeared a bit surprised but not at all startled to be addressed. He set his glass on a nearby table and peered short-sightedly about him. "What's that you say, m' dear?"

"The wine, my lord. Is it not to your liking?"

"It's fair enough. But I cannot help thinking that a claret straight from France would be even better."

He raised his quizzing glass and stared directly at Annie. "You wouldn't know if a delivery has been made yet, would you, m'dear?"

She blinked, trying to erase the image of that enlarged eye trained on her. It was quite disconcerting—as though he actually, truly *saw* her!

He put the glass down. "Didn't think so," he said resignedly. "Pretty little thing like you. What would you know about a wine delivery?"

Annie swallowed. "But, sir . . . my lord! Can you see me, then?"

" 'Course I can see you. May not have perfect eyesight, but I'm not blind," he said indignantly.

"But *no one*—"

No one can see me, she had been about to say. She had been sure of it. Dash it! She was a *ghost!* Yet she had been heard, and she had made her presence felt when she wanted it. Could she possibly be visible as well?

Was this also something she could make happen at will? She didn't think she had *wanted* Lord Decimus to see her.

He frowned and peered more closely at her. "Have

we met, m'dear? I don't offhand seem to recall your name."

Flustered, Annie rose with more haste than grace. She curtsied. "I'm Annie, my lord. Annie Tuck, junior nursery maid. And if you'll pardon me, I must be off immediately."

"Wait!"

Decimus stretched out a detaining hand but encountered only thin air. The comely young girl in a blue-and-white striped gown had vanished.

"Upon my word!"

Screwing the quizzing glass once more to his eye, he looked about the room. His gaze fell on the decanter and his empty glass.

"Upon my word," he repeated. "My capacity is not what it used to be."

Chapter Thirteen

Leaning out the window, Elizabeth could hear the faint toll of the Seaford church bells. The four Astleys had left some time ago — and so, she assumed, had the rest of the company and most of the servants — to attend church on this fourth Sunday in Advent, the day before Christmas Eve.

Elizabeth had planned to go to church as well, but Lady Astley and Juliette had both protested. They wanted her to stay in bed — as though the little adventure yesterday had turned her into an invalid! And Juliette, who called herself a friend, had bluntly refused to lend her a cloak or a pelisse.

Overnight, the temperature had dropped considerably. The rain had stopped and not a cloud marred the pale sky, but the sunshine that had lured Elizabeth to the window was deceptive. It did nothing to mitigate the biting chill of the air. Having grown up on the coast, she knew this for an unusually severe cold, and if the sky had been dark and gray she would have looked forward to a rare December snow.

When the cold raised goose bumps on her arms, Elizabeth closed the window. Now what was she to do until the others returned from Seaford? She started to pace. She would *not* go back to bed, for she was quite well except for a slight woolliness in the head, which she attributed to the effects of laudanum. She might read, but, somehow, the notion of sitting still did not appeal to her.

There was a restlessness in her, an unfamiliar agitation that could be alleviated only by some form of brisk physical exercise, such as a long walk — or by the confrontation with Stenton, in which she would tell him to stay away from the beach.

What presumptuousness! No wonder she felt hot and cold at the prospect of facing him.

Truly, her agitation had *nothing* to do with dark gray eyes that had looked at her with concern, with a voice that had soothed and reassured when she came to her senses by the landing stage.

Neither had it to do with awaking suddenly in the middle of the night from a laudanum-drugged sleep and wishing she could see Stenton and make a clean breast of it, explain that she had allowed pique and vanity to rule her common sense when she denied a previous acquaintance with him.

Later, in the gray light of morning, she had admitted it was a foolish wish. For one thing, there was that wager between Lord Nicholas and Juliette. Reprehensible the bet might be, but *she* had invited it when Stenton suspected he knew her and she denied it. No true-blooded Englishman or woman could have resisted a wager under the circumstances. The deed was done and, as Nicholas said, she mustn't spoil sport now.

But what had clinched the matter was the realization that she wanted Stenton to look upon her as a woman, not a puzzle piece that did not quite fit the picture.

"So?"

Elizabeth stopped in her tracks. She was alone in her chamber, yet someone had spoken to her.

"Tell me this, Miss Elizabeth! If you're too proud to set his grace straight, how will you get him to see you as a woman?"

The voice was female. Elizabeth was sure of it. Possibly that of a young girl.

Her heart beat in her throat. Turning slowly, she scanned the room. "Who is there?"

She heard a giggle, hastily stifled. The swish of skirts, then silence.

"Who is it?" she asked again, but all she heard in reply was her own rapid breathing.

Elizabeth hugged her arms to her chest. Snippets of tales about ghosts in old houses whirled in her mind. Was that what she had heard? A ghost? A ghost, speaking to the point as though it—she?—had known Elizabeth's every thought.

The possibility that there might be a ghost at Stenton Castle was not half as disconcerting as the alternative: that she had been talking aloud to herself.

She shook her head. All this nonsense came from

159

being cooped up in a room when she should be out walking, letting the wind blow the cobwebs from her head.

She could borrow a cloak from one of the maids and explore the village of East Dean where, she suspected, a great many of the smugglers lived. The notion was intriguing, but, reluctantly, Elizabeth abandoned the plan. She had no idea when the church party would return from Seaford, and when they did, she wanted to be on hand to intercept the duke. She would not back out of the responsibility Dr. Wimple had placed on her reluctant shoulders.

Stopping only to provide herself with a spencer, she left her chamber to explore the castle. Since she had spent the first day cowering in her room because she could not decide whether she did or did not want to face Stenton, and the second day fast asleep in her bed, she had seen nothing of the castle but the Great Hall, the Crimson Drawing Room, and the dining room. She was sure a tour of exploration would be worth her while.

And who could tell? She might even encounter her ghost again.

She started with the rooms adjoining her own, which she knew to be unoccupied. She counted four sitting rooms; the rest were bedrooms, beautifully furnished, but none with a canopied fourposter as splendid as her own.

In two of the bed chambers she noted towels and pitchers of water set out by the wash stand and wondered if the duke expected still more visitors.

160

But the significance of the towels faded beside another discovery: every one of the chambers she had seen was wainscoted. And wainscoting with tiers and panels, with richly carved and bossed friezes, was perfect for the concealment of secret compartments and priest holes.

Elizabeth chuckled. Lady Fanny and Lady Harry, if they still planned to go treasure hunting, would have their work cut out for them. It could take *years* to find a hidden treasure in this place.

She reached the stairs marking the halfway point of the long hallway, the end of the east wing and the beginning of the south wing. Slowly, she walked past the stairs to the first door in the south wing. She gave the same cursory knock she had applied to all the doors and jumped almost out of her skin when a male voice impatiently bade her enter.

Stenton had *not* accompanied his guests to church.

This was so unexpected that she stood blinking at the wooden panel in front of her. She had wanted to see him, but this was too soon. And, lud, what if this was his bedchamber?

Before she had quite collected her wits, the door was jerked open.

"Elizabeth! I dared not hope to see you before luncheon."

For a moment he stood motionless, letting his eyes roam over her face, assuring himself that she truly had suffered no harm.

"Are you quite recovered?"

"I am well, thank you."

161

He opened the door wide. "Come and sit down."

Stepping past him, she was absurdly relieved to note the bookcases lining the walls, the desk by the windows, and several easy chairs drawn up to the hearth. As though he'd have invited her to enter if she had indeed stumbled upon his bedchamber!

"I was exploring," she told him. "I didn't expect to find anyone at home, so if I'm intruding, pray do not hesitate to say so."

"You're not intruding."

He settled her in a chair, then positioned his own so he could look straight at her. "I am glad we have this occasion to speak privately. There are certain questions I wish to put to you. In fact, I should have done so yesterday."

Questions. An ominous word. Unconsciously, she stiffened her back. She had wanted the charade to end. She was ready for his questions.

"And what is it that you want to ask, your grace?"

He did not miss the brittle edge in her voice, the defensive posture.

"What have I said to make you go all prickly, Elizabeth? I've even sunk to your grace again. You called me Stenton yesterday, and I liked it just fine."

"Did you?" It was difficult to smile under that suddenly watchful, guarded look. Indeed, she did not know what had caused the change in him. "Is that why you took the liberty of calling me by my first name?"

"My apologies. I could not ask your leave when I searched for you and found Miss Gore-Langton

162

quite a mouthful to call out every twenty paces or so. Now, I'm afraid, it has become a habit impossible to break. Do you mind very much?"

"Not at all," she said politely. If he wanted to question her, she wished he'd get it over with so that she could deliver Dr. Wimple's warning and be gone.

Her wish was granted, at least a part of it. He sat forward suddenly. "Elizabeth, whom did you go to meet by the landing stage?"

"What?" It took her a moment to comprehend that the question had nothing to do with their former acquaintance.

"Come now! Don't play the innocent. You had a tryst, didn't you?"

She was torn between laughter and indignation. A tryst! How ridiculous. And how impertinent. But she'd forgive his impertinence since it gave her just the opening she needed.

"I daresay you think I went to meet a smuggler on your beach?"

"Yes."

The bald confirmation took her aback. It was not at all what she had expected.

"Did you know, then, that free-traders use your landing stage?" she asked, incredulous. "I believed you unaware of the smuggling traffic."

"I'd have to be as blind as a bat or extremely dull witted not to have noticed the path leading to the landing stage, or that the planks have been kept in excellent condition."

163

"But if you know, why do you walk on the beach so much? And along the estuary?"

His eyes narrowed. "And how would you know what I do?"

"Your groom told me." She leaned forward, saying earnestly, "Don't you realize how dangerous it is to show too much interest? Especially now, when the moon is on the wane."

"I realize that *you* are extremely well informed."

"Naturally I am informed. I grew up near Lydd."

He rose abruptly and went to the bookcase near his desk, where decanters and glasses were set out on one of the shelves. He stood in need of a drink, something to wash away the taste of bitterness in his mouth.

The towns of Lydd and nearby Rye were notorious for their involvement in smuggling activities. If that was where she grew up—

He checked his thoughts. Mustn't jump to conclusions. Just because he knew she was hiding something didn't mean she was hand-in-glove with smugglers and, worse, with French spies.

Carrying a glass of brandy for himself and sherry for Elizabeth, he returned to the fireplace.

He handed her the glass. "Do you know who hit you, Elizabeth?"

"No."

"Yet, if he approached you from behind, wouldn't you have heard footsteps on the planks?"

Her brow wrinkled in thought. "I should think so. But, I assure you, I heard nothing. If I had, I

164

would have turned around and seen him. On the other hand, I was rather intrigued by the boat, and someone could have sneaked up on me if he took care not to make a sound."

"The boat . . . you said it was a cutter. A revenue cutter."

"Yes, that's what I believed at the time. But preventive officers are not the only ones using the small, swift craft. I realize now that it must have been a smuggling vessel and, I daresay, it was one of the free-traders who gave me that bash on the head."

He took a swig of brandy, rolling it in his mouth before swallowing. If she was hand-in-glove with the smugglers, she was doing a superb job of strewing sand in his eyes. She had almost convinced him that she simply happened to be at the wrong place at the wrong time.

There was just one thing—he knew that it had not been a free-trader who assaulted her.

"Don't go back to the beach," he said curtly.

His tone made her bristle. "Is that an order?"

"Yes, Elizabeth, that is an order."

"Then I wish you'd follow your own orders and stay away, too! At least for the next few nights."

Again he tasted bitterness. "What do you know about the nights ahead, Elizabeth?"

"Gracious!" she said impatiently. "Every child on the coast knows that smugglers sail on moonless, cloudless nights."

"But I did not grow up on the coast. That should excuse my ignorance."

165

"It might, if you didn't know about the free-traders. But you do know! And you assured me but a moment ago that you're not dull witted."

"*Touché.*" A gleam lit in his eye, but with a hint of steel in it. "I must request, however, that no matter what I do on my property *you* will restrict your movements to the castle yard and gardens."

She opened her mouth to utter an indignant protest, but he continued in that same imperative tone of voice, "Or, if you feel the need for more exhilarating exercise, take one of the hacks and go riding. A groom will accompany you."

"Thank you," she said tartly. Had he always been so toplofty and overbearing? "You are very generous."

"Not at all. There are a dozen horses in the stables, all eating their heads off and not getting any exercise."

She set down her untouched glass and rose. Immediately, he got to his feet as well.

"You are not leaving so soon?"

She gave him a level look. "There's no purpose to my staying since you're unwilling to listen to advice."

"And you?" His gaze held hers. "Would you heed it if I gave you a piece of advice?"

"But of course. If it is good counsel."

"It is the best I can give, and it is quite for your own good." He paused. "*Do not cross me, Elizabeth!*"

She was shaken, but said with admirable cool, "I don't intend to, but *someone* will have to make certain you don't come to harm."

"What harm?" He frowned. Damn, but she could turn him upside down. "Elizabeth, I ask you once again. What do you know about the upcoming smuggling operation?"

"A great deal more than you do, I daresay. You were born and bred in London. You have no notion how dangerous the free-traders can be when they believe their livelihood threatened."

"Are you afraid for my safety, then?"

"Is that so incredible?" Again his tone set up her hackles, which did not escape those keen gray eyes.

"No need to fly up into the boughs, Elizabeth. If you weren't so dashed secretive about yourself, I might not find it quite so difficult to believe in your concern."

Her face stung. Taking a deep breath, she made a quick decision.

"I shan't pretend any longer that we have never met. But I cannot at the moment tell you of our previous encounters."

"And why not?"

"Lud! Are you never done with questions?"

"Not until I have the answers."

"I will tell you who I am as soon as . . ."

As soon as the wager was settled. How foolish that would sound! She'd bite her tongue before she'd explain Lord Nicholas and Juliette's silly bet. But she had never excelled at evasion and found it difficult to gather her wits under that steady gaze.

She snapped, "I'll explain as soon as I'm at liberty to do so."

167

"I see."

But he did not. He only had a new suspicion. Devil a bit! Could she be another Whitehall agent?

It wouldn't be the first time that two government agents unbeknown to each other had been sent out on the same mission. A woman, however, in either of the Whitehall offices' employ was rather unusual. But, then, Elizabeth was unusual. And intriguing.

He wondered if Chamberlain had seen Elizabeth. If she was an agent, Chamberlain might recognize her.

"Very well," he said. "Play it your way. But in the meantime, rest assured that I am perfectly capable of looking after myself, which is more than can be said for you."

"You're wrong. When it comes to smuggling, you're not at all up to snuff, whereas *I* am."

"Indeed. Yet you allowed yourself to be caught unawares and rendered unconscious."

"Dash it, Stenton! I did not know *then* that your beach was a smugglers' haven!"

"I wonder," he said softly, provocatively. "Is this another lie, Elizabeth? Or are you for once speaking the truth?"

Chapter Fourteen

Stenton's words cut, but Elizabeth would not show hurt. Her look was one of pure outrage. "How dare you! I *never* lie!"

"Don't you?" He raised a mocking brow. "Aren't you lying when you say you never lie? What about the denial that we have met?"

"What a low, underhanded thrust!"

"The truth, nevertheless."

Fighting the urge to turn and run from his mocking presence, she inclined her head and, with great dignity, walked to the door.

He was reluctant to let her go and, strangely, regretful for having pressed her so hard. He shouldn't be, of course. It was his business to make her tell him what she knew.

He followed her. "I hope your cloak could indeed be salvaged. Or does it still smell of the marsh?"

"My cloak?" She whirled to face him. "What do you mean?"

"Mrs. Rodwell assured me it could be cleaned and dried. Has she not returned it to you?"

"You did go back to the landing stage! I knew it!"

Her mouth and jawline firmed with disapproval in just the way he had known they could when he first saw her. He thought she'd walk off without another word, but curiosity was obviously stronger than displeasure.

She gave him a sidelong look. "Did you see any sign of the smuggling vessel?"

"No sign of the boat or your attacker. But I met an old gager from East Dean, who warned me away from the estuary."

"Then you were already warned! I needn't have bothered. . . ." She let her voice trail, aware that neither two nor two dozen warnings would stop him from doing what he wanted to do.

She shook her head. "Either you have changed, or I never truly knew you. I didn't expect you to be obstinate to the point of foolishness."

"When did you know me, Elizabeth? Was it five, six years ago?"

Five years ago, he had still been working under the Secretary for War, but even as he formulated the questions, he realized it was not suspicion that drove him to find out about her, but pure, personal curiosity.

"Was it in London, or did we meet abroad?"

"Abroad?" A sudden smile softened her mouth, giving it a tilt he found enchanting.

"If you traveled on the war-torn continent, I suppose I mustn't be surprised that you see no danger in visiting a beach claimed by smugglers. But how

170

do you think I could have gone abroad, Stenton? The ladies I serve don't generally travel farther than Bath to drink the waters."

"I daresay a companion's movements are somewhat restricted, but I didn't know you were a companion five or six years ago."

"I've been with Lady Astley for five years, and I've held three positions before that."

She spoke matter-of-factly, without regret or self-pity, and he could not help but admire her. By now, he was also more or less convinced that for whatever reason she was secretive about their prior meeting, it had nothing to do with smuggling or spying.

Intuition and common sense confirmed his judgment, but for once he did not know if he could trust his intuition. Never before had personal interest intruded while he was on an assignment. It did now. He could not deny that he was intrigued by Elizabeth Gore-Langton. For some reason it was important to him that she be nothing more than she claimed.

She resumed her course toward the door, and again he felt compelled to detain her — compelled and prodded by some inner demon of whose existence he had been unaware until this day.

"A companion's life must be a humdrum one. Don't you ever long for change? For excitement? Adventure?"

Very slowly, she turned to face him. Tilting her head to one side, she gave him a searching look.

"This morning you have raised my hackles more

171

than once, you strained my credulity to the limit, and on top of that you insulted me. Now I am puzzled. And it occurs to me that quite possibly we have been talking at cross-purposes."

He wanted to ask her to sit down again, to sip the sherry he had poured only to have it ignored by her, and to talk to him for as long as she pleased. About anything she pleased. Instead, he folded his arms across his chest, very much in the manner of an inquisitor.

"What cross-purpose, Elizabeth? You had better explain."

"I came as an envoy of Dr. Wimple, the Seaford physician you sent to me yesterday."

It was Clive's turn to be puzzled. "What does Wimple have to say to anything?"

"He bade me warn you off the beach. As did I, Dr. Wimple believed you unaware of the smugglers' presence and the danger you court by early morning and late night excursions to the beach and the estuary."

"Ha! Two warnings. One from a Seaford physician, and one from an East Dean ancient. It appears the smugglers are an uncommonly nervous lot!"

"Be that as it may." Her voice took on an edge of tartness. "But it appears to me that *you* believe a yearning for excitement and adventure has lured me into the smugglers' camp!"

He began to feel warm beneath his collar. "Is it so strange I should have believed that? You grew up on the coast and—"

172

"Oh, fiddle!" She was torn between laughter and annoyance. He certainly had a knack for rousing ambivalent feelings. "I haven't been near Lydd in over a decade. And even if I still lived there, the smugglers *never* employ females."

"Where did you live this past decade, before you were employed by Lady Astley? You may as well tell me now, for sooner or later I will remember where we've met."

So they were back to the charade, and he believed he met her at the home of one of her employers.

She made the mistake of meeting his eyes. All those years ago she had been caught in a spell woven by his eyes — mysterious she had thought them to be. And now she knew that the spell still held her fast. She stood motionless, hardly daring to breathe. And she found herself wishing that he *would* remember and put an end to the game she should never have started.

"Afraid, Elizabeth? Afraid of what I'll remember?"

The low, deep voice held a challenging note. Common sense demanded that she ignore him. But common sense had deserted her before with regard to Stenton. Or, perhaps, the streak of recklessness that had possessed her father after the death of his beloved wife ran in the blood of the Gore-Langtons and took hold of her now.

"I am not at all afraid," she said haughtily, and then, discarding hauteur and dignity, she flung at him such words as she had deplored when they were uttered by Lord Nicholas.

173

"Would you care to wager on your memory?"

A gleam lit his eyes, a devilish gleam that made her question the wisdom of having answered his challenge with a challenge of her own. But she would not back down. She had her pride.

"Name the stakes, Elizabeth."

The blood raced through her veins. It was exhilarating—and not a little frightening. She must be mad!

"If you can convince me by Christmas Eve, midnight, that you remember where and when we met, I owe you . . . what? A guinea?"

"Chicken stakes."

Still reckless, she said, "Five guineas?"

"No, Elizabeth. When I wager with a lady I expect her to stake no less than a kiss."

Her breath caught. "Out of the question!"

"Under the mistletoe, of course. Quite unexceptionable, I assure you."

She had to admire his smoothness. "Unexceptionable to you, perhaps, but not to me."

"Why? Are you so certain you'll lose?"

She was, but she wouldn't admit it for anything. And it had been she who proposed the wager. Why kick up a dust over the stakes? She categorically denied that the particular stake he suggested added a dimension of breathless excitement she had not known since she first made his acquaintance.

"And what," she said, trying to look indifferent, "would you stake against a kiss?"

"Anything you like. The treasure of the first fourth duchess—"

An involuntary chuckle escaped her. "Which may or may not exist."

"A suit of armor?"

"What on earth would I do with it?"

"You name the prize."

A sudden notion took hold of her mind. It was ridiculous. Impossible. And quite improper. But no more so than the proposed wager.

"The canopied fourposter bed in my chamber."

"Done."

He blessed Margaret, the kissing bough, and the greenery she had lugged all the way from Bath. And he prided himself on his wits that had so timely recalled the convenient Christmas trappings.

"And you'll answer any questions I put to you, Elizabeth?"

"*More* questions? You've done nothing but interrogate me all morning!"

"You've presented yourself as the mystery woman. If I'm not permitted to ask questions, how do you expect me to jog my lamentable memory?"

"You were dashed certain of your memory a moment ago!"

"That was before the wager. In all fairness—"

"Gammon!"

Fairness . . . Lord Nicholas and Juliette had preached fairness. They expected her to protect their wager. But this was between her and Stenton.

She suppressed a sigh. Whatever made her do it?

"Very well, Stenton. I shall answer any *legitimate* questions. Nothing that smacks in the least of 'where and when have we met?' "

"That goes without saying," he replied with just a hint of stiffness.

He held out his hand, and slowly she placed her hand in his. The bargain was sealed.

Christmas Eve, midnight. When she was a child, her parents had presented her with a surprise each Christmas morning. She wondered what she'd wake up to this Christmas. She could only hope it'd be a wager won.

She thought about Stenton's guests. Lord Nicholas and Juliette had their own reasons for not giving her away, and the others, with the exception of Lord Decimus, had not known her eleven years ago. She had been introduced to Lord Decimus at Rosalind and Clive's wedding, but he was such a bumbling, vague old gentleman, he seemed to remember only that he had known her father.

She became aware that her hand still rested in Stenton's warm grip and that he was looking at her quizzically.

"What are you thinking, Elizabeth?"

"Oh, no! That is *not* a legitimate question."

She withdrew her hand just as a knock fell on the door.

"What the deuce?" He strode to the door, jerking it open in very much the same manner he had opened it for her.

176

MORE PASSION AND ADVENTURE AWAIT... YOUR TRIP TO A BIG ADVENTUROUS WORLD BEGINS WHEN YOU ACCEPT YOUR FIRST 4 NOVELS ABSOLUTELY *FREE* (AN $18.00 VALUE)

Accept your Free gift and start to experience more of the passion and adventure you like in a historical romance novel. Each Zebra novel is filled with proud men, spirited women and tempestuous love that you'll remember long after you turn the last page.

Zebra Historical Romances are the finest novels of their kind. They are written by authors who really know how to weave tales of romance and adventure in the historical settings you love. You'll feel like you've actually gone back in time with the thrilling stories that each Zebra novel offers.

GET YOUR FREE GIFT WITH THE START OF YOUR HOME SUBSCRIPTION

Our readers tell us that these books sell out very fast in book stores and often they miss the newest titles. So Zebra has made arrangements for you to receive the four newest novels published each month.

You'll be guaranteed that you'll never miss a title, and home delivery is so convenient. And to show you just how easy it is to get Zebra Historical Romances, we'll send you your first 4 books absolutely FREE! Our gift to you just for trying our home subscription service.

BIG SAVINGS AND FREE HOME DELIVERY

Each month, you'll receive the four newest titles as soon as they are published. You'll probably receive them even before the bookstores do. What's more, you may preview these exciting novels free for 10 days. If you like them as much as we think you will, just pay the low preferred subscriber's price of just $3.75 each. *You'll save $3.00 each month off the publisher's price.* AND, your savings are even greater because there are never any shipping, handling or other hidden charges—FREE Home Delivery. Of course you can return any shipment within 10 days for full credit, no questions asked. There is no minimum number of books you must buy.

4 FREE BOOKS

TO GET YOUR 4 FREE BOOKS WORTH $18.00 —MAIL IN THE FREE BOOK CERTIFICATE T O D A Y

Fill in the Free Book Certificate below, and we'll send your FREE BOOKS to you as soon as we receive it.

If the certificate is missing below, write to: Zebra Home Subscription Service, Inc., P.O. Box 5214, 120 Brighton Road, Clifton, New Jersey 07015-5214.

FREE BOOK CERTIFICATE
4 FREE BOOKS

ZEBRA HOME SUBSCRIPTION SERVICE, INC.

YES! Please start my subscription to Zebra Historical Romances and send me my first 4 books absolutely FREE. I understand that each month I may preview four new Zebra Historical Romances free for 10 days. If I'm not satisfied with them, I may return the four books within 10 days and owe nothing. Otherwise, I will pay the low preferred subscriber's price of just $3.75 each; a total of $15.00, *a savings off the publisher's price of $3.00.* I may return any shipment and I may cancel this subscription at any time. There is no obligation to buy any shipment and there are no shipping, handling or other hidden charges. Regardless of what I decide, the four free books are mine to keep.

NAME

ADDRESS   APT

CITY   STATE   ZIP

TELEPHONE
(   )

SIGNATURE   (if under 18, parent or guardian must sign)

Terms, offer and prices subject to change without notice. Subscription subject to acceptance by Zebra Books. Zebra Books reserves the right to reject any order or cancel any subscription.

GET
FOUR
FREE
BOOKS
(AN $18.00 VALUE)

ZEBRA HOME SUBSCRIPTION
SERVICE, INC.
P.O. Box 5214
120 BRIGHTON ROAD
CLIFTON, NEW JERSEY 07015-5214

"Chamberlain!" he barked. "I'll be with you in a moment."

He was about to shut the door again when Elizabeth stepped past him.

"No, Stenton. Please don't postpone your business on my account."

He had sent for Chamberlain over an hour ago and had been annoyed when the footman returned with the news that the gardener was not in his cottage. Now he wished Chamberlain to the devil.

He bowed. "I shall see you at luncheon."

"Yes. And thank you for rescuing my cloak," she said politely.

He shrugged, very much aware of Chamberlain's covert looks. "Since Mrs. Rodwell has not returned it to you, I fear it may be spoilt after all."

"It's made of wool and must be dried very slowly to prevent matting. No doubt, I'll have it by tomorrow."

She gave him a nod and smiled at Chamberlain, who stood in the corridor with his head bowed and his cap in hand, the way any respectable gardener would stand in the presence of his betters.

As she walked off, a thought occurred to Clive—a notion that was as unpalatable as it was unwelcome. He wondered if Elizabeth with her seeming frankness about smugglers and about her years as a lady's companion had expertly and quite ruthlessly led him by the nose.

Chapter Fifteen

The "gardener" sprawled in the most comfortable chair by the library fire, his feet crossed on the hearth, and a glass generously filled with Clive's best brandy in his hands. They had discussed Jed Beamish, innkeeper, constable, and mayor of East Dean; they had speculated about the cave Clive had been unable to locate; and now they had reached the topic of Miss Elizabeth Gore-Langton.

Clive had explained about Elizabeth and had briefly outlined his suspicions. What he did not mention was that while she was with him, giving him those clear looks that made him believe he could read her every thought, she had convinced him she was in no way connected with smuggling or with Whitehall. For once he could not trust his judgment. He needed Chamberlain's cool head, his unbiased view on the matter.

"Well?" he asked. "What do you think?"

"Didn't recognize her," said Chamberlain, sniffing

the brandy. "And I can't say the name means anything to me. Elizabeth Gore-Langton. It's the kind of name one doesn't easily forget."

"I did." Clive went to stand by the fireplace and leaned a shoulder against the high mantel. "And when I think I'm on the brink of remembering, I want to attach the name to some young girl, which is ridiculous."

"It is, if you believe you might have met her while you were on an assignment. The government don't employ schoolroom chits. How old do you think she is?"

"Twenty-eight, she said."

"You *asked* the lady her age?" Chamberlain's lean face registered astonishment. "Stap me, but I thought you had better manners!"

"Oh, I have. Told her she couldn't be more than four-and-twenty, and she corrected me."

Chamberlain shook his head. "No matter what the provocation, *I* wouldn't dare bring up the subject of age when speaking with a female. Makes 'em demmed tetchy."

But Elizabeth hadn't been tetchy. Clive well remembered the occasion. On the day of her arrival they had been alone in the Great Hall after Margaret left with the children. Elizabeth was seated by the fire, her dark brown hair catching the glow of the dancing flames.

He remembered the acerbic edge to her voice when she took him to task about his handling of the twins, but until he asked her if they had met before, she had been quite calm and composed. And those wide green eyes had not sparked anger until he called her an abominable little liar.

"In any case," said Chamberlain, recalling him to the matter at hand, "you finished your last mission just prior to your father's death, when Miss Gore-Langton would have been—"

"She was twenty-four. Said she was employed as a companion even then."

"A lady's companion. Not a bad cover for a government agent. She could've been blond or raven haired if you saw her then. Her name might've been Letitia Smith or Sarah Brown." Chamberlain grinned. "All females in the government's pay are masters of disguise."

Clive did not like the way the conversation was going. Chamberlain was supposed to confirm his judgment, not raise arguments showing she *could* be an agent.

"She is too transparent to be one of us. I knew she was lying the moment she denied—"

Clive broke off, listening intently. He couldn't be certain he had heard something, but he definitely had the feeling that he and Chamberlain were not alone.

"What is it, Stenton?"

Clive glanced at his partner. Chamberlain looked curious but not disturbed, which he would have been if he suspected someone was listening to their conversation. He was a man renowned for an acute sixth sense. He always knew when he was followed,

180

even if his pursuer was as soft-footed as a cat. He knew when a pistol was trained on him, without having heard the betraying click of the hammer drawn back.

"It's nothing." Clive relaxed muscles which had tensed at the first feeling of unease. If Chamberlain did not sense anything amiss, then nothing was. "I'm a bit jumpy. That's all."

"I've never known you to suffer from a nervous disposition."

"No, but when we last worked together, I hadn't been retired for four years. You've quit government service less than six months ago, so you wouldn't know what inactivity and boredom do to a man. But you will in a year or two."

Chamberlain raised a skeptical brow. "If you say so. Tell me, is it because of the mysterious Miss Gore-Langton that you feel jumpy?"

"No. Mind you, I shan't feel easy about her until I know what game she's playing at, but she has nothing to do with my feeling on edge."

"Then I can only assume it's this ancestral pile of yours that's getting on your nerves. Old houses, especially castles, do that to some people."

Clive looked from Chamberlain's face, which was perfectly grave, to the glass in the older man's hand. "You can't be foxed. You've hardly tasted the brandy. I must assume you're touched in your upper works. Dammit, Chamberlain! What's the castle got to do with anything?"

"You should hear the talk in the servants' hall

181

when your butler and housekeeper aren't around to put a stop to it. There's a ghost here at Stenton. Didn't you know?"

Again, Clive was aware of something—it wasn't unease exactly, but a sensation he couldn't define. It was a feeling he'd had before. Here in the library, when he was talking with Nick. And in the corridor, when he imagined he was accompanied by a silent shadow.

He shrugged the feeling off. "Next you'll be telling me that you believe in ghosts."

"*I* don't, but . . ." Chamberlain stretched in the chair and rested his gaze suggestively on Clive.

"Rot! Not I," said Clive, more amused than annoyed. "Ghosts and spooks are for old women like Nurse Gertrud. She didn't want Adam and Grace to stay in the former nursery wing in case it's haunted. Insisted that they all be moved to the west wing instead."

"I've met the nurse. Splendid woman. No nonsense about her."

"She's foolish enough to talk of ghosts. I only hope she has the sense not to do it in front of the children."

"No need to worry about that. Nurse Gertrud don't want the nipperkins alarmed. Threatened dire consequences if the nursery maids so much as breathe a word in their presence."

Clive gave a snort. "They wouldn't be in the least afraid, those imps. Quite the contrary. Day *and night,* just when we want them underfoot the least, they'd be all over the place trying to catch a glimpse of a ghost that doesn't exist."

Annie Tuck, having slipped into the library and seated herself in the chair behind the desk some time earlier, pursed her mouth. So she didn't exist, did she?

"About Elizabeth," said Clive, bending to put another log on the fire. "We cannot overlook the possibility that she's in league with the smugglers."

"Gudgeon," muttered Annie.

Clive did not drop the piece of wood, but it was a near thing. He might agree that he was a gudgeon, even if he had raised the argument only as a devil's advocate. But the dark mutter had come from the back of the room, from the direction of the desk, and not from Chamberlain in his chair by the hearth.

Just in case, however, he asked, "Did you say something, Chamberlain?"

"Not yet. Was about to tell you, though, that this is a devilish fine brandy."

"And not smuggled either," said Annie.

Clive's hand tightened on the grip of the long iron poker. Dammit! There was that voice again. And Chamberlain just sat there, quite unconcerned. What the deuce was going on? With vicious thrusts, Clive stoked the glowing embers.

"About Miss Gore-Langton," said Chamberlain, "I'm inclined to believe she is what she claims to be. A lady's companion."

"Well, now." Annie nodded approvingly. "There's a sensible lad."

Clive's hand jerked, but Chamberlain was unmoved by the praise. It seemed he was unaware of the voice Clive heard so clearly.

"Smugglers are a strange lot." Chamberlain paused for a swallow of brandy. "They don't like to involve womenfolk. Not even as a land contact. And it seems a bit farfetched to suspect the young lady as a go-between for Bonaparte's agents."

Listening grimly for another uninvited comment, Clive said, "I certainly don't want to suspect her of treason."

"No need to, I'd say. Hertfordshire is hardly the place where spies congregate, and didn't you say she's lived with the Astleys several years?"

"Five years."

Or so Elizabeth said. At the time, he had seen no reason to disbelieve her. But he had remembered something that might shed a different light on the matter.

"The devil of it is, when the Astleys came to town two years ago for Juliette and Stewart's wedding, Lady Astley did not have a companion. At least, she didn't have Elizabeth with her. I would *not* have forgotten in just two years."

"Humbug!" said Annie. "Forgetting is what gentlemen do best."

Clive had had enough. Dropping the poker, he turned swiftly to face the desk.

Suddenly, the library seemed stifling hot. So hot

that he had difficulty seeing clearly. How else could he explain the sight of a pen moving across a sheet of paper without a guiding hand to steady it?

"Chamberlain!"

Chamberlain raised a lazy brow.

"Look at the desk!"

Clive strode across the room, but before he reached the desk, before Chamberlain had shifted in the chair to observe him with a look of astonishment, the pen dropped onto the blotter in a splattering of ink.

Clive stopped abruptly, his eyes on a sheet of crested vellum. In an unformed hand someone had written, *Goasts Do Eggsist!*

"Stenton?" Unhurried, Chamberlain crossed to his side. "Do you care to explain?"

Clive heard a gleeful chuckle, the whisper of skirts moving around the desk, passing so close to him that he could almost feel the material brushing against his leg. Then the sound seemed to be swallowed by the bookcase on his right.

Knowing he'd see nothing, no secret door or panel, he didn't even turn his head but snatched up the sheet of paper and thrust it at Chamberlain.

"Explain?" he said hoarsely. "I? Not on your life! I'll leave *you* to explain the voice that joined our conversation. *You* may explain the writing. After all, it was *you* who told me there's a ghost at Stenton."

"You heard a voice? Then you *do* believe in ghosts."

"Devil a bit! I don't. Out with it, Chamberlain!

185

What fiendish tricks did you employ to make me see a pen writing on its own accord and to make me hear someone I cannot see?"

Chamberlain frowned. "It's a strange thing about ghosts. I don't believe in 'em. Never heard one and never saw one. Yet this is the second time I was in the same room with someone who did encounter a ghost while I was right there."

Against his will, Clive was intrigued. "When was the first time?"

"In '02, just before the Treaty of Amiens. I was in Venice with Bunting and Weatherby. You know them, I believe?"

Clive knew the men. They were two of the wiliest government agents. They still worked for the Secretary for War.

"We were staying at one of the palazzos. With friends, we believed. We were about to have dinner with our host. Suddenly Weatherby rose from the table and made our apologies. Said we were dead tired and could we take some food to our rooms."

"Weatherby is *never* tired."

"Exactly. But Bunting and I knew better than to contradict him. Our host was very obliging. Had a servant pile most of the food on a tray. Also several bottles of wine. Once we were in Weatherby's room, with the door locked, Weatherby opened the window and tossed all the food to the dogs roaming in our host's garden."

"He suspected it was poisoned."

Chamberlain shook his head. "He didn't suspect.

He *knew*. A lady whose portrait hung in the gallery and who'd been dead for close to a century told him the food was poisoned."

"Are you saying Weatherby encountered a ghost?"

"Must have. He swore he saw her and heard her as clear as if she were a living person. Bunting, too, finally admitted he'd heard whispers about the food, but he didn't see anyone. The dogs, by the way, were dead an hour later, and we made good our escape."

"Dammit, Chamberlain, and you accused *me* of believing in ghosts. It's you who believes."

"I don't," Chamberlain said apologetically. "That's why, I suspect, I never hear or see anything when others do."

Clive gave a shaky laugh. "Have you looked at the paper I gave you? *I* didn't write it."

His face inscrutable, Chamberlain gazed at the writing for a long moment. Finally, a low, rumbling laugh shaking his lean frame, he handed it back to Clive.

"I'm willing to believe that you heard some ghostly voice, just as I was forced to believe Weatherby and Bunting heard a warning. But this writing . . . how old are your niece and nevvy, Stenton?"

"Nine, but—"

"You ought to check the credentials of their tutor and governess. The spelling is atrocious."

Clive nodded absently. Adam's spelling was exemplary, but Grace would never be accused of being a bluestocking. The explanation was comfortable—or would be if he could forget seeing the pen move by itself. And what about the voice he, but not Chamberlain, had heard?

He inserted a finger behind the band of his collar and tugged. The library *was* stifling. Enough to cloud a man's brain. What with the heat and all that talk of ghosts and spooks, he must have imagined the whole.

Or Chamberlain—although Clive had never known him to be a jokester—had played a trick on him after all.

He looked at the pen, the ink stains on the blotter. Slowly, he stretched out a hand and touched the nib of the pen. A faint blue mark graced the tip of his index finger. *The deuce!*

Chamberlain finished the last of his brandy. Setting the glass on the desk, he said, "I'd best be going. Even an impudent dog like me wouldn't dare take up more than an hour of your time discussing the gardens."

With an effort, Clive turned his attention to matters more mundane and also more important than the improbable existence of a ghost.

"Yes, go. Come dusk, Nicholas or I will be on the southeast tower watching for your signal."

"So your indolent friend is still set on taking part in the operation?"

"He'll definitely help keep watch. I won't let him back off from that. As for the second phase . . ." Clive shrugged.

"A third man might come in handy," said Chamberlain. "I don't like it that we don't know exactly where the cave is located."

"I don't like it either. But there's nothing to be done about it—unless *you* would like to knock out a couple of toothless ancients?"

"No, thanks. Not if it's old Will," Chamberlain said dryly. "He's been uncommonly kind to me. Always lets me buy him a drink. And there's another one—I forget his name—but he has a granddaughter."

This made Clive grin. "I cannot tell you which of the old gagers is presently on guard. There seems to be no end of them. I've sneaked down to the estuary three times since my meeting with Will, and every time I encountered a different set of ancients."

Chamberlain started for the door. "They're sent by Beamish, but even though the innkeeper may have been in charge of the smuggling operation at one time, he is not now. He's as afraid as the rest of the men I've met in the village. And Jed Beamish, I'd say, is not a man easily frightened."

"I've crossed the Channel many a time in a smuggling vessel," Clive said pensively. "But not once did I encounter a frightened or timid free-trader. I very much suspect this lot went in way over their heads."

"The men don't talk about it, but the granddaughter I mentioned, she let slip that there've been two deaths recently. Two young men, come to grief on the cliffs they'd been climbing since the day they were breeched."

Clive's mouth tightened. "I don't suppose the

189

deaths can be blamed on a falling out among the smugglers, or on a rival gang?"

"In that case, the men would be furious but not afraid. No, Stenton. It's my belief that Bonaparte's agents have taken command here."

His hand on the door knob, Chamberlain hesitated.

"What is it?" Clive's eyes narrowed as he watched the lean, craggy face. He had never seen Chamberlain uncertain or hesitant. "Is there something else I ought to know?"

"That's what I cannot decide." The older man met Clive's searching look. "A carriage broke down this morning a mile or two east of the village. The gentleman and his niece came to the Crown and Anchor, and they'll be there until tomorrow because the wheelwright—a West Dean man—refuses to work on the Lord's day."

"Did you see the gentleman?"

"No. According to Beamish, he surpasses the Prince of Wales in stoutness and is exhausted after walking a mile. He hired two bedchambers and Mrs. Beamish's parlor and hasn't moved from his chair since his arrival. Sounds logical enough, I thought."

"But?"

"That's just it. I cannot find a but. Went to look at the carriage, and it's true enough that one of the wheels is splintered."

"What brought him here? After all, East Dean is not Brighton."

190

"Told Beamish he's from Shropshire, visiting relatives in Bournemouth. This morning, seeing the sun for the first time in days, he decided to go for a drive."

Which sounded reasonable enough. Bournemouth wasn't a great distance away, and visitors to the harbor town had always been attracted by the chalk cliffs of Beachy Head.

"Did you learn his name?"

"Morton. Anthony Morton."

"And the niece?"

"Caught a glimpse of her on the stairs. A real beauty, if you like the dark, exotic kind. She ran back upstairs as soon as she saw me. She's shy, Mrs. Beamish said. Hardly opens her mouth."

Clive considered the matter. "Offhand, I'd say about Mr. Morton and his niece what you said about Miss Gore-Langton, that they are what they claim to be. But I wonder why Jed Beamish didn't press the wheelwright to repair the carriage. It cannot be convenient to have to cater to customers at this time."

Chapter Sixteen

After taking leave of Stenton, Elizabeth continued her tour of exploration in a half-hearted fashion. Preoccupied with the wager and even more so with the eventual outcome, she peeked into one or two of the chambers on the unused second floor. The shrouded furniture, the faded drapes on windows and beds were not enticing, and she quickly returned to the first floor.

When she discovered Stenton's niece and nephew in the west wing, she was quite content to visit awhile. Grace and Adam were with their nurse Mrs. Gertrud Schwerdtfeger. *Schwerdtfeger!* Impossible to remember; difficult to pronounce. No wonder the good woman was called by her first rather than her family name as was her right.

Soon, Elizabeth was helping the children place a quantity of slim white candles in silver holders which had a clip attached to the base. She learned that the candles were destined for the Christmas tree, a beautiful fir Grace and Adam would fetch with their uncle the following day.

Nurse Gertrud, her knitting needles clicking away with alarming speed, shook her head. "I feel snow in my bones. A storm. I will not be surprised if we cannot push the door open in the morning."

"Oh, no!" Grace looked at the old woman imploringly. "Dear Nurse Trudy, for once your bones must be wrong!"

"I want it to snow," said Adam. "But Mr. Ponsonby said it doesn't on the coast."

"It does." Elizabeth wriggled a candle into one of the narrow holders. "But usually not until later in the season."

"There will be snow for Christmas," Nurse Gertrud said firmly. *"Eine weisse Weihnachten."*

Neither of the children argued, but Grace said, "Uncle Clive promised we'd have a Christmas tree—two trees—and a yule log. And he promised to take us to fetch them. He'll think of something if it snows."

Adam nodded, then started to tell Elizabeth that in Germany the *Christkindl*, accompanied by its helper *Knecht Ruprecht*, came to every house late on Christmas Eve. The *Christkindl* lit the candles while *Knecht Ruprecht* placed a toy from his pack beneath the tree for boys and girls who had been good throughout the year.

"And they'll come here, too," the boy concluded. "Because we'll have the Christmas tree, and the candles must be lit."

Elizabeth's eyes twinkled. "Will the *Christkindl* and its helper overlook a toppled suit of armor and still leave a toy?"

"Oh, yes!" said Grace. " 'Cause that was an acci-

193

dent. They wouldn't expect us to know how to walk in all that clanking chain."

"It wasn't chain," Adam protested, and immediately a lively squabble erupted between the siblings.

Exchanging a smile with the nurse, Elizabeth left the children's quarters. But as soon as the high, excited voices faded behind the closed door, she wished she had stayed. At least, the twins had kept her from thinking about the interview with their uncle. About the wager.

And the disconcerting questions he had asked about her visit to the landing stage. He suspected her of something. That she was a member of the smugglers gang? That she arranged the sale of their goods? Ridiculous. Well, he planned to ask her further questions. This time, she'd have some questions of her own.

That subject dealt with, she had nothing to do but think once again about —

Giving herself a mental shake, she took the nearest set of stairs down to the Great Hall, crossed it, and, cowardly or not, returned to her chamber by a route that did *not* take her past the library.

Her thoughts awhirl, she closed the door and leaned against the wooden panels.

Her eyes swept the room. "Hello," she said softly, breathlessly. "Are you here, ghost?"

Silence greeted her.

"I made a bet, ghost. With Stenton. And he demanded a kiss as the stake. What do you say? Does he think of me as a hard to fit puzzle piece, or has he started to regard me as a woman?"

Still only silence.

She pushed away from the door. There was no reason to feel disappointed. She had not truly expected a reply.

Preparation for luncheon did not take long. Elizabeth merely had to remove her spencer, a serviceable garment of dark blue merino that blended with the grays and dull blues she had chosen for her day gowns. These past years as a companion she hadn't given much thought to colors and how they suited her, but as she checked her hair in the dressing mirror, she stopped for a good, long look.

Lud, she was the veriest homely Joan! Her face looked thin with her hair all scraped back. The soft gray of her high-necked gown, unrelieved by even the tiniest scrap of lace or ribbon, drained her of color. No wonder Stenton did not recognize her. She was but a shadow of her former self.

Her fingers tugged at the pins holding the tight knot at the base of her neck until her hair fell free. It was long and straight and heavy. Without hesitation, she took a pair of scissors from a drawer. A thin strand at a time, she cut off a good twelve inches all around. Released from a heavy weight, her hair bounced around her shoulders, and after she had brushed it a hundred strokes it even showed a hint of waviness.

She repinned it, but much looser, and had the satisfaction of seeing the thinness of her face transformed into elegant slenderness with arresting high cheekbones.

There was no point in changing her gown. With

195

the exception of three evening gowns, all her dresses were of some drab, shadowy color. But she had the jewelry, unworn since her mother's death. She could have sold the pieces and thus might have postponed the necessity for employment by a few years. But she could never bring herself to part from these mementos of her past life.

Slowly, Elizabeth unlocked the box and opened the first tier. Diamonds. A necklace, a bracelet, ear drops. Quite unsuitable.

The second tier held a pearl necklace and an assortment of brooches and pins. Her hand hovered over the necklace. Pearls and gray. 'Twould be just the thing. But so insipid.

Feeling quite daring, she picked out a brooch, a fine emerald nestled in a web of wrought silver. When pinned to the neck of her gown the gem reflected the green fire in her eyes.

But perhaps the light in her eyes was not due to the emerald after all. Perhaps it was due to the realization that she was deliberately, willfully setting out to catch Stenton's attention.

Possibly, the wager had been the start of this purposeful scheme. She did not know. When she thought back on that moment, she did not recall a feeling of deliberateness, just recklessness and the urge to prove that she was not at all afraid of what he might remember.

Staring at her image in the mirror, she asked herself what had happened to the sensible, levelheaded woman of the past decade. Common sense had become submerged in uncertainty and embarrassment during the journey to Stenton Castle. Uncertainty had given way to pique, and thereafter her emotions and feelings had resembled a fleet of small fishing craft caught in a storm on the Channel, bounced and tossed and quite without direction.

She had found the direction she wanted to go, and nothing would turn her back. Not the small voice trying to shame her with a reminder of the impropriety of setting her cap so blatantly for the Duke of Stenton. Not the knowledge that she would in all likelihood end up as hurt as she had been eleven years ago.

Footsteps sounded in the corridor. Juliette's and Lady Astley's voices. Elizabeth draped a shawl around her shoulders, the beautiful paisley shawl Sir John and Lady Astley had given her last Christmas. She had hardly worn it, believing it too elegant for a companion. But today things were different. And the pattern contained a touch of emerald.

She went to Lady Astley's chamber. Minter, Lady Astley's maid was there, helping her mistress change.

"Elizabeth, my dear! How well you look." Louisa Astley sat down at the dressing table to allow Minter to brush her fine gray hair. "I always said you needed a touch of color, and now I see I was right. You are positively glowing."

"Thank you, ma'am. Is there anything I can do for you? Would you like your neck massaged?"

A neck massage had become a routine on Sundays when Lady Astley often returned from church with a throbbing ache at the back of her head. She said it came from sitting still so long in a hard pew and staring up at the pulpit, but on this day she declined Elizabeth's offer.

"It's not necessary, my dear. I have never felt better. Either sea air is the benefactor, or it's having Stewart and Juliette with me."

A look of sadness crossed her delicate features. Hesitantly, she said, "Something is not quite right between them. They try to hide it from me, but I can feel it. Do you know what it is, Elizabeth?"

Elizabeth did not consider it her place to tell Stewart's mama of his plans, especially since she knew of her employer's weak heart. But she had never been good at dissimulation and could only pray that she met Lady Astley's searching look with unconcern.

"I wouldn't be surprised if they have run into some of the difficulties all newly wed couples experience. Stewart and Juliette may have been married two years, but for all practical purposes, their union is only a few weeks old."

She encountered an approving look from Minter—servants always knew more than one expected!

"Of course, that's it," Louisa Astley said, relieved. "They need to get used to each other."

She smiled at Elizabeth. "Run along, my dear. I intend to give you a holiday while we're at Stenton. If I want my neck rubbed, Juliette can do it. And if I want someone to read to me, why, there's Stewart. He has a very pleasant reading voice, you know. And I never lack for entertainment while Lord Decimus keeps me amused with tales about the Prince of Wales and his set."

Thus dismissed, Elizabeth knocked on Juliette's door. Since she had slept all of the previous day, she'd had no occasion to find out whether Juliette had made progress in changing her husband's mind.

Juliette, already changed from her walking dress into a gown of soft, rose-colored wool, opened immediately. A shadow of disappointment crossed her face, but she caught herself and smiled.

"Come in, Elizabeth. You look lovely. What have you done to your hair?"

Stepping into the room, Elizabeth closed the door. "I'm sorry I'm not the one you expected."

Juliette turned her back. It seemed as though she would not reply, but after a moment she blurted out, "I wish I weren't so damnably foolish!"

"Why are you foolish? Because you hoped it was Stewart knocking on your door when it would have been more logical for him to have used the connecting door?"

Juliette swung around. "He locked it. Yesterday. After I asked him to button up my gown. I didn't bring my maid, you see, because I wanted him to help me. I wanted him to remember our honeymoon. But it didn't work!"

"You quarreled?"

"It takes two to quarrel. I tried my best to shake him out of that reserve he shows me." Juliette threw her hands up in a gesture of exasperation. "Stewart won't quarrel. He won't explain. He merely walks off, shuts the door and locks it."

Elizabeth searched her mind for something encouraging to say. She could think of nothing. Her heart ached for her friend. She wanted to help but did not see how. Quite possibly it was nothing but a misunderstanding that kept the couple apart. Juliette was young and inexperienced.

But Stewart . . . he could not claim youth or inexperience to account for his behavior. Since Elizabeth had written the congratulatory letter for Lady Astley, she knew for a fact that Stewart had turned eight-and-twenty this past spring. And from remarks dropped by his fond parents she had gathered that before his marriage he enjoyed a certain reputation among the ladies of the muslin set.

No, Major Stewart Astley was not inexperienced. But he had lost an arm. Elizabeth felt sure there was not a man alive whose state of mind would remain unaffected by the gruesome surgery. Why, her body was racked with shudders at the mere thought of the surgeon's saw.

"While I was sitting in church this morning," said Juliette, "it was brought home to me that I have never celebrated a Christmas with Stewart. With his mother and father, yes. But never with my husband."

"Stewart must feel it as you do. Tomorrow is Christmas Eve. Make him go with you to help bring in the yule log and the Christmas tree Grace and Adam told me about. Will there be carolers or mummers, do you suppose?"

"I don't know."

Juliette pulled a shawl of Norwich silk from a dresser drawer. She looked at it and frowned as if she couldn't decide what to do with it and finally dropped it onto the bed.

"I don't know *what* Clive has planned. I never had a Christmas with him either."

200

"How can that be? You lived so many years at Stenton House."

"Yes, but Clive was never home for Christmas. Before I married, I spent the holidays with Cousin Flora and Cousin Amelia. They're dears, but quite old and set in their ways."

It sounded as dreary as the Christmases Elizabeth had spent in the various houses where she had been employed as a companion. She shouldn't complain, though. The past five years with Sir John and Lady Astley had made up for many a snub and indignity and for loneliness suffered in previous years.

"We'll do our own caroling, Juliette. Let's consult with Lady Harry. I'm sure she'll want to make the holidays a happy occasion for her children."

"When we drove down from London," said Juliette, "I thought about miracles. I wondered if they still happen. For, surely, it's a miracle I need to make this a happy Christmas."

"Miracles do happen," Elizabeth assured her and wished for just a very small one for herself.

The two young ladies were silent, each pursuing her own thoughts.

Juliette was the first to break the somber mood. She pushed Elizabeth toward the dressing table.

"Whatever you did to your hair, I like it. But it needs something . . . a bit of *je ne sais quoi*. Will you trust me?"

"I don't dare. The last time you offered a suggestion on my hair, you wanted me to wear it flowing down my back."

"No, nothing spectacular like that." Juliette tilted

201

her head this way and that in an attempt to catch every angle of Elizabeth's coiffure. "Although I still say you ought to pin it up high and allow long curls to fall down the back of your head."

"I don't have curls."

"There are such things as curl papers and curling irons."

With one hand Juliette nudged her onto the stool in front of the dresser and reached for a pair of scissors with the other. "Let me see now."

Elizabeth clasped both hands protectively to her head. "Juliette, don't you dare! I'm afraid I've cut off too much as it is, and if I move my head, the hair will all come unpinned."

"You didn't do badly for a start."

Juliette tugged a strand of hair from beneath Elizabeth's fingers and shortened it to two inches. It hung straight and lifeless in front of Elizabeth's right ear. Before she could protest, Juliette had cut a strand near the other ear.

Elizabeth suppressed a groan. It was awful!

"All we need now is a bit of water," Juliette said cheerfully.

She dipped into the water pitcher and went to work, dampening the short strands, snipping a bit more, dampening again, then twisting the hair, and within moments short, wispy curls clung to Elizabeth's ears and temples.

"Now, what do you say?"

"Thank you," breathed Elizabeth. The girl she had once been was beginning to reappear. Surely Stenton would recognize her now.

Juliette picked her shawl off the bed. "Let's go down, shall we? If we want caroling tomorrow night, we'll have to find singers and practice."

"Perhaps we ought to discover first what Stenton may have planned."

"Clive?"

Juliette looked so astonished that Elizabeth laughed. "Yes, your cousin Clive. It's his party, you know!"

"Not a bit of it. If Fanny and Margaret hadn't decorated the Great Hall yesterday, we wouldn't even know this is a Christmas party. *I* don't know why he asked us here in the first place. He's forever off doing what he pleases and leaves his guests to fend for themselves. You must have noticed that yourself."

"Well, no. But, then, I haven't been here as long as you have."

"And all day yesterday," said Juliette with a quick, sympathetic smile, "you were asleep. Believe me, you missed nothing but Uncle Decimus's stories about smugglers."

Smugglers. All of a sudden Elizabeth understood what must have happened. Stenton had heard of the smugglers' activities on his property and had come to put a stop to them. Foolish man! He should have notified the Home Office. Catching smugglers was the business of the Revenue Service, not of a single, inexperienced man.

Juliette misunderstood her silence. "I am sorry, Elizabeth. I shouldn't have mentioned the free-traders. It was one of them who attacked you, wasn't it?"

"So your cousin believes."

He also believed that she'd had a tryst with that same smuggler! Elizabeth deemed it advisable to change the subject.

"Never mind about the smugglers, Juliette. There's something I want to ask you. But first you must promise not to mention it to a soul."

Juliette, who had started for the door, stopped and gave her a wide-eyed look. "I promise. What is it, Elizabeth? Oh! Have you found the treasure Fanny and Margaret are always carrying on about? Was it hidden in your room?"

"Surely you don't think I would keep that to myself!"

A roguish look lit Juliette's eye. "I would if I were you. Just think! You'd never have to be a companion again."

"True. But on the whole," Elizabeth said dryly, "I prefer the life of a companion to that of a convict in New South Wales."

Juliette giggled. "Dear Elizabeth. Always so prosaic. But pray don't keep me in suspense. What is it you wanted to say? Or ask?"

"Have you ever had it happen that someone spoke to you here at the castle—I mean, someone you could not see?"

"Of course." Juliette looked puzzled and disappointed. "When I was in a different room from the speaker."

"No, that's not what I'm talking about. Someone in the same room, but you couldn't see anyone." Elizabeth hesitated. "A . . . ghost."

Chapter Seventeen

"A ghost?" Juliette's eyes widened. "I take back everything I ever said or thought about your being sensible or prosaic. Have you encountered a ghost here at Stenton?"

Feeling rather foolish, Elizabeth admitted that she might have.

"Unless," she said, "I have started talking to myself. Which, you must agree, would be worse than speaking with a ghost."

Juliette nodded absently. "Do you remember when we believed we heard someone clap and you said it must be wood beetles?"

"*You* said it was wood beetles. I merely suspected the timbers of creaking and crackling with age."

"What did he say to you, the ghost? Oh, I wish I could have met him, too!"

"It's a female. Sounded quite young, I thought."

"Piffle!" said Annie, feeling obliged to make her presence known. "I'm not all that young. And you *have* met me, Miss Juliette. I called you and your husband a set of silly gudgeons."

Juliette dropped her shawl. The ardent wish to meet the ghost forgotten, she drew closer to Elizabeth and grasped for her hand.

"Did you hear that, Elizabeth?" she whispered.

Elizabeth could only nod. Her throat was dry; her skin cold. She wasn't sure whether she was glad or terrified to have the presence of a ghost confirmed.

She looked toward the bed; the voice had come from there. "Who . . ." She swallowed and cleared her throat. "Who are you?"

"I'm Annie. You aren't afraid of me, are you?"

"I don't know," Elizabeth said truthfully. She could feel Juliette trembling and, perversely, became quite calm. "Certainly the notion of having a ghost around takes some getting used to."

Annie chuckled. "Oh, you'll get used to me. I've no doubts about that."

"Don't you?" asked Juliette, gathering courage. "Are you planning to visit us again?"

"Of course. I'm going to help you make up with the major."

Juliette took a step toward the voice. "You are? Truly?"

"Wait and see if I don't."

"But how?"

"Wait and see," said Annie, flitting off soundlessly.

"Won't you give me a hint of what you're planning to do?" asked Juliette but, of course, received no reply.

Elizabeth pulled her shawl tighter. She was neither cold nor afraid. It was rather that she suddenly felt

. . . alone. But she wasn't. Juliette was still with her.

"I think she's gone, Juliette."

"Oh. How do you know?"

"Something is . . . different. I wonder who she is. She said her name is Annie."

Juliette retrieved her shawl and slung it around her shoulders. "Let's see if we can find Decimus. He knows the castle's history like no one else. He must know about the ghost. And I shall be very cross with him for not telling me."

No longer afraid, Juliette was as excited as a child. Taking Elizabeth's hand, she dragged her into the corridor. When they were even with the door to Stewart's room, she hesitated, then stopped.

"Excuse me a moment, will you, Elizabeth? I just had the most famous notion."

Without waiting for a reply, Juliette knocked on the door. John Piggott opened.

"John." She directed a brilliant smile at the batman. "Is the major in?"

"No, ma'am. Haven't seen him since he left for church."

"Oh, well. I don't suppose it matters."

She brushed past him into Stewart's chamber. In less than a minute, she was back in the corridor.

"Thank you, John," she said graciously, but Elizabeth was quick to note the triumphant glitter in her eyes.

"What did you do, Juliette?"

Putting a finger to her mouth, Juliette shook her head and hurried off. She did not reply until they reached the stairs.

"I unlocked the connecting door and pocketed the key."

"Good for you. I doubt you'll need the assistance of a ghost. You're doing quite nicely on your own."

"It doesn't do to sit still and wait for miracles to happen," Juliette said sagely. "Mind you, I'll accept all the help I can get, but in the meantime I'll fight with every weapon I have."

"An excellent resolution." Elizabeth touched the emerald brooch at the neck of her gown. "There are many weapons at a woman's disposal, not the least of which are resolve and determination."

Juliette gave her a sidelong look. But they had reached the Great Hall, and Elizabeth was quick to change the subject before Juliette could follow up on that look with questions.

"Now where do you suppose we can find Lord Decimus? Shall we ask the footman?"

The footman stationed in the hall professed ignorance. He had come on duty only a few minutes ago and had not seen any of the guests.

Starting with the Crimson Drawing Room, Juliette and Elizabeth peeked into several chambers before they ran their quarry to ground in one of the smaller salons, where he was sampling a Madeira recommended by Sir John. When taxed by Juliette, Lord Decimus denied all knowledge of a ghost. He was quite indignant.

"No, no, my dear! We Rowlands don't have ghosts. Quite beneath our dignity!"

Dignity? The two young ladies exchanged looks. Just how much of the wine had Decimus sampled?

"Uncle Decimus, what does dignity have to say to anything? I asked you about a ghost."

Lord Decimus poured himself a third glass of Madeira.

"Tolerable," he muttered after a mouthful. "Quite tolerable. But then I never doubted Clive's ability to pick a wine. Couldn't have been better if we'd received a delivery from the 'gentlemen.' "

Elizabeth stiffened at the mention of the "gentlemen," but before she could ask a question, Juliette demanded, "Uncle Decimus, what would you say if I told you that there *is* a ghost at Stenton? That Elizabeth and I have met her!"

"Impossible. Here, have a glass of wine, Juliette. It'll put the bloom back into your cheeks. You've been looking mighty peaked lately." He leaned toward her chair and peered shortsightedly at her. "What's the matter, puss? You in an interesting condition?"

"No."

Blushing furiously, Juliette almost snatched the glass from him. She might have finished the wine in a gulp if Decimus had not protested.

"Here, I say! Stop! That's no way to treat a Madeira." Having poured another glass, he turned to Elizabeth. "And you, Miss . . . ah . . . beg your pardon. Never was any good with names."

"Gore-Langton, sir. Pray call me Elizabeth."

"Ah, yes. Poor Arthur's daughter. Don't know how I came to forget. Try the Madeira, Elizabeth."

She took a small sip. "Sir, do you deny the existence of ghosts?"

"*Deny*—" He gasped indignantly. "Upon my soul! If

I denied ghosts, I might as well deny the sun and the moon and the stars."

"But you said—"

"I said, my dear young lady, there are *no ghosts at Stenton.*"

"But you're wrong, Uncle Decimus! I told you, Elizabeth and I met a ghost. Her name is Annie—"

"If you met the same Annie I met, you're out of your head to call her a ghost. Annie is the nursery maid, m'dear."

"Well, our Annie is not a maid." If Juliette had been standing, she might have stamped a foot. "And I don't know why you're so set against admitting there's a ghost at Stenton."

"And I don't know why you shouldn't understand." He fixed his myopic gaze on Juliette. "Surely you remember my brother, your cousin Edward?"

"Of course I do. But, Uncle Decimus—"

"You never called *him* uncle," Decimus said musingly. "Not that he was your uncle, but, then, neither am I."

"You're a courtesy uncle." Juliette gave him an affectionate look. "Cousin Edward was my *guardian.* But about the ghost—"

"Well, d'you think he would have tolerated a ghost? No, no, m'dear. Edward had too much consequence, too much pride, to allow a ghost in any of the Rowland homes."

"But Cousin Edward has been dead these past four years!"

Decimus dismissed the interjection with a wave of his hand. "Clive's as proud as his father was. Wouldn't tolerate a ghost either. Think on it, m'dear! A ghost would draw the vulgar as they're drawn to Hampton Court to catch a glimpse of the wives of that rascal Henry. Now, which one was it? The fifth?"

"Henry the Eighth." Elizabeth struggled to preserve a straight face. What odd notions Lord Decimus took into his head! "So you believe it is possible to deny a ghost entrance into one's home?"

"Stands to reason, don't it?"

Decimus paused to finish his wine while the luncheon gong sounded in the Great Hall. When the last resounding bong died away, he favored Juliette and Elizabeth with a benign smile.

"Now what do you think I'd do if my man were so unwise as to allow anyone into my chambers I didn't care to see? Not that Whatmore would dare, but just *supposing* he did. I'd dismiss him. That's what I'd do."

Exchanging looks, the two ladies rose. Clearly, Decimus had dipped too deep to make sense.

"Are you coming to luncheon, Uncle Decimus?"

"Aye. I'll just have another sip of this Madeira. You two run along."

When they reached the door, they heard him say, "Ah! There you are, m'dear. I was wondering what had become of you."

They turned, staring at Decimus. His face was pink with pleasure and wreathed in smiles, and he was leaning toward the chair vacated by Elizabeth.

"A glass of wine?" he asked.

They were quite certain they heard a soft giggle and again exchanged looks.

Lord Decimus slewed his bulk to fully face the

empty chair. He reached out and patted the air above the chair arm.

"Now don't be shy with me," he coaxed. "Annie, isn't it? I'm no good with names, but I do remember yours. Annie Tuck. And that's a very becoming gown you're wearing, m'dear. Reminds me of my youth, when females knew how to dress and didn't wear the shapeless sack that goes for a gown nowadays."

Elizabeth sat through luncheon without tasting any of the food she put into her mouth. *Annie.* First, Lord Decimus had denied the existence of a ghost at Stenton. Then, he had conversed with Annie as though she were a real person. Someone he could see and touch.

She glanced around the table which was quite informally arranged. Sir John, Stewart, Lord Wilmott, and Nicholas were discussing the possibility of taking out their guns in the morning. Lady Astley conversed with Stenton, and Lady Harry and Lady Fanny enjoyed a skirmish over the rights of a younger brother's widow versus the rights of a sister. Each insisted *she* should sit in the hostess chair during the formal Christmas dinner.

Only Juliette was quiet. She looked as dazed as Elizabeth felt. Every now and then Juliette would look at Lord Decimus, who had come in a little late. But he was quite unconscious of her stare. He was bubbling over with cheerfulness as he claimed everyone's attention and announced that a keg of cognac had finally been delivered.

212

"Has it?" Clive's tone was repressive. "I am glad for your sake."

"Aye, Symes caught me as I was leaving the salon, and he told me. It arrived while we were all at church."

"What excellent timing," said Lord Nicholas, a sarcastic edge to his voice.

Lady Fanny complained, "I don't understand. What's all this about a silly keg of brandy?"

Lord Wilmott, patted her hand. "Smuggled brandy, my love. Genuine cognac. You remember, I told you about the free-traders who land their goods on Clive's beach."

Elizabeth's eyes locked with Stenton's, at the head of the table. Her heart skipped a beat. She had expected to encounter one of the guarded, suspicious looks he had given her in the library when they discussed the smugglers. But the smile in those gray eyes was unmistakable.

It was a smile that showed appreciation and approval of a woman's looks. Of her looks. It was a smile that made her feel beautiful.

"I'll be glad to oversee the decanting, Clive, my boy," said Lord Decimus. "Unless you want the honors?"

"I don't."

Clive did not take his gaze off Elizabeth. He had known the first time he saw her that with a very little effort she could be stunning. What he had not known was that she could rouse the wish to pull the pins from her hair and—

The butler thrust open the dining-room door and

announced, "Miss Flora and Miss Amelia Rowland, your grace."

Part regretful, part relieved, Clive rose to greet the elderly sisters, his father's cousins twice removed. His thoughts were turning wayward with regard to Elizabeth Gore-Langton. Not that he minded thinking about her, but the timing was wrong. Today of all days, he needed no distractions.

"Clive, my dear." Miss Flora, plump and soft-spoken, advanced to have her rosy cheek kissed.

Miss Amelia, trim and stern looking, shook hands. "What's this we hear from your butler, Clive? Why can Flora and I not have the first fourth duchess's chambers? I particularly asked you to arrange it."

"Did you? I'm afraid I don't recall. In fact, I'm not sure I know which were the chambers of my father's first wife." Clive looked at the butler. "Symes? Do you know? Can something be arranged?"

"Lady Fanny and Lord Wilmott are in the ducal suite, your grace."

"Odds are they won't be in it much longer," Lord Decimus muttered in an audible aside.

No one acknowledged his words, and Juliette covered the worst of a fit of giggles with the scrape of her chair as she rose to greet the spinster ladies.

Confusion reigned for the next half-hour while the members of the Rowland family welcomed the sisters and everyone talked at the same time. Miss Flora patted and kissed and Miss Amelia bestowed nods. Even Lord Nicholas seemed to be considered a part of the family and had his hand patted by Miss Flora and shaken by Miss Amelia.

Amidst the greetings, the sisters managed to scold Lady Harry for looking worn, Juliette for not having paid them a visit since Stewart's return, and Fanny for not offering to move out of the duchess's chambers. Finally, after a brief introduction of the elder Astleys and Elizabeth, all but Clive returned to the table and relative calm was restored.

"No, we shan't require luncheon," Miss Amelia said in reply to a question from Clive. "Just tea and toast in our room, if it isn't too much trouble."

"If we *have* a room, dear sister," said Flora, smiling wistfully. "Fanny, my love, Amelia had her heart set on sleeping in the dear duchess's chamber. Surely—"

"Lud, Flora!" Decimus said disgustedly. "Must you always be kicking up a dust? I tell you this, my girl! If I had known you were coming to Stenton, I'd have spent Christmas in debtor's prison rather than accept Clive's invitation."

Flora's soft mouth puckered, but Amelia rounded on him. "There's no need for rudeness, Decimus. Flora and I shall be quite happy wherever Clive has put us."

Elizabeth, feeling as if she were watching a poorly written play, saw the look of helpless inquiry Clive sent his butler.

Symes did not let his master down. He bowed majestically. "If you will follow me, Miss Flora, Miss Amelia. Mrs. Rodwell has prepared two very nice connecting chambers in the east wing."

"The east wing?" Flora and Amelia said in unison.

Flora added, "But we've always stayed in the south wing when we visited before!"

"You would find the south wing sadly changed, Miss Flora." Symes held the door invitingly open. "No doubt the craftsmen did their best when they copied the wainscoting, yet one cannot help but judge the carvings inferior to the original design."

The sisters exchanged glances.

"Lead the way, Symes," Amelia said briskly. "We don't want to stand in the dining room all day."

"Whew!" said Fanny when the door had closed. "And what do you bet they wanted to stay in *my* room because they know that's where the first fourth duchess kept her jewels?"

Chapter Eighteen

No one lingered over luncheon, and as soon as Lady Fanny rose, Elizabeth slipped away, determined to recover her cloak from the kitchens across the Great Hall.

"Elizabeth, a word with you, please!"

Stenton's voice brooked no refusal. It wasn't that he was peremptory, but he was firm. And in truth, she had no desire to disoblige him.

She stopped just short of the door leading into the north wing and turned to face him as he closed the distance between them with his long stride.

"If you're on your way to the kitchen, you may save yourself the trouble," he said. "The cloak is still damp. I spoke with Mrs. Rodwell before luncheon."

"Thank you. How thoughtful of you."

But appreciation was leavened by a certain suspicion. She could not forget that just as she had warned him off the beach, he had warned—nay, commanded—that she stay away from the waterfront.

"Or was it precaution that made you check on the cloak?" she asked. "I suppose if it had been dry, you would have dampened it again?"

A gleam lit his eye.

"You don't deny it! And you think it amusing!"

"You should wear emeralds more often, Elizabeth. They ignite a green fire in your eyes."

She was caught off stride but made an immediate recovery. "That fire, as you call it, is indignation. How can you still suspect me of being a part of the smuggling gang?"

"I don't."

"You don't?" This time, recovery was slower. "Then, why—"

He placed a hand beneath her elbow and gently steered her out of the way of footmen bearing the remains of luncheon toward the kitchens.

"You expressed concern for my safety. You said that *someone* will have to make certain I don't come to harm. I'm afraid you mean that someone to be yourself."

"But you believed my concern a sham!"

"I apologize."

He frowned as another footman hurried past with a tray of glasses. "Dash it! I wish you did have your cloak. At least we could step outside for an uninterrupted talk. Why the deuce did it have to turn so cold?"

"It's winter. That's why."

A corner of his mouth curled upward. He motioned to the settle in front of the fireplace. "In that

218

case, let's draw closer to the warmth. Isn't that what sensible people do in winter?"

"And sensible animals."

She knelt by the hearth and gently stroked the large tabby curled up on the warm stone. The cat began to purr.

Continuing to stroke the soft fur, an exercise as soothing to her as it was to Madam Tabby, Elizabeth glanced up at Stenton. "I did not know you had a cat."

"Neither did I."

Her eyes brimmed with laughter. "Perhaps an early Christmas surprise for you?"

He thought of all the "surprises" that had come his way lately—Decimus's knowledge of the smugglers, the inclusion of the twins and their mentors in the Christmas party, Nicholas's hankering for adventure. A ghost? And Elizabeth herself.

"Don't you like surprises?" she asked.

"Some more than others."

"Others, meaning a cat?"

He shook his head. "Some, meaning you."

Her eyes widened. "If I understand you correctly, I suppose I ought to thank you for the compliment."

"You ought to. But I shan't press you."

Very much aware of the teasing light in his eyes, she returned her attention to the cat. "Something tells me that Madam Tabby is no surprise, pleasant or otherwise."

"The kitchen mouser?"

"Yes. She's sleek and fat and undoubtedly did her duty before she sneaked out of the kitchens.

He watched red and golden lights dancing in her hair as she bent over the cat, and he once more knew the urge to pull out the pins confining the thick, dark brown tresses at the nape of her neck. He wanted to touch the short, feathery curls at her ear and temple.

And why shouldn't he?

He flicked a silky curl with one finger. "You did not have these earlier."

She looked up. A delicate glow tinted her face. It might be a blush. It might be a reflection of the dancing flames in the hearth.

"Juliette just cut them."

He frowned at the chignon. "I wish she had done something about all those pins. Have you always worn your hair pulled back like that?"

"I have not."

"How did you wear it?"

She had worn it cropped short, very short, as had Rosalind and most young ladies of the *ton*. The fashion had started in France, some said in sympathy for the victims of the revolution whose hair was shorn to make work easier for the executioner and his guillotine. But it could not be denied that the fame of Josephine Bonaparte's beauty had contributed vastly to the popularity of the style.

She rose. "More questions to jog your memory, Stenton? I see that I'll have to be on my toes or be caught unawares."

220

"Devil a bit! This has nothing to do with my memory."

"No? Did I misunderstand your question?"

"I asked about your hair because I want to picture you without the trappings of a lady's companion."

"But, then, if we met before I became a companion, the information might help you to remember."

"I'm beginning to think that I don't give a straw whether I remember a previous meeting or not. What does it matter who you were? I want to know the woman you are."

Her heart beat in her throat. She didn't dare stop to analyze his words.

"But . . . the wager?"

"The wager stands," he said, a disquieting light in his eyes. "I'm looking forward to claiming my prize."

"I wonder why that assurance makes me distrust you profoundly?"

"I cannot imagine."

His gaze swept the Great Hall. He did not see a kissing bough or a sprig of mistletoe anywhere among the garlands and ribbons. But, no doubt, it'd be there on the morrow. Christmas Eve.

One of the logs in the cavernous fireplace crumbled amid a shower of sparks, and the cat dived for the protection of Elizabeth's skirts.

Elizabeth picked her up. Two pairs of reproachful green eyes stared at Clive.

"There ought to be a screen or a fireguard of some kind," said Elizabeth.

"Gammon! No medieval fireplace has a screen.

The grate is set so far back that there's no danger from flying sparks."

"The cat thought otherwise."

"That cat is a mountebank."

Meeting Madam Tabby's wide, innocent gaze, Elizabeth gave a peal of laughter.

"No doubt you're right. But, Stenton, would not coal be a more efficient fuel? Coal doesn't spark as much as wood, and it doesn't burn as fast. The castle is huge. It must take mounds of wood to heat it."

"Aye," he said dryly. "Since October, when I gave the orders to open the castle, half a dozen West Dean men have labored continuously to supply the necessary fire wood."

Returning Madam Tabby to the warm hearth, Elizabeth gave him a sidelong look. "At least, you are providing employment for villagers who now won't have to join the smugglers."

"They still smuggle. All of them. Unless something drastic is done, Stenton alone cannot support the families in West and East Dean. Not even if I kept the castle open all year."

"If you know that, why do you want to put a stop to the free-trading?"

She caught an arrested look on his face.

"Is that what you believe I'm up to?" he asked. "My poor deluded girl!"

She should take exception to his tone and form of address, but, somehow, it did not seem worth the effort.

"I believe," she said, meeting his look squarely,

222

"that you learned of the smuggling activities on your property. You arranged the Christmas party and came to Stenton with the express purpose to stop the 'gentlemen.' "

She came so close to the truth, and yet was quite wrong.

"Elizabeth, I swear I have no interest in the smuggling of wine or silk or tea."

Her mouth turned down at the corners. "No doubt, you mean to be reassuring. For some reason, however, your words have just the opposite effect."

He did not stop her when she walked away. Since he could not tell her the truth—not yet—it was better to say nothing at all.

She looked over her shoulder. "Please be careful, Stenton."

"Elizabeth—"

He couldn't remember when he had last allowed impulse to govern judgment. Not since his salad days, for sure. Yet here he was, striding after her when he should be priming Nick so there wouldn't be a slipup that night.

"Elizabeth, will you ride with me?"

She gave him a smile so dazzling it stirred another impulse, one to which he must not give way until Christmas Eve, midnight.

"Thank you, Stenton. Shall I meet you at the stables, say in half an hour?"

It was a little past four o'clock when they returned

223

by the Great North Gate. "I'll take the horses to the stables," he said, steering toward the castle's main door. "You run along and get inside."

"Thank you." If her teeth were not exactly chattering, she *had* felt quite chilled the past ten or fifteen minutes. "The wind has shifted, hasn't it? It seems to be blowing from the northeast."

A good wind for a crossing to France, he thought. But it'd be a long, cold night if they had to wait for a boat sailing against the wind.

Their eyes met. He was certain she, too, was thinking of boats crossing the Channel, but she did not say so. Not once during their ride had they touched upon the subject of smugglers—or a former meeting—and apparently she wanted it to stay that way.

"A good wind for snow," she said, dismounting quickly and gracefully before he could assist her. "Perhaps Nurse Gertrud is right after all. She told the children we'd have a white Christmas."

"They'd like it, those imps," he said, thinking that snow meant clouds. If it must snow, he hoped it wouldn't be for a day or so.

He wanted to get his business over and done with. Wanted to catch the blasted spy, send him to London with Chamberlain, and let the gentlemen at Whitehall worry about the spy's contact at the Horse Guards and the Admiralty. His mission accomplished, he could then pay proper attention to his guests . . . one guest in particular.

He gathered both horses' reins. "Thank you, Elizabeth. I don't know when I've enjoyed a ride more."

"Or I."

Her face, already pink with cold, turned a shade darker. Catching the short train of her habit, she quickly mounted the steps to the door.

Clive watched her disappear inside, then led the horses across the courtyard. He and Elizabeth had been out for two hours. No matter what happened that night, whether he succeeded in his mission or not, those two hours, snatched on impulse, made his visit to the ancestral home worthwhile.

They had talked. And if he could not recall many instances of having given in to impulse before, he could recall even fewer occasions when he had truly appreciated a conversation with a woman.

Ladies delighted in social chitchat, an exercise that wore him out faster than a bout of serious sparring in Gentleman Jackson's Boxing Saloon. With Elizabeth, he had discovered, he could talk in much the same way he talked with friends when they met at White's and discussed Wellington's progress on the Peninsula, the growing unrest among industrial workers, or hypothesized on the possible changes in government if and when the Prince of Wales was made Regent.

Except that he could never forget Elizabeth was a woman, and this awareness added to the intellectual experience an exciting twist of sensuality.

"Uncle Clive! Uncle Clive!"

The twins erupted from the stables and raced to meet him. Adam might generally be a little behind

225

his sister, but not when running some distance.

"Sir! Mr. Nutley says there's a sleigh in the old coach house."

"And he promised to have it all fixed up and ready by tomorrow." Panting, Grace tugged at his sleeve. "Can we go in the sleigh to fetch the Christmas trees and the yule log, Uncle Clive?"

He laughed. "You're that sure of your nurse's prediction? Miss Gore-Langton was telling me that she forecast a white Christmas."

"It's Nurse Trudy's bones, Uncle Clive." Grace skipped beside him. "They always know the weather. I guess it's on account of their being German bones."

"Gammon!" said Adam. "Cook in Bath can also tell the weather. And she has Wiltshire bones."

Margaret and Fanny, followed by Sam Nutley, came out of the stables. The groom took charge of the horses, and Margaret immediately swooped on her children, hurrying them back to the castle and out of the cold wind.

"You said you'd go straight to the schoolroom," Margaret scolded. "And here I find you standing in this bitter cold! Clive, I wonder at you! You know Adam always gets an earache from the wind."

Since Adam and Grace both wore knitted caps that fitted tightly over their ears, and mufflers that hid most of their faces, Clive did not think that even sensitive Adam would come to harm. But he knew better than to argue with Margaret when she was in a stew. Keeping beside Fanny, he allowed his sister-in-law and the children to draw ahead.

226

"Mama, only listen!" Grace's voice was shrill with excitement. "Uncle Clive says we can go in the sleigh tomorrow!"

Fanny's eyes danced. "Clive, you didn't, did you? Those silly children think there'll be snow tomorrow. But how can there be?"

"Apparently, Nurse Gertrud's word is law. If she says there'll be snow for Christmas, then it will be."

"I admit the old woman is often uncannily right. But look at the sky! As clear as it can be."

Clive's look at the sky was grateful. "Tomorrow is only Christmas Eve. Mayhap she predicted the snow for Christmas Day."

Fanny had slowed her steps until she could be certain that Margaret and the children were out of earshot. When Clive steered toward the nearest kitchen door, she said, "Let's go around to the front, shall we? I've been cooped up inside too long to shy away from a little cold air."

"The rain was a nuisance. I apologize."

She laughed. "I didn't say it was your fault!"

Fanny was still dawdling, and Clive, knowing his sister, said, "Open your budget, Fanny. You may not be eager to get inside, but I am."

"You went riding, didn't you?" she said with such deliberate casualness that he was instantly put on the alert. "With Miss Gore-Langton."

"Yes."

"I haven't had much of a chance to get acquainted with her, but she seems to be a very nice young

227

lady. Louisa Astley cannot sing her praises high enough."

"Indeed."

"She's prettier, too, than I first thought. I like her hair, don't you?"

"Yes."

"She doesn't smile much, but when she does, her eyes light up. Have you noticed their unusual color?"

"Yes."

Fanny stamped a foot. "Dash it, Clive! Can you not say something other than yes and indeed?"

"Certainly I can. And since you're about as subtle as a street vendor hawking her goods, I'll be blunt as well. Mind your own business, Fanny."

"I asked for that," she acknowledged wryly. "But, seriously, Clive. I've been meaning to speak to you for a long time, only George thought I ought not to meddle."

"Splendid man, George. You may be a silly little widgeon most of the time, but you proved you had some sense when you picked him."

Fanny was not to be diverted. "Clive, you must marry!"

"Must I?"

"You'll be six-and-thirty in three weeks!"

"In fact," he said dryly, "I'll be an ancient."

"I am planning a ball in your honor. I've invited Miss Sedgewicke and Miss Marple. Lady Sarah Wilton has accepted—"

"Devil a bit, Fanny!" he exploded. "Haven't I told you over and over that I have no interest in being paraded before a gaggle of females on the catch?"

She stopped, arms akimbo. "And how do you propose to meet *any* female if you don't make an effort to attend a ball or a soiree once in a while? You cannot meet young ladies at your club!"

"No, thank goodness. Fanny, listen. I want you to stop thrusting me at your friends—or your friends at me. I am no great matrimonial catch. I have nothing to offer a wife, save for a title. The young ladies won't thank you for wasting their time on an unworthy object for their ambitions."

"Unworthy!" She gave a snort. "You have a very nice income from the Shropshire farms."

"Income that must go right back into the land if I want to have anything at all to leave my heir besides an expensive townhouse and a great hulk of a castle."

"But you won't have an heir if you don't marry! And don't say that Adam is your heir. Dash it, Clive! Isn't it enough that George must leave his title and land to some cousin or other?"

He gripped her shoulder. "Fanny," he said gently. "You mustn't give up hope."

"Six years, Clive! And may it be a lesson to you. What if *you* have to wait six years or longer before your wife presents you with a child? Why, you'd be forty-two years old!"

"Father was forty-five when I was born."

This was unanswerable.

"Come along, Fanny." He firmly took her by the elbow. "You're shivering."

But his sister's comfort was not the only consideration that drove him to hurry. The shadows were lengthening. Before long, he and Nick must take up positions on the southeast tower to wait for Chamberlain's signal from East Dean.

"Clive? You didn't mean it, did you, when you said you had nothing to offer a wife?"

"I meant it."

Silent, Fanny mounted the steps to the portico. There she stopped.

"Why, then, did you renovate the south wing, Clive? It must have cost a fortune."

"It did."

The money had come from the government, however, for services rendered in the past. Perhaps tomorrow, if it still troubled Fanny, he could explain.

He encountered her puzzled look.

"I felt obligated," he said solemnly, "to put the castle to rights for my heir."

"Indeed." Her tone was caustic. "I just wish I could believe you."

He opened the door. As Fanny preceded him into the Great Hall, he thought about his father who had remarried for the sake of an heir. But . . . perhaps not merely for the sake of an heir.

As though Fanny read his thoughts, she said, "Our father loved Mama. I may have been only seven, but I was old enough to see that he was heartbroken when she died. And he loved us. I believe he'd have considered his life empty, even wasted, without a wife and children."

Clive frowned. Was his life empty? It had certainly been boring since he resigned from government service and had nothing but crops and fertilizers to occupy his mind. When offered the opportunity to pit his wits once more against a French spy, he had snatched at it as eagerly as a youth.

But he was no longer a young man. He was fast approaching middle age, as aching muscles had proven once or twice. And now he couldn't wait to complete his mission so he'd be able to devote his time to a certain intriguing young lady.

The heels of Fanny's half boots tapped busily on the tiles. "Just think, Clive! If Papa hadn't married again, Decimus would be the duke now!"

"Don't you think he'd make a noble duke?"

"An expensive one," she said dryly. "I love him dearly, but you cannot deny that within a year he'd have run through the inheritance. And since he never married, who'd have inherited the title after him?"

"Juliette's father. I don't know of any other male Rowland."

"There you are, then! He doesn't have a son either. The title would have been extinct with his demise. And if you count on Adam to be *your* heir, who's to say that he'll marry? Or, perhaps, he'll have only girls!"

Clive burst out laughing. "And who's to say *I* will sire boys? Or that my son will marry? Give it up, sister dear. Let me decide for myself whether I want to get buckled. And," he added after an almost imperceptible pause, "for what reason I'll marry."

They had reached the first-floor corridor of the south wing. Clive's chamber was at the end of the hallway to the right, Fanny's around the corner to the left. She smiled and raised her hand in a gesture of farewell before turning away.

Not a word more would she utter. In contrast to some occasions, when he had simply stalked off while she was still talking, Clive had been amazingly good-natured about her nagging. Anything she'd say now would only annoy him. And besides, there was no need to say anything else, was there? The arguments he had raised were proof that he had at long last given some thought to marriage.

She listened to his footsteps — quick, impatient steps. She wondered if he was in a hurry to change because he had decided for once to join his guests in the Crimson Drawing Room where tea and cakes were served for the ladies at five o'clock and wine and sandwiches for the gentlemen. Miss Gore-Langton would be one of the party today, wouldn't she?

Fanny turned the corner and stopped in midstride at the sight of the plump, gray-haired lady tiptoeing out of the nearest chamber.

"Cousin Flora! May I ask what you were doing in my room?" Fanny said indignantly and gasped when Flora was joined in the doorway by her sister. "And you, Cousin Amelia!"

Chapter Nineteen

"And bold as brass, they admitted they were looking for the treasure!" Fanny confided a short while later to the ladies gathered around a low table in the Crimson Drawing Room.

Margaret presided over the tea urn, but for once Fanny did not mind. She had more important matters to consider than her sister-in-law's usurpation of hostess duties.

"They said there was some jewelry the first fourth duchess had bequeathed to *them!*"

"How can that be?" Margaret handed cups of tea to Lady Astley, Juliette, Fanny, and Elizabeth. "The duchess didn't leave a will, did she?"

"I don't know." Fanny looked at Juliette. "Did you ever hear of a will?"

"I never even heard of the treasure until you mentioned it the other night."

Fanny cast a quick look over her shoulder. The four gentlemen standing at the credenza could not possibly hear what was said among the ladies at the opposite side of the room; nor would they be interested in the talk since they were happily occupied sampling the smuggled cognac. Decimus had boasted it was the smoothest cognac he ever got his tongue around, and, naturally, the pronouncement had to be verified.

Nevertheless, Fanny lowered her voice. "George says I'm silly. But I suspect Flora and Amelia intend to make off with *all* the jewels when they find them."

Juliette uttered a protest, but Fanny ignored her.

"I think we should go ahead with the treasure hunt I suggested on Friday. Remember, it's a small chest we're looking for, a miniature sea chest about fifteen inches long and ten inches high. The lid is inlaid with marquetry work. We ought to be able to find it. And then we can give it to Clive as a Christmas present!"

"Pardon me, Lady Fanny," said Elizabeth. "I was under the impression that there is no treasure. That a servant made off with the jewels after the fire."

"And I don't believe Cousin Flora and Cousin Amelia would cheat Clive." Juliette reached for a mincemeat tart. "They may be crotchety and as poor as church mice, but they are not *grasping.*"

"Be that as it may,"—Fanny directed her reply at both Elizabeth and Juliette—"but Amelia and Flora were here at the time of the tragedy. If *they* believe the jewels are at Stenton, it's a guinea to a gooseberry that they are. And if Flora and Amelia don't mean to pocket the jewels, why sneak into my room—the first

234

fourth duchess's room—behind my back?"

"Like you, they may wish to make a Christmas gift of the jewels to Clive," Lady Astley suggested gently.

Fanny was too polite to pooh-pooh the older woman's suggestion but managed to convey her doubts by maintaining a discreet silence.

"Lady Fanny," said Elizabeth. "Does Stenton know about his cousins' . . . odd behavior?"

"Why don't you say snooping?" Fanny's smile made Elizabeth feel a part of the family. "Yes, I told him. And typically Clive, he had other, more important business to attend than the recovery of a treasure that could make him a rich man."

As Fanny had done earlier, Juliette glanced at the gentlemen. Her gaze lingered for an instant on Stewart, in animated conversation with his father.

"Where *is* Clive?" she asked. "And Lord Nicholas?"

"Engaged in Clive's infernal *business*," Fanny said bitterly. "He warned me they may not even be in for dinner."

Since Miss Whitlock and Mr. Ponsonby chose this moment to usher the twins into the drawing room, no one noticed that Elizabeth's hand started to shake and that a few drops of tea spilled into her saucer.

A scarce two minutes later, Miss Flora, dressed in a flounced and ruffled gown of pink silk that would have better suited a young girl, tripped into the drawing room. Sharp on her heels trod Miss Amelia in a severely cut gown of dark gray wool.

235

Taking advantage of the confusion caused by Grace, who caught a foot in one of Miss Flora's many trailing scarves, Elizabeth left the Crimson Drawing Room.

Stenton had important business to attend. And he might not be in for dinner. To her mind, there was no might be about it. He would be on the beach when his guests sat down at the table.

She pressed her hands together in an attempt to still the trembling. So silly of her to be upset. She had known that he would try to stop the free-traders. Not for a moment had she believed him when he said he had no interest in the smuggling.

She glanced down the hall at the kitchen door. Her cloak . . .

But what if Stenton had left orders not to give it to her? He had made it quite clear he did not want *her* on the beach. He might even have warned Mrs. Rodwell not to let her borrow a cloak from one of the maids.

Elizabeth's mouth tightened. Chin and nose assumed a determined tilt. Without a second glance at the kitchen wing, she hurried to her room.

Flinging open the wardrobe doors, she dragged out a walking dress of thick wool, a pair of sturdy boots, and the jacket of her riding habit.

"Annie! If you're here, speak up."

There was a whisper of a sound, a breathless little laugh. "Goodness me! Aren't you in a pelter? I had a hard time keeping up with you."

"Did you?" Elizabeth's voice was muffled by folds

236

of fabric as she changed gowns. "Were you looking for me, then?"

"I thought you might like to know that the duke and his friend just left for the estuary."

"I suspected that much."

A part of Elizabeth's mind registered the fact that she had totally accepted the presence of a ghost, that she was talking to her as though it were an everyday occurrence. The other part was busy sorting the most pertinent questions from those that could wait.

"Annie, what do you know about the smugglers?" Buttoning the bodice of the walking dress, she turned toward the dresser, near which Annie had spoken. "Will they be setting sail from here, or is a boat expected to land?"

"From what I've heard, I expect they'll be crossing to France," said Annie from the bed.

Elizabeth swung around. "Pray don't change places. It's very confusing."

"Sorry. Miss Elizabeth, there's a lot of whispering among the local girls today. I think it's something his grace should know about. Only he left before I could get to him."

Elizabeth stared harder at the bed. Was that a shadow, the outline of a human shape, she saw?

"Annie, why can Lord Decimus see you when I cannot?"

"I don't know." Annie sounded wistful. "Can you not see me at all?"

"A moment ago, I thought I saw a shadow." Elizabeth sat on a chair to button her boots. "But, I daresay it was my imagination. Tell me what it is you heard."

"There's a gentleman arrived at the Crown and Anchor. And he plans to kill the French spy."

Elizabeth had half risen, but, at Annie's words, sank back onto the chair.

"The French spy," she repeated numbly.

"Aye, the spy his grace is planning to catch."

"So that's it! Heavens, what a goose I've been!"

Elizabeth bustled into action. She forced the tight riding jacket over the thick walking dress, snatched a pair of lined gloves from a drawer, and, after a slight hesitation, draped an old knitted shawl around her head.

It did not matter that she cut a fine figure of fun. This was not the time to think of her appearance. Besides, it was dark. No one would recognize her. And the important thing was to make sure Stenton did not get hurt. And, of course, Lord Nicholas.

When Lady Fanny mentioned Stenton's "business," Elizabeth had only had a vague notion of preventing his getting hit over the head by the smugglers as she had been. Annie's news about the spy put the matter in a totally different perspective. A spy encountering someone bent on catching him did not hesitate to stab or shoot that someone dead.

Despite the double layer of thick outdoor clothing, Elizabeth shivered. There was also the gentleman at the Crown and Anchor Annie had mentioned. He planned to kill the spy, but in the dark it was easy to mistake one's man.

Facing the bed, she vaguely noted the shadow again. "Quickly, Annie. Tell me everything you know."

Clive knew that Chamberlain would be following the smugglers from the Crown and Anchor, where the men from East and West Dean and from Seaford gathered before a trip across the Channel. They would approach the estuary by way of the narrow strip of beach along the Channel coast.

Nicholas had gone down the carriage track. He was bringing Rambunctious and two fast mares, their hooves muffled with sacking. The horses were a precaution — just in case they needed to make a quick getaway.

Clive himself used the cliff path to approach the estuary. It was dusk when he and Nick had seen Chamberlain's signal, two short flashes of light and two long, repeated twice. By the time they had collected the horses from Sam Nutley, darkness had fallen swiftly and suddenly. But it didn't bother him to negotiate the cliff path in the dark. He was familiar with every step of the way.

Still, he went slowly. He had plenty of time before the smugglers would get here, and in the meantime all that mattered was not to alert the guard stationed somewhere below.

He thought of old Will and his comrades and hoped that the ancients had been replaced by men with a few years less in their dish.

When he reached the bottom of the path, he stretched out behind a large boulder of chalk rock. This was the difficult part. The waiting. It was cold, icy cold. But Chamberlain had provided thick knitted caps like those worn by the smugglers. Also smocks to hide their coats when they must mingle with the men from East and West Dean.

They were as certain as could be that a boat—the sloop Elizabeth had seen anchored at the landing stage—would leave that night. This did not exclude the possibility that a second craft was crossing from France, but with the wind blowing offshore, no vessel would land before morning.

For the time being, they were concerned only with a departure, with the spy who would embark and carry with him copies of documents pilfered from the Whitehall offices. Clive was willing to wager next year's crop that the spy had been hiding in the cave these past two days. There could be no other reason for the attack on Elizabeth and for the guards when, during the previous days exploration, no one had tried to stop him.

The plan he and Chamberlain had hatched was simple—and safer than forging into the cave and getting shot by the spy who, if he knew his business, must have made preparations to defend the entrance.

They would simply meld with the band of smugglers as they approached the estuary, then seize the man who would be waiting there. The smugglers, once they understood that Clive, Chamberlain, and

240

Nick were not revenue officers, wouldn't lift a hand for the Frenchman who had terrified even Jed Beamish, the powerful landlord of the Crown and Anchor.

Pushing the knitted cap off one ear, Clive raised his head. He thought he had heard something, some small sound that had not been made by the wind or by the choppy waters of the Channel.

It was too soon for the smugglers. Every sense alert, every muscle taut, he strained to hear a repetition of the sound. And there it was. He heard it clearly this time, a scrape and then the spatter of gravel. And it came from the cliff path rising steeply behind him.

Biting down an oath, he got to his feet. It must be Nicholas. Something had gone wrong on the carriage track. But Nick, the indolent fellow who had refused to practice a stealthy descent on the cliff path, would have the guard on them in no time at all if he didn't proceed more cautiously.

Swift and soft-footed as a cat, Clive started to climb. He had gone almost a third of the way when he saw a dark shape ahead, a black shadow against the gray of the chalk cliffs. He heard a small piece of rock trundle down the path toward him and knew that the shadow was indeed his clumsy friend, Lord Nicholas Mackay.

Nick, apparently, saw him too. He stopped.

Before Clive could feel relief at his friend's good sense, Nick turned and started back to the top of the cliffs, this time with even less regard for stealth than before.

241

Again, Clive bit down an oath. Increasing his pace, he caught up with Nick in a few steps, but just as he gripped his quarry by the coat, Nicholas turned and planted him a facer that made his jaw crack and his ears ring.

"Nick, you blasted idiot!"

Even as he ground out the low-pitched curse, he realized that he was not dealing with Lord Nicholas. His friend would have worn over his tight-fitting coat the short, voluminous smock supplied by Chamberlain. And he'd have had on a knitted cap, not what appeared to be a scarf wound around his head.

"Stenton?" whispered an incredulous female voice.

A second knock to the jaw could not have hit him harder.

"I'm sorry I hit you," Elizabeth whispered. "I thought you were one of the smugglers. That cap you're wearing, and that bulky blouse . . ."

She faltered as he tightened his grip on her jacket and pulled her closer until they stood breast to breast, nose to nose, on the steep, narrow path.

"What the *devil* are you doing here, Elizabeth?"

Perhaps it was because he spoke in an even lower voice than she had done that his tone hit her as particularly menacing. Perhaps it was relief making her heart pound. Relief that it was he and not a smuggler she had encountered on the path. And then again, it could simply be his presence alone that had this curious effect on her.

The treacherous soles of her boots began to slide

on the slippery rock. She put out a hand, bracing herself against his shoulder.

"For goodness' sake, Stenton! Let's go down before the matter is taken out of our hands and we end up tumbling down like two kegs of wine."

He scarcely hesitated. "Grip my arm."

She did, feeling his muscles like bands of corded steel. Slowly but surely, he guided her downward.

He had no choice but to take her. The distance to the top of the cliffs was twice that to the beach. He could not let her go alone in the dark, and by the time he had accompanied her *and* returned to his hiding place behind the boulder, the smugglers might have passed.

Damn! He hated having his hand forced. He did not doubt that she had what *she* considered a perfectly good reason for being here. Neither did he doubt that when everything was over he would wring the neck she was risking so foolishly.

They did not speak until they reached the boulder.

"Lie down." He pulled her with him as he stretched out, stomach down, on the damp sand.

She followed his example without protest but wriggled and squirmed in a manner that reminded him of Grace at her most restless.

He put an arm across her shoulders. "Dash it, Elizabeth! Can you not be still?"

"Not until I'm more comfortable. There's a piece of driftwood digging into my waist, and the sand has mounds where it should have hollows to fit my anatomy."

This time, instead of an oath, he had to bite down laughter. Why had he ever thought of her as timid or shy? And he should have known it would take more than the lack of a cloak to keep her off the beach. The cut of her mouth and chin had told him she could be willful, and she had made it clear she believed the smugglers too dangerous for him to handle alone. It was foolish of her to have come, but it was also touching.

Gone was his anger. He had to force a note of sternness into his voice. "Let this be understood, Elizabeth! No matter what happens, no matter where I go, *you* will stay here until I come for you."

She finally lay still. His order hung between them, but she was reluctant to make a promise she might not want to keep.

"Is it safe to speak?" she asked softly. "Are you certain no one can hear us?"

"The smugglers have a guard posted at the mouth of the estuary. But the breakers are noisy, and if we keep our voices low we should be safe."

"I daresay you're right." She raised her head a little, listening. "The tide's in, isn't it? The waves crashing ashore sound very close."

"Elizabeth."

She heard the softer note in his voice and was immediately, disquietingly aware of certain circumstances she had tried hard to ignore: the arm across her shoulders and the length of muscled leg pressed against hers.

"Why are you here, Elizabeth?"

244

Lud! She must be mad to allow herself to be distracted by his touch. She had a reason for lying beside him in this intimate way, and it was not a romantic reason.

"I came to warn you, Stenton. There's a man, bound and determined to shoot the spy you want to deliver to Whitehall."

He was silent. Even though it was a moonless night, the light of the stars was sufficient to show her the sudden tightening of his mouth, the crease between the dark brows.

"How did you find out about the spy, Elizabeth?"

She stared at him helplessly.

"Say something," he said gruffly, angrily. "Dammit, Elizabeth! Can you not understand that I don't want to be suspicious of you again?"

"Hush!" Distracted by some faint noise, she raised her head higher. "What is that sound I hear?"

He briefly put his ear to the ground.

"The smugglers are coming."

"What are you going to do, Stenton?"

His hand gripped her shoulder. "Elizabeth! How did you know about the spy?"

He sounded so grim, clearly the truth alone would serve.

"Annie told me. The ghost at Stenton. She knew you had come here to catch the spy and take him to Whitehall. And she heard the maids—local girls— talking about a gentleman stopping at the Crown and Anchor. He has come to *kill* the spy."

She had no notion how he would react to her

news. When he remained silent, she steeled herself against another of his quick bursts of anger. She was quite unprepared for a chuckle.

Even less did she expect the swift movement of his hands, which suddenly cupped her face. His mouth brushed hers. Then, just as swiftly as he had taken hold of her, he released her.

Chapter Twenty

It hadn't been a kiss, not the kind of kiss Elizabeth dreamed of as a young girl. But whatever it had been, it left a warmth that the coldest gust of wind could not extinguish.

"And what was that all about?" she asked in a voice that was not quite steady.

She caught Stenton's grin, wide and boyish.

"A ghost," he murmured. "It's madness to believe in ghosts, but it's a madness I'll gladly share with you."

"I don't understand."

He placed a fingertip against her mouth, silencing her. "I cannot explain in a few words," he said, his voice a mere breath. "But, remember! Whatever I do, *you* stay here."

He rose to his knees and crouched thus, a shoulder pressed against the chalk rock.

And suddenly the smugglers were there, dark shadows in the gray night, their footsteps muffled by the sand and the wind and the smacking of the breakers.

One of the men spoke. Elizabeth could not make out the words, tossed about in the wind and carried seaward. But they all stopped, at least two dozen men, and huddled briefly in one great black knot. The knot dissolved into shadows once more. They moved on, swiftly and silently.

She felt a stir beside her, the touch of a hand on her shoulder. Then Stenton was gone, one more shadow blending with the others.

She lay motionless. Did she imagine it, or had the night grown darker, the wind fiercer, the crashing of the waves louder? Without Stenton's warm body beside her, she felt the dampness of the sand. It seeped through the thick, coarse wool of her skirt and even penetrated the stiff material of her riding jacket.

As Stenton had done earlier, she crouched behind the rock. She'd wait a few moments, but then she'd follow him. She would not stay here — alone, prey to the elements and her imagination.

And a good thing it was that she had waited, for out of the dark materialized two more shadowy figures from the direction of East Dean. Straggling smugglers, she believed them at first. But as they passed her hiding place, she knew herself mistaken.

The one closest to her wheezed alarmingly with every step he took, which was not surprising since he was nearly as stout as he was tall. Definitely not a smuggler. And his companion, all but hidden by his bulk, wore a hooded cloak — a woman's garment.

Heart pounding, Elizabeth followed at a short distance. That the stout one was the man who wanted to kill the spy, she did not doubt. No one without a serious purpose would be out on the beach on this bone-chilling, dark night. But Annie had not said a word about a female accompanying the man.

The two stopped suddenly, turning toward each other. If they turned just a bit more, they must see her. Without hesitation, she dropped full-length onto the sand.

She did not hear what they said, but that they spoke—indeed, argued—was clear from the woman's expressive gestures. Perhaps she wanted the man to turn back, forget about killing the spy. And perhaps she was trying to hurry him on. If only the wind and the breakers weren't so noisy!

When the stout man began to gesticulate as well, Elizabeth crawled closer. The two were so involved with each other, they wouldn't see or hear an elephant approach.

Suddenly she stopped. She was no more than six paces distant from the couple, and she saw that what she had taken for a misshapen hand on the stout man was, in fact, a pistol. A short, snub-nosed pistol that could be hidden in a coat pocket or in the top of a boot. And it looked as if he was threatening his companion with the deadly toy.

Lud, what a bumble-broth! She could understand that he wanted to shoot a spy. Many Englishmen, including good-natured Sir John Astley, had very strong views on spies and French agents. But shoot his companion merely because they had a falling-out?

Her fingers dug into the sand. Most likely, she quite misunderstood the situation. But if she did not? Confound it! She couldn't just do nothing. She might be a bloody fool, confronting an irate man armed with a pistol. But at least she would not, later, have to face that, but for a want of pluck and determination, she might have saved the woman's life.

"Stop it!"

She had not shouted. Indeed, she had not spoken above a loud, urgent whisper. But the two swung around as though a cannon ball had exploded at their feet.

With sublime disregard for the pistol that now pointed its nose at her, Elizabeth scrambled to her feet.

"Sir, you mustn't shoot now!"

"Hell and damnation!" He had a deep, cultured voice. "Where the deuce did you spring from?"

Clutching the skirt of her gown, she hurried toward him. She must keep talking. And it didn't matter whether she made sense or not as long as she could distract him.

"Sir, the smugglers! They'd overpower you before you had time to reload. And then where would you be when the spy turns up?"

Breathing noisily, he positioned himself in front of his companion.

"Who the devil are you?"

"I'm Elizabeth Gore-Langton. And I strongly advise you to put away that pistol. You'd go to the gallows for sure if you were to shoot two women."

"He will not shoot *me*." The woman's voice, low and angry, had a curious inflection. "But if you do not leave this very instant, it will be *you —*"

"Hush, Gabrielle!"

"No, my friend, I will not hush. It is my fault that we find ourselves in a situation most awkward. Had I not raised this great big argument about staying behind, she would not have caught us. So, naturally, it is *I* who must make her go away."

Elizabeth had listened to the impassioned speech with some interest. As soon as Gabrielle — the name had already given her a clue — paused for breath, she said, "You're French. But not, I take it, the spy."

"Go away!" Stepping around the stout man who tried in vain to silence her, Gabrielle advanced on Elizabeth. "You are quite mad with all that talk about spies. And you are very much in the way, let me tell you! We have come on an errand that is most important."

"I know," Elizabeth said placidly. The longer she kept the pair talking, the more time Stenton would have to do his duty by the spy. "And, like you, I have the greatest dislike of being told to stay behind."

"Ah, that is something I understand well."

Elizabeth wished she could see Gabrielle. The voice was that of a young lady of good family, one who had lived in England for a long time. An *émigrée* who hated Bonaparte? That would explain why she was with an Englishman determined to kill one of Bonaparte's agents.

Gabrielle faced the stout man. "My friend, if she won't go away, this Elizabeth Gore-Langton, she will have to come with us."

Even the sweeping gusts of wind could not drown the ominous click that told Elizabeth the pistol was now cocked.

"Just what I was thinking, my dear." The man drew a wheezing breath. "Come along, Miss Gore-Langton."

He sounded more resigned than menacing, but Elizabeth decided not to take chances. Besides, if she could not keep the pair away from the spy, she might as well go with them. For where the spy was, there, too, would be Stenton. And Stenton, Annie had assured her, needed the spy alive.

Walking ahead with Gabrielle, she heard the stout man mutter, "Had it all planned, down to the smallest detail. Where the devil did I go wrong?

One of the smugglers in front of Clive gave him a hard stare over his shoulder. After a moment, he stopped and bent, fiddling with his boot until Clive caught up, then, quite naturally, fell into step beside him. It was Chamberlain.

"What's going on?" asked Clive. "Far too many hands to man one sloop."

"Can't figure it out," Chamberlain said grimly. "Half of the men are land-smugglers, yet no cargo is expected. That much I did learn, but no more. They're as close as oysters about tonight."

"At least it won't immediately be obvious that their number has increased by two."

"Hmm," Chamberlain said absently. "What I don't like is that Beamish is here. The way I understand it, he never comes down to the beach. Directs every operation from the Crown and Anchor."

"Is his unexpected guest here as well?"

"The fat man whose coach broke down? No. What makes you ask?"

"Elizabeth warned me that the gentleman at the inn plans to kill our man."

Chamberlain stared. "What the devil does *she* know about the business?"

There was no time for long explanations. The ground was subtly changing and the gale, instead of blowing from the right, hit them full in the face. They had made the turn north along the estuary. He and Chamberlain must soon split up to be certain they'd catch the spy as he joined the smugglers gang.

So he said only, "The maids, the local wenches, were gossiping."

"The deuce! A dead spy cannot talk. If it's true—" Chamberlain contemplated the implications in silence. "Beamish bedamned! He had me convinced the gent was too stout to walk from his chamber to the common room."

"Which one is Beamish?"

"The tall one in front."

"Do you join him, then. That way, you'll see our man first if he's already at the landing stage, and you can drop a word of caution in the innkeeper's ear. I'll walk on the right flank, in case the Frenchie is coming from the cave."

"Aye. We'll just have to play our cards as they're dealt."

Clive waited until Chamberlain had made his way to the front of the band before he edged to the right, toward the cliffs. What a mission this had turned out to be! He did not know whether to curse or to laugh.

His plan had called for two experienced agents to catch the spy: himself and Chamberlain. It should have been simple and straightforward. They had done it often enough.

But before they ever reached Stenton, Nick had demanded his share in the "adventure," as he called it. And just when Clive believed Elizabeth safely out of the way, she must needs thrust her pert nose into the business once more—on the instigation of a *ghost!*

Then there was the man who, if the ghost could be believed, planned to kill the agent. Clive did not like to engage in idle speculation, but two possibilities came to mind without any effort on his part. The man could be an assassin employed by the smugglers, or the traitor at Whitehall had gotten wind of the operation and decided to eliminate the French agent who could point a finger at him.

Whichever was the case, he and Chamberlain would do their damnedest to keep the blasted spy alive until—

He was brought up short by a shout from the front.

"Beamish, *mon ami!* I did not expect you, but since you 'ave come all the way from your so 'ospitable inn, tell me if this man is a friend of yours."

The smugglers had all come to a stop. No one

spoke, but Clive felt unease and tension surrounding him like some tangible matter. Pushing past a dozen or more of the free-traders, he saw Nicholas, hands raised high, facing them. Behind Nick, barely visible since he was clad all in black, stood the man who had challenged the innkeeper.

The French agent. Clive had instantly recognized the voice, as must have Chamberlain. They had encountered him before. Jean-Pierre Duval, the wiliest, most ruthless of French agents, originally trained as a police spy by Josef Fouché, the notorious French Minister of Police. If Duval realized what a trump he held in Lord Nicholas Mackay, it would be very difficult to bluff him. Impossible, if he recognized Chamberlain or Clive.

Clive touched his coat pocket beneath the concealing smock, but made no attempt to withdraw the small gun hidden there. It could serve no purpose.

He saw Chamberlain whisper to the tall free-trader he had pointed out as Beamish. When the innkeeper stepped slowly forward, Chamberlain retreated into the ranks of the smugglers.

"That is quite far enough, Beamish, *mon ami.*"

The Frenchman's right hand remained hidden behind Nicholas's back. His left pointed a pistol at Beamish.

"It's a pepperbox pistol," whispered Chamberlain, stopping at Clive's side. "Eight blasted shots. That's what has everyone petrified."

The innkeeper from East Dean took one more step. "Put up your barking irons, Duval. That's one of my men you got there. One of the guards I

255

posted for your protection."

"Ah, well. In that case, I think, 'e will not object to boarding the sloop with me, *n'est-ce pas?*"

"Not in the least," said Beamish. "But I do not see what good he would do on the boat. He's a land-smuggler."

The pistol in Duval's hand prescribed a circle. "As are most of your friends, eh?"

"Aye. We're expecting a cargo in an hour or so."

"Not with this gale," the Frenchman said softly.

"We'll wait however long it takes. But if the *Louise* has arrived, you ought to prepare to sail. The tide's turning."

Clive nudged Chamberlain. "Let's go. I'll warn Nicholas."

"Will he react quickly enough?"

"He had better," Clive said grimly.

Swiftly, the two men pushed forward. As they reached the front line of smugglers, who had not moved or made a sound, an excited, unmistakably female voice cut through the night.

"Monsieur Duval! Wait! I have another dispatch for you."

Clive knew the voice did not belong to Elizabeth, yet for a moment he stood paralyzed. He did not like females in this business. Never had. Never would. Even Chamberlain was caught by surprise and hesitated.

Waving a folded paper, a slender, cloaked figure swept past them.

"Here you are, *monsieur*. I am so glad I was in

256

time."

"Sacre-bleu!" Duval took a hasty step backward. "Get out of the way, *mademoiselle.*"

She kept going despite the Frenchman's threatening gestures with his pistol.

Clive and Chamberlain started to move toward Duval at the same time.

"Nick!" shouted Clive, but the warning was lost in a sudden uproar of voices and the blast of pistol shots. Three shots.

He had seen one flash from Duval's pepperbox but neither knew nor cared who had fired the other two shots. For, etched in his mind as he leaped at the Frenchman and pinned him to the ground, were two voices rising above indistinguishable shouts.

He had heard Nicholas exclaim, "Gabrielle! Great Scot! I must be going mad."

And he had heard Elizabeth, her voice fierce if a little breathless. "I am sorry, sir. But I *cannot* let you shoot that spy."

Elizabeth, who was supposed to have stayed hidden behind the boulder until he came for her.

Chapter Twenty-one

"Bête!" Duval struggled weakly. "Get off, you fool. Do you not know that I am 'urt?"

The clamor at Clive's back rose to a crescendo. Fear for Elizabeth, who for some reason was in the smugglers' midst, twisted his insides. But he must keep his attention on the French agent. Chamberlain would have to look after Elizabeth. And after Nick, who should have been somewhere nearby but wasn't.

Clive eased his weight off Duval, but kept the man's arms pinned to the ground. "Where are you hurt?"

"My shoulder."

"Your grace." Beamish, innkeeper, mayor, and constable of East Dean, dropped down on one knee beside them. "You can let him go. I've got his pepperbox and he knows I'll gladly use it."

"He had two guns."

Beamish stepped around them and after some groping in the dry marsh grass found the pistol Duval had held at Nicholas's back. He pointed that gun also at the Frenchman.

"Chamberlain explained, your grace. I won't let him get away, I swear. And you needn't fear neither that I'll blow his brains out. Although," he added ruminatively, "it'd give me great pleasure, it would."

Clive waited no longer. He sprang to his feet and swung around, his eyes anxiously searching among the smugglers. The shots—or the downing of the French agent—had released the men from immobility. They tromped about, shouting and arguing like merrymakers at a fair and making it difficult to pick out the one person he sought.

He saw Nicholas standing off to the side with the cloaked woman. But not even the startling sight of his friend's hand beneath the woman's chin and his arm around her waist made Clive forget his purpose.

And then he saw her. Elizabeth. She knelt beside the prone figure of a large man, whose upper torso was supported in Chamberlain's strong arms.

In a few long strides he was at her side. He gripped her shoulders, pulling her to her feet.

Her eyes widened. "Stenton! How you startled me."

"You deserve worse." His grip tightened under an onslaught of jumbled emotions. "Elizabeth, are you all right?"

"Yes, of course I am. It is the gentleman who is injured."

"Nothing but a scratch," said the corpulent man on the ground. "I'll be fine as soon as I'm on my feet."

Clive took a good look at the fleshy face, the broad forehead topped by a full head of longish gray hair which gave the man a leonine appearance.

"Sylvester Throckmorton! I'll be damned!"

"You know him?" Elizabeth faltered. Had she made a mistake? Perhaps it was not the stout man, after all, Annie had warned her about. "Was he not, then, trying to interfere with your business, Stenton?"

Chamberlain answered. "He was, indeed, Miss Gore-Langton."

To Stenton he said, "Meet Anthony Morton, the gentleman from the Crown and Anchor who took such care not to be seen by anyone. Very clever. Had I caught a glimpse of him, I'd have recognized him as Mr. John Smith who engaged me in late October to trace a certain young gentleman in France."

"Help me up!" demanded Throckmorton.

His mind seething, Clive gave him a distracted look. Sylvester Throckmorton was the man who had lured Nick's latest flirt away, the young French lady, the diamond of the first water. Sylvester Throckmorton had friends in the Horse Guards as well as the Admiralty.

He said, "You have some explaining to do, sir. But let's get you to the castle first. Explanations can wait until the physician has seen you."

"Don't need a physician to quack me. The ball only grazed my hand. Duval's doing, I suppose. He's a damned poor shot. Reason I'm down is that Miss Gore-Langton *pushed* me."

"You were going to shoot the spy," Elizabeth said indignantly. "Even though I explained that Stenton must take him to Whitehall."

Chamberlain grinned appreciatively. "Well done, miss! Don't you agree, Stenton?"

The painful twist of fear for Elizabeth still sharp in his memory, Clive was in no mood to praise her for what he considered ill-judged interference. Yet he could not help but acknowledge that she was as resourceful as she was willful.

He met her quizzical look. "No doubt I would agree—had there been a need for such heroics."

She took this in good part. "You're miffed," she said, smiling a little, "that I did not do as you bade me."

Despite himself, his mouth twitched. "That is something we shall discuss later."

"Take the advice of an older man," said Throckmorton. "Don't have anything to do with a hurly-burly miss who doesn't think twice about knocking a man down. Caught me off balance, she did, for I never expected anything like it. Now, will somebody help me up?"

Clive gripped him under the right arm, Chamberlain under the left, and together they hauled him to his feet.

"Duval is hit." Clive looked at Chamberlain. "Do you think one of Beamish's men will fetch Dr. Wimple from Seaford?"

Throckmorton gave a grunt. "So I got him, did I? Well, I hope I hit a vital spot."

"No, you didn't get him," Chamberlain said curtly. "I did."

He turned, saying over his shoulder to Clive, "Couldn't risk having him lose more shots out of that pepperbox. Aimed for the left shoulder. I trust that's all I hit?"

"You hit a shoulder, and if it isn't the left, it's the first time you missed what you aimed for."

Chamberlain nodded. "I'll see what I can do about the physician. No doubt about it, though. The men would as soon drown Duval as render him assistance."

Throckmorton, who had been peering about him in some agitation, asked, "Where is Gabrielle?" He wheezed in a quite alarming way. "Mademoiselle de Tournier—if anything happened to her—"

"Nothing happened to her," Elizabeth assured him. "She is coming this way with Lord Nicholas Mackay."

"Mackay, eh? Planned to offer her *carte blanche,* the young dog!"

"Sylvester, my friend!" Gabrielle, with Nicholas in tow, pushed through the throng of smugglers. "Nicholas says I must confess all to the Duke of Stenton. And he also tells me that it would not at all be proper to shoot Duval. What do you think? It seems to me a great piece of nonsense—"

"Hush, child!" Throckmorton spoke with such severity that Gabrielle for once did as she was bid. "*I* will make the explanations. But first, let us remove ourselves from this damnably cold and damp place."

"Well spoken, sir," said Nicholas. "Never could abide a beach. Too much sand and water."

"And gales. Blasted wind took my hat before I'd gone ten paces from the Crown and Anchor."

"Nick." Clive's voice had an impatient edge. "You brought the horses, I take it?"

"Left 'em at the end of the carriage track, just as you told me."

During the next few minutes, while Clive instructed

262

Nicholas to place two of the horses at Gabrielle's and Mr. Throckmorton's disposal and to accompany them to Stenton, while he conferred with Chamberlain and with Beamish, who still held two pistols trained on the French agent, and while the main body of smugglers huddled together in a debate of some kind, Elizabeth felt very much *de trop*.

Not one glance did Stenton spare her. She did not doubt that he was annoyed with her. Gentlemen never liked to have their orders ignored. But, surely, he might have suggested that she leave with Gabrielle.

She watched his strong profile, the straight nose and square chin exposed against the night sky. His shoulders shook a little; she supposed he was chuckling at something the innkeeper from East Dean said to him. From Chamberlain's talk with the stout man who answered to three different names she understood that Beamish was the smugglers' leader, and why Stenton should be amused by anything *he* said was more than she could see.

The icy wind plucked at her skirt and at the shawl around her head. Her feet and hands grew numb, and her temper rose. She did not expect gratitude from Stenton, but he could at least show her the consideration he had shown Mademoiselle de Tournier. And a little respect would not hurt either. After all, she *had* spoiled Mr. Throckmorton's aim when he leveled his pistol at the spy.

Resolutely, she turned her back on the men and started northward, in the direction of the landing stage and the carriage track. Stenton had not said she should *not* leave.

She regretted the impulsive act before she had gone twenty paces. It was so very dark and so very lonely with the gray shadows of the cliffs to her right and the churning waters of the Cuckmere estuary to her left.

When she had ventured down the cliff path earlier, she'd been driven by a purpose, and although she had been fully aware of the danger, she had not been frightened—except for that brief moment when she believed one of the smugglers was climbing up to meet her.

And neither was she frightened now, she told herself. It was the northern gale sweeping unimpeded down the Cuckmere valley that made her shiver since the heat of temper had cooled. It had cooled sufficiently to make her wish Stenton would call her back.

Slowly she walked on, dividing her attention between the ground and the chalk cliffs on the right. If she kept close to the looming gray wall, she could not possibly miss the way.

Once, she stopped to look up at the sky. Most of the stars had disappeared. Behind clouds? If that were so, the twins would have their white Christmas.

Since she was walking into the wind, she did not hear the men until they had caught up with her and suddenly appeared beside her, two on the right and one on the left. Her heart seemed to stop for a sickening instant when the man on her left gripped her elbow.

"Dash it, Elizabeth! Why didn't you wait?"

Her hand, balled in a tight fist, stopped in midair. She could not speak, for now her heart sat in her throat.

"So you would have slugged me again."

She heard the laughter in Stenton's voice. Firmly, he pushed her hand down.

"I fear Throckmorton was right," he said, still sounding amused. "Behind that very prim and proper exterior hides a hurly-burly miss."

"You have a habit of startling me that is not at all endearing." She tried to be stern. "Why did you not warn me?"

"I called out, but you did not hear."

The grip on her arm which had frightened her almost out of her wits, now soothed and reassured. She hoped he would not let go.

She glanced at the other two men. She recognized Chamberlain and Duval, the spy, whose left arm rested in a sling.

"Will you take the spy to Whitehall immediately?" she asked as the other two men drew ahead.

And how long will you be gone? she wanted to add.

"Chamberlain will take him to London as soon as the physician has dug the ball from his shoulder. *I* have unfinished, important business here at Stenton."

She gave him a fleeting look. Even in the dark she could see the smile that left no doubt as to the nature of the business.

"Do you?" she murmured. "Allow me to wish you success."

"Thank you. However, there's no doubt at all about the outcome of my venture."

They passed the landing stage, marked by the tall, slim mast of the sloop *Louise*.

She wanted to ask why he was so certain but changed her mind. It wouldn't do to let him see just how interested she was.

Instead, pointing back to the mast, she asked, "Will the smugglers still sail tonight?"

"No. They voted to celebrate Duval's capture."

"I could not help but notice that your smugglers kept very quiet until everything was settled."

"*My* smugglers? Yes, I suppose they are mine at present. Another legacy to pass on to my heir."

She felt his gaze on her but did not look up. Chamberlain and Duval had disappeared in the dark. She was alone with the man who had caught her girlish fancy more than a decade ago, and she suddenly realized how very much she wanted her share of a miracle.

Miracles, she had assured Juliette, still happened. But did they?

"Do you know what a pepperbox is, Elizabeth?"

"No," she said, resigning herself that, at least tonight, a miracle was not in the making.

"It is a pistol with a mechanism that makes it possible to fire six or more shots, depending on the number of barrels and firing pans. I once saw a twenty-four-shot pepperbox. All one has to do is recock and rotate the barrels."

"I take it, Duval had such a pistol?"

"Yes, an eight-shot model. And since the Stenton smugglers don't own a gun among them, they found it impossible to refuse Duval passage across the Channel."

He did not add that two young men had been shot,

then pushed off the cliffs after an attempt to over-power the Frenchman.

"It is too bad," she said with a little sigh, "that free-traders distrust the government so much they will not even ask for help in a desperate case like this. I know there are dragoons stationed near Bournemouth and, I believe, also near Brighton. They would have been only too happy to have caught a spy."

"Three months ago, Beamish sent his son into Bournemouth to speak with a Colonel Ryder of the First Dragoons. The lad never returned."

"Is he in gaol?"

"No, in the navy. The colonel handed him over to a recruiting officer."

"You're saying he was impressed into the navy!"

"Yes. The colonel did not believe the boy's story about the spy and decided to punish him for trying to lead the dragoons on a wild-goose chase."

"But that is dreadful!"

"Colonel Ryder obviously did not think so. In fact," Clive said sarcastically, "he was kind enough to let Beamish know where his son was."

"Infamous!"

"Think of it from the colonel's point of view. While a lad is in the navy, he cannot turn free-trader."

"But, surely, the boy did not admit—"

"There was no need. Beamish told me that the pre-ventive officers and the dragoons have known of the smuggling activities here at Stenton for some time. But *my* smugglers are small fry. They have only one boat and go out only when the village coffers are empty. So they have been left alone while the preventives went after gangs with a regular traffic pattern."

"Would a French agent be aware of that?"

"Most assuredly he would."

"You are so certain!"

She stared at him in dawning understanding. "It wasn't chance, was it, or the circumstance that you happen to own Stenton that *you* were sent to catch the agent? You are an agent yourself. An English agent."

"Do I detect a trace of loathing?"

"For myself, for having been so dense."

He said ruefully, "No more so than I was with regard to you. I daresay you noticed I was extraordinarily glad to hear that it was a ghost who told you about Throckmorton."

The reminder of the kiss that hadn't quite been a kiss drove warmth into her face. Or, perhaps, it was annoyance that he should still have harbored doubts about her.

She was granted no opportunity to explore her feelings, for he stopped, giving a low whistle.

"What are you doing?" As soon as they stood still, she felt the cold again. "Whom are you signaling, Stenton?"

"My horse. Unless Chamberlain decided to make off with him, Rambunctious should be right here at the foot of the carriage track. Ah, yes." Tightening his grip on her elbow, he moved on. "There he comes."

She neither heard nor saw anything to substantiate his conviction until the roan pressed his nose into her side.

Stenton mounted swiftly, then stretched his right arm toward her. She gripped his wrist, placed a foot atop his in the stirrup and swung herself up in front of him.

"This will be a bit uncomfortable," he said, wrapping an arm around her waist. "But at least I'll get you back in time for dinner, even if you'll be pressed for time if you want to change your gown."

Dinner? It was difficult to believe that she had not spent all night chasing smugglers and spies. And the stout man and his companion, the mysterious Mademoiselle de Tournier.

"Stenton, how does Gabrielle fit into the picture? And Mr. Throckmorton?"

"I don't know yet." He shifted in the saddle as if to put distance between their bodies. "But I hope to find out before long."

She relaxed against the broad chest behind her—he might call it an uncomfortable ride; to her, it was a delight. An unexpected and, perhaps, forbidden pleasure, all the more to be enjoyed for its element of impropriety.

And the sensible, levelheaded Elizabeth who had governed her life for the past decade might go to the dickens with her goodwill.

Chapter Twenty-two

Disappointed and uneasy, Juliette turned away from Elizabeth's door. She had knocked once before, over an hour ago, to invite her to a game of hide-and-seek with Adam and Grace. She had thought nothing of it when Elizabeth did not answer. But now, with only thirty minutes to go until the dinner hour, she could not help but wonder where her friend might be. Not in the castle, or she and the children would have come across her.

She had seen her leave the Crimson Drawing Room shortly after Flora's and Amelia's entrance. It was dusk then. But Elizabeth had a penchant for taking walks at the oddest hours and might have gone out. Surely, though, she must have returned by now. It was completely dark. Juliette had peeked out the window and had seen nothing but the deepest blackness. Even the stars had disappeared.

Making a sudden decision, Juliette hurried toward the south wing.

A door opened. Her plump shoulders draped as

usual in a number of shawls, Miss Flora Rowland peeked into the dim corridor.

"Juliette, love. Just the person I wanted to see! Won't you come in? Amelia and I have hardly had an opportunity to visit with you."

"Cousin Flora, have you seen Elizabeth — Miss Gore-Langton?"

"No, love. But do come in. We don't want to be conversing in the corridor."

"Some other time." Juliette reached out to adjust a chiffon stole that trailed perilously close to the ground. "I want to find Elizabeth. She's not in her chamber, and I'm beginning to worry about her."

Miss Amelia's spare frame appeared behind Flora. "She's Louisa Astley's companion, isn't she? No doubt she's with your mama-in-law."

"No. Mother Astley is downstairs with Fanny and Margaret."

"Poor, dear Fanny!" said Flora. "She's getting more crotchety every year. If only she could have a child. A dear little baby."

"It's not the lack of children that makes Fanny snap at us." Amelia gave her sister a wry look. "She suspects we're trying to cheat her brother out of a fortune."

Flora's rosy complexion turned a shade darker. "Gracious! If that isn't crotchety —"

Juliette interrupted. "Did the first fourth duchess truly bequeath you some of her jewelry?"

"Yes, she did," said Flora.

But Amelia shook her head. "There was no bequest. How could there be? Sarah—the duchess—didn't know she was going to die. But she had promised Flora a sapphire brooch for her eighteenth birthday—"

"Which, as it turned out, was exactly a month after dear Sarah died," said Flora.

"And she promised me a string of pearls." Amelia's stern features softened. "She knew I'd never have pearls otherwise. Flora, as the elder, would have our mother's. But I—" She shook her head. "However, that's neither here nor there. Juliette, if you're worried about your friend, you want to go looking for her, not for some old pieces of jewelry."

Juliette hesitated. "Fanny and Margaret are also hunting for the duchess's jewelry chest, but Clive believes that someone, a servant perhaps, made off with it after the fire."

"Why would he think that?" asked Amelia. "The staff was devoted to Sarah and Edward. Besides, what would a servant—or *any* thief—do with jewels worth a king's ransom?"

"Sell them?" suggested Juliette.

"Easier said than done. Even a less than respectable jeweler—"

"A fence," Flora interjected.

Amelia looked annoyed. "Even a dishonest jeweler might think twice about buying. Sarah's diamond set and the rubies were too well known. They would have to be recut and reset at a great expense. No, I think if Sarah's jewels had been offered for sale, the prospective buyer would have turned to Edward for a reward."

"Hush!" Flora peered up and down the corridor,

272

which was quite dim and shadowy even though every candle was lit in the wall sconces. "We really should not be discussing the matter out here, where we can be overheard!"

"Rubbish!" said Amelia. She looked at Juliette. "Clive is a sensible man. He must know the jewels cannot be easily sold, so what convinced him they were stolen?"

"Uncle Decimus said the duchess kept her jewels in a secret compartment behind the wainscoting of her chamber. But all the woodwork was gutted and the compartment was empty when Cousin Edward came back to Stenton to look for—"

"Edward returned to Stenton after Sarah's death?" Flora gave her sister an agitated look. "I didn't know that. Did you, Amelia?"

"I did not, but it hardly matters. If he had found the jewels, he wouldn't have had to scrape for pennies all these years."

"Nor would Clive," said Juliette.

Amelia frowned, mulling over something. "It was such an awful, confusing night. I wonder if Sarah had time to take the chest to a safe place?"

"We slept in one of the chambers next to the ducal suite," said Flora. "It is now the muniment room, I believe. I was frightened to death when I awoke to screams of 'Fire! Fire!' "

"It was one of the maids." Amelia's sallow skin turned paler. "She was hammering on Sarah's door and shouting at the top of her voice. By the time Flora and I had donned wraps, Sarah had already gone. Down to the Great Hall, we believed. We didn't know then that the children were trapped in the nursery, and that Sarah . . ."

"Had gone to the nursery?" Juliette finished gently.

Flora drew her shawls closer. "A footman told us to hurry. The fire was spreading our way, he said. And we could see it was true. We could scarcely breathe for the smoke! So we went with him. The Great Hall was crowded . . . there were so many friends Sarah had invited for the weekend . . . and the servants . . . and everyone was in hysterics. Edward's steward and Decimus tried to organize the men. A bucket brigade, I think they called it."

"There's a pump in one of the kitchens," said Amelia. "But there weren't enough men. Or buckets. The maids helped, and Flora and I. All we could do was try to stop the fire from spreading into the east and west wings. Then, fortunately, help arrived. A band of smugglers, who had just landed a cargo in the estuary, saw flames shoot out a window. They left their casks of wine and came immediately to the castle."

Flora nodded. "They worked like demons. And they looked like demons from hell, for they took over the positions closest to the smoke and the fire, which made their skin look red, and they had wet kerchieves tied around their mouths and noses."

"But it was too late," Amelia concluded, her voice gruff. "When the fire was finally put out, the south wing was destroyed. And when we wanted to tell Sarah how very sorry we were, we realized that she and the children were missing as well as eight of the staff."

"How awful." Juliette's throat was dry, as though

she, too, had been breathing the smoke and heated air.

"Yes, it was. But it was a long time ago. More than four decades." Stepping around her sister, Amelia gave Juliette a little nudge. "Now it's your friend who is missing, and you're worried. So, run along, dear. Flora and I will just step into the muniment room and do a bit of reading until dinner."

"It's a good thing the muniment room was on the second floor at the time of the fire," said Flora. "Or all the records would have been destroyed."

Juliette nodded absently. Falling into step beside Amelia, she said, "I am going in the same direction. To the billiard room. I want to ask Stewart and George to look for Elizabeth outside."

"It's pitch dark, and there's a gale blowing." Flora's heeled sandals tapped on the oaken floorboards as she followed Juliette and Amelia. "It'd be folly to venture out on a night like this!"

"But Elizabeth is not a foolish woman," Juliette said quietly. "That is why I'm worried. I do not understand what has become of her."

They passed the library and were approaching the billiard room.

Amelia briefly touched Juliette's arm. "It's a pity that Clive is not here. But, no doubt, George and Stewart will know what to do."

The door to the billiard room was ajar, and the faint click of the ivory balls could be heard in the corridor.

Flora whispered, "Poor Stewart. How much he used to like a game of billiards! If I heard it once, I must have heard it a dozen times when Clive teased you that Stewart came to Stenton House not to court you but to challenge him to a game. It must be painful for the dear boy to be reduced to a spectator role."

"Nonsense." Amelia did not lower her voice. "Of course Stewart is playing! Don't you remember old Admiral Comstock? He, too, had lost an arm up to the elbow. Only his was the right arm. But he was a devilish sharp billiard player."

The door opened. Stewart, a cue stick under the stump of his arm and a hard glint in his eye, sketched a bow.

"You're quite right, Miss Amelia. I am indeed playing. A few more practice sessions, and I shall be in excellent trim." He glanced at Flora. "Miss Rowland, would you care to watch?"

"Thank you, dear boy." Flora fluttered her shawls. "I'm honored. But some other time, perhaps? Juliette was wanting a word with you and George."

The sisters walked on, past the estate offices, and disappeared into the muniment room.

Stewart finally met Juliette's eyes. "I don't want to seem disobliging, but George was called away. Some emergency, I believe, with the treasure hunt."

"I don't care about George," Juliette blurted out.

Her heart hammered. She knew her unruly tongue would most likely play her false, but she could not stop herself.

"Stewart, I am so proud of you! And if there were time, I'd like very much to watch you play billiards."

His mouth tightened. "You're too kind. But don't worry, I was not about to ask you to miss your

276

dinner for the sake of watching my clumsy attempts."

"Dinner . . . what are you talking about? Oh, I see! That there is no time."

She pressed a shaking hand to her forehead. "Stewart, I could shake you! But there's no time even for that. I cannot find Elizabeth, and I'm very much afraid she may have gone out at dusk and . . . and something must have happened because she is nowhere in the castle!"

As the hardness left his eyes, she caught a glimpse of the old Stewart, the man who had captured her heart.

"I shan't ask you the obvious, whether she is with Mother or one of the other ladies. But the castle is huge. Are you sure you've looked everywhere, Juliette? What about the second floor?"

"I haven't made a conscious search," she admitted. "But, Stewart! I was playing hide-and-seek with the twins this past hour. Believe me, we were *everywhere*."

Frowning, he took the cue stick he still held clutched under the stump of his arm and returned it to the rack on the wall.

"I suppose you want to go looking for her? Well, I'm game." The hint of a smile softened his mouth as he rejoined her. "This has been a devilish dull afternoon and evening."

"Thank you!"

She felt like skipping or dancing. She wanted to throw her arms around his neck and give him a hug. But for once, mind prevailed over heart. She walked sedately at his side, determined to do nothing that would bring back his coldness.

"I don't know where to look for her if she's not in the yard or garden," she said. "I ventured out the Great North Gate this morning and followed the road. It forks three ways after just a little bit."

"We'll go about this methodically."

He let his gaze linger on her. How beautiful she was with the candlelight dancing in her hair. It looked like spun gold.

"How do we do that?"

Sharply, he recalled his wandering mind. "First we'll find out if anyone saw Elizabeth leave. For all we know, she may have told the butler or one of the footmen where she was going. If not, I'll appropriate lanterns and Clive's curricle, and you and I will search the road to West Dean. Some of the stable lads can follow the lanes to East Dean and to Seaford."

"That's a capital plan. I'm afraid I would have simply rushed off. And, most likely," she added pensively, "it would have turned out that Elizabeth wasn't lost at all, so everyone would have had to come looking for me."

They stopped at her door.

Gently, he ran a fingertip along her cheek and jaw line. "You always were impulsive."

"And you always had the orderly mind. I daresay that's why you rose so quickly to brigade major."

She caught his hand and held it captive against her face. Taking courage when he did not try to withdraw it, she said, "And I wish you would wear your uniform."

"Why? I'll resign as soon as I return to town. What

278

difference does it make whether I wear the uniform a few more days?"

A certain stiffness of tone warned her that he was pokering up again. But now that she had said this much, she might as well speak her mind. Slowly, she released his hand. Better give it up voluntarily than have it snatched from her.

"For one thing, it would please your parents if you wore regimentals. You cannot deny that your father was just a little disconcerted when he arrived and saw you in civilian clothes. Stewart, he is so very proud of you. Could you not indulge him?"

"And you, Juliette? Do you want to see me in uniform again?" His voice turned harsh. "A reminder of the days that used to be?"

"A reminder wouldn't hurt. I have begun to wonder if those days of courtship and the honeymoon happened only in my imagination."

"It wasn't imagination. But I am no longer the man who courted you."

"No." She met his gaze squarely. "The man who courted me would not have discarded uniform and wife as though he blamed them for the loss of his arm."

"Julie, I don't blame you. Never have!"

She went on as though he had not spoken. "Something happened to that man I fell in love with, and I wish I knew what it was. It is damned difficult having to go to battle when you don't know what you're fighting."

"It is impossible. I should know."

"It is also unfair."

279

When he made no reply, she turned abruptly and opened the door to her chamber. "I had better fetch my cloak."

He watched her go inside and fling open the wardrobe. Deep in thought, he went to his own room for his driving coat and gloves.

Unfair. Unfair.

The accusation still rang in his ears when he rejoined Juliette. In silence, they descended to the Great Hall, where he spoke briefly with the footman on duty. But James could not help. He had not seen Miss Gore-Langton leave.

Stewart turned to Juliette. He saw that she had not closed the frogging at the neck of her cloak and reached out to fasten it. She held quite still, but her pulse was agitated and fluttered against his fingers.

"The shortest way to the stables is through the kitchens," he said while his mind once more grappled with the concept of fairness. Or unfairness. "On our way out we can question the rest of the staff."

She did not answer. In fact, she could not. She hardly dared breathe until he was done and she no longer felt the touch of his fingers against her throat.

She took a deep breath then, but before she could speak, one wing of the great front door crashed open, admitting an icy blast of air and three disheveled, windblown figures, their faces red with cold.

"You there, James!" Nicholas, whom Juliette almost did not recognize in his homespun smock and knitted cap, grinned at the footman. "Don't stand there gaping. Fetch the housekeeper. We need chambers prepared. And have someone take care of the horses."

"Horses?" gasped James.

"Yes. Outside. Now be a good fellow and run along."

Juliette cast a quick look at the cloaked woman with Nicholas—not Elizabeth—and at the stout man, whose right hand was wrapped in a bloodstained handkerchief.

Stewart said, "Nicholas, I thought you were with Clive."

"Where is Elizabeth?" demanded Juliette. "And who are these people?"

"Elizabeth will be along," Nicholas said cheerfully. "So will Clive. And a French spy."

"The devil you say!" Stewart looked grim. In a reflex motion, his right hand reached for the sword he no longer carried at his side.

Juliette could only mutter weakly, "Gracious! Whatever does Clive want with a spy?"

Chapter Twenty-three

The Great Hall was crowded with Clive's guests and as many of the staff as could invent an errand that would take them into the vast chamber where they might take a peek at the French spy.

Chamberlain had ordered Duval to sit on a straight-backed chair near the western fireplace, had bandaged his left shoulder and, finally, tied his right wrist to the chair back. Sylvester Throckmorton and Gabrielle de Tournier received their share of curious looks, while Clive and Nicholas were peppered with questions about the spy's capture. Even Elizabeth was interrogated about her part in the affair.

It was well past the dinner hour, but none of the company had a thought to spare for the meal spoiling in the kitchens or for the chef, whose heart was breaking as he dismembered and deboned the roasted pheasants, done to a turn. With an expression of utter disgust, Monsieur Maurice tossed the scraps of meat into a sauce.

"A *fricassée!*" He glared at the most junior of kitchen

maids, who started to tremble and wished she had dared sneak off with the others to take a look at the spy. "If his grace is content to eat *fricassée,* he need not have engaged me, the best chef in all of England and the Continent."

And while Monsieur Maurice grumbled and swore he would give notice if his grace did not sit down to dinner within the hour, Annie flitted around excitedly.

From the strip of second-floor landing below the oriel window above the great front door, she gazed down into the crowded hall and was reminded of the days when the fourth duke and his wife—his first wife—entertained at Stenton. For a moment her gaze lingered on Miss Juliette and the major. She was glad to see they were still together.

Earlier, when the major fastened the frogging on Miss Juliette's cloak, Annie had been sorely tempted to try her hand at peacemaking. But she had hesitated too long, and when she was about to give Miss Juliette a little push, Lord Nicholas and his companions had burst into the hall.

Annie moved among the company, turning up her nose at Lady Harry's sensible wool gown, touching the velvet of Lady Fanny's elegant dinner gown, and thinking wistfully of the glittering, stiff brocades that prevailed in the olden days. But, overall, this night was the best, the most lively, she had seen in many a year.

And it was getting livelier, since Mr. Symes, the dignified butler who would never admit to vulgar curiosity, had struck upon the notion to serve brandy and Madeira to the gentlemen, ratafia and sherry to the ladies. It was a masterful stroke to keep him and the footmen occupied in the Great Hall.

Annie stopped behind a settle, where Lord Decimus sat with the Misses Rowland.

"Isn't it grand?" she said gleefully. "Better than a raree show."

For once, Decimus paid her no attention. His myopic gaze was fixed with painful intensity on Sylvester Throckmorton, who stood not too far away talking with Clive, Sir John Astley, Lord Wilmott, and Elizabeth.

It was Miss Flora who turned around, saying, "But that man, the spy, he doesn't look at all dangerous. I am quite disappointed. I remember, when I was a child, my parents took me to the hanging of a highwayman. . . ."

Her voice trailing, Flora blinked at the emptiness behind the settle.

Annie looked the plump, elderly lady over, assessing the blond-turned-gray crimped curls, the complexion that owed some of its rosiness to the rouge pot.

"You may no longer be in your salad days, Miss Flora, but you're not old enough to have known Dick Turpin. And that's who my da saw hanged. He said Dick Turpin was the fiercest, meanest-looking highwayman he ever clapped eyes on."

Flora's rouge spots flamed in her suddenly pale face. "Amelia," she whispered. "Who is that talking to me?"

Amelia broke off her conversation with Grace's governess.

"For goodness' sake, Flora. Are you turning blind?" She looked over her shoulder. "Well, whoever it was, she's gone. And what can you have been thinking of, comparing a spy to a highwayman! This Frenchman may look harmless—that, I'm sure, is his stock-in-trade—but he's far more dangerous than Dick Turpin ever was."

Flora was about to protest that it wasn't she who mentioned Dick Turpin, when Decimus muttered something under his breath. He set his brandy glass on the floor and rose lumberingly to his feet.

"What I want to know," he said loudly as he made his way toward Throckmorton, his old gaming companion of Watier's Club, "is how *you* came to be mixed up in this spying business, Sylvester."

A hush fell over the Great Hall. Heads turned, and more than a dozen pairs of eyes fixed on the two stout gentlemen.

"Decimus, my dear fellow! Don't look at me as though you've already convicted me of high treason." Throckmorton drew a wheezing breath. "I did nothing I need be ashamed of—save for missing that cad Duval when I finally had him at firing distance."

Gabrielle de Tournier, standing nearby and yet not a part of the group surrounding Throckmorton since she had been talking exclusively with Nicholas, swung around.

She said sharply, "But that was altogether the fault of Miss Gore-Langton, and I still think we should have been permitted to shoot Duval later."

Most of those who heard Gabrielle looked startled by her vehemence, and Decimus voiced the sentiments of many. "My dear young lady! Can't shoot a man who's down. It's not done. And he *was* down. Shot by Chamberlain. I distinctly heard Clive say so."

"Ah, bah! You English have so much phlegm. All you can say is, 'It is not done!' " In a dramatic gesture, Gabrielle pointed at Elizabeth. "Then *you* should *not* have meddled. That also is not done. It was, in fact, a great piece of impertinence."

Elizabeth merely smiled. There was something about the raven-haired young Frenchwoman that appealed to her. Perhaps it was Gabrielle's liveliness, a trait Elizabeth lacked. Rosalind, however, had possessed that same spirited quality. . . .

Clive said coldly, "Mademoiselle, if you're quite done venting your spleen, perhaps you will allow Mr. Throckmorton to speak."

Throckmorton nodded. "I am willing, nay, eager to say my piece. And if everyone would draw a little closer so that I won't have to exert myself?"

While others drew near, Elizabeth retreated to a chair flanked by suits of armor at the back of the Great Hall. She was beginning to feel a little dizzy, perhaps a result of the sherry Stenton had pressed on her as soon as Symes appeared with a drink tray. Or, perhaps, it was merely the warmth from the fireplaces penetrating her chilled body. Whatever the cause of the light-headedness, she was quite content to stay in the background.

Juliette joined her a moment later. "Clive wants to know if you're all right. He says I should take you upstairs and see that you have dinner sent to your room."

Startled, Elizabeth looked up. Her eyes met Stenton's, and across the distance she was aware of his concern.

"Are you tired, Elizabeth?" asked Juliette. Her voice implied that she would think it quite poor spirited if Elizabeth were to admit fatigue. "Would you like to go to your room?"

Smiling a little, Elizabeth shook her head. But her gaze was still on Stenton.

"Now, if everyone can hear me," said Throckmorton, "I shall begin."

Clive turned to the older man and, reluctantly, Elizabeth followed suit.

"And I tell you to your faces," said Throckmorton, "there's no need to send for the dragoons or the justice of the peace. Gabrielle and I have done no wrong."

Taking advantage of Throckmorton's pausing for breath, Gabrielle said, "We . . . how do you say? We diddled the spy and, indeed, Napoléon Bonaparte himself. That is what we did!"

"Hush, Gabrielle! *I* will explain. Every document I copied for Duval, and there were about a dozen of them these past three months, had the contents altered. None of the information Bonaparte received through me was ever quite correct."

"In fact," Gabrielle said with satisfaction, "we led the upstart emperor by the nose."

Duval on his chair near the fireplace made a strangled sound.

"Three months?" said Clive, his eyes narrowing. "But Liverpool and Yorke both have proof that information has been leaked far longer than three months.

287

And some of it at least was correct, as certain maneuvers of the French army and navy have shown us."

"By God!" Stewart said grimly. "And weren't we made to feel it in the Peninsula when the French had gotten hold of Wellington's plans!"

Throckmorton remained unruffled. "I was obviously not Duval's only source."

"Very well." Clive gave the older man a hard look. "But why give information at all? Were you blackmailed?"

"Gabrielle was."

Elizabeth became aware of Lord Nicholas close to Gabrielle. In fact, he had been near the young Frenchwoman since the moment he had recognized her on the beach and shouted, "Gabrielle! Great Scot! I must be going mad."

But now there was pain in his face. He said, "And you turned to Throckmorton. Dash it, Gabrielle! Why didn't you come to me?"

"But, Nicholas! Surely, you must understand. You do not have friends at the Horse Guards."

"And what was the blackmail?" asked Clive.

"The *canaille!*" said Gabrielle, lapsing into French in her fury. "The cad, he told me that my brother was imprisoned in the cellars of some old house outside Boulogne. And that Pierre would be shot if I did not give Duval what he wants!"

Until now, the assembled company had listened in silence. But at Gabrielle's disclosure, some muttering could be heard among the gentlemen, and a whisper here and there among the ladies.

Nicholas captured Gabrielle's hand. "If only you

had confided in me. Duval would have been dead three months ago."

"Young hothead," said Throckmorton. "And what would you have asked of Gabrielle in return?"

A flush stained Nicholas's face. "No more than you asked of her."

"Ah! But, you see, I ask nothing. I am an old friend of the family. I courted Gabrielle's mother before she ever met de Tournier. And it was for the mother's sake that I helped the daughter—and, as I believed for some time, the son."

Nicholas stared at Gabrielle.

"But there was no son who needed to be saved," said Chamberlain from his guard position behind Duval. "Throckmorton here, in the guise of Mr. John Smith, engaged me to travel to Boulogne to check out Duval's claim."

"Aye," said Throckmorton. "Young Pierre de Tournier returned to France two years ago to throw in his lot with Bonaparte—like so many other young Frenchmen have done. The family had two letters from him, the last one intimating that he would try to get back to England."

"I told Pierre he would not be happy in France!" Gabrielle said passionately. "But he had no future here, save being a dancing master or marrying some merchant's fat daughter with a squint and a fat dowry. He believed that in France under the new order he could rise to a position of importance."

"He did make the attempt to return to England," said Chamberlain. "Four months ago, Pierre de Tournier arrived in Boulogne, where he tried to get a passage across the Channel. But someone informed against him, and before he could make contact with a gang of smugglers from Rye who were about to sail, he was arrested and shot."

"The poor young man," said Flora.

She stepped back to search her reticule for a handkerchief. Two of her shawls slipped off her shoulders. Elizabeth and Juliette both started toward her, but before they had taken more than three or four steps, Flora, a lace-edged handkerchief in her hand, looked up. Her gaze fell on one of the footmen who still balanced a drink tray in his hand.

Flora's eyes widened. Her mouth opened in a startled, inaudible cry. Slowly, she crumpled on the floor in a dead faint.

Elizabeth and Juliette rushed forward. Elizabeth gathered several shawls and placed them under Miss Flora's head while Juliette chafed her elderly cousin's hands.

They did not look at each other. And when Miss Amelia, Lady Fanny, Lady Harry, and Lady Astley all gathered around, they said not a word. Without a protest, they accepted Miss Amelia's explanation that Flora had always been sensitive, and, no doubt, poor Pierre de Tournier's sad story had caused her to swoon.

But like Miss Flora, Elizabeth and Juliette had seen the footman's tray. And they had seen the brandy glass, raised by an unseen hand, tilted toward an invisible mouth, the contents disappearing at an alarming rate.

And while Miss Flora took refuge in oblivion, they

saw the empty glass switched for a full one that rather shakily weaved its way toward the south wing passage. They heard a stifled sob and a hiccough and Annie saying, "Oh, the poor young gentleman!"

Chapter Twenty-four

"Miss Elizabeth, wake up! Gorblimey! Are you going to sleep all day?"

Elizabeth did not stir. She did not want to give up a dream in which Clive Rowland swore that he had never forgotten her, had in fact scoured the earth looking for her. And now he was taking her hand, and he led her into the Great Hall, which was festooned from one end to the other with garlands of mistletoe.

He cupped her face with his hands. He bent his dark head toward her. She could see the fine streak of white in his hair. His mouth came closer. . . .

"Get up, Miss Elizabeth!"

Annie's voice. Surely, one should be able to ignore a ghost. But the dream was shattered. She was awake, and it was Christmas Eve.

"Miss Elizabeth, don't you want to help bring in the yule log and that fir tree the twins are forever chattering about?"

"I dreamed about mistletoe and Stenton." Elizabeth

292

sat up and frowned at the foot of the bed, where she had heard the persistent ghost. "I'm sure it was an omen. If you had not roused me, I might have learned whether he will win the kiss tonight."

Annie giggled. "He'll get his kiss."

"How do you know? Has he remembered? Oh, surely he must have!"

"Why must he? Think how few occasions he's had to be with you. This is Monday. When you arrived on Friday, you hid in your room until dinner. You slept all of Saturday —"

"Which was hardly my fault!"

"He had only yesterday to jog his memory. And then he was preoccupied with catching the spy."

The spy . . . a jumble of impressions flashed through Elizabeth's mind. The beach, the icy wind, the crashing of the breakers. She and Clive hiding behind the boulder of chalk rock, walking along the estuary, sharing a ride on Rambunctious. Gabrielle and Throckmorton. Gabrielle and Lord Nicholas. The smugglers. The spy.

Clive again, the look she could not mistake when he told her he would not accompany Duval to London because he had unfinished important business at the castle.

The assembly in the Great Hall. As Miss Flora recovered from her swoon, Dr. Wimple arrived. The crusty physician did not blink an eye at the confusion but prescribed a dose of hartshorn and a small glass of wine for Miss Flora, dusted the graze on Sylvester Throckmorton's hand with basilicum powder and bound it, then, after a brief consultation with Stenton, had Duval removed to a chamber in the north wing where he dug the ball from the Frenchman's shoulder.

"Have they left yet, Chamberlain and Duval?" she asked.

"Oh, aye. At the crack of dawn. But hurry now, Miss Elizabeth. They'll be putting the horses to the sleigh within the half-hour."

"The *sleigh?*"

Aware suddenly of the quiet outside, a thick silence after the blustering gale of the previous night, Elizabeth slid out of bed and hurried barefoot to the windows. She raised a corner of the gauze curtain and blinked at the dazzling whiteness in the garden below.

"Miss Grace and Master Adam got their wish." Annie sounded wistful. "I wonder if it snowed in London?"

"I imagine so. There was a trace of snow on the ground when we traveled through."

"I remember my last Christmas at home. Icicles on the eaves of every house and the trees in the parks. The snow a foot thick. Even the meanest streets and squares looking clean and crisp and pretty. I took the little ones caroling that Christmas Eve, and afterward I treated them to roasted chestnuts."

Elizabeth let the curtain drop. She turned toward the soft voice that held such a mixture of happy memories, of sadness and longing.

"Can't you just smell it all, Miss Elizabeth? The chestnuts. The spice cakes. The hot cider. Can't you just hear the cries of pedlars and crossing sweeps, the rattle of carriages, the hustle and bustle? And all the church bells ringing on Christmas Day."

"Why, Annie! You sound homesick."

"I *am* homesick. For London. All these years, I've wanted to go home. And now I will!"

"But . . . can you? A ghost?"

"Oh, yes." Annie's voice now came from the center of the large fourposter bed. "All I need is a human to take me up in her carriage."

"*Her* carriage? I take it you have someone particular in mind."

"I want to go with Miss Juliette."

Her eyes on the milky shadow in the middle of the counterpane, Elizabeth slowly walked toward the bed.

"But Miss Juliette may have to go to Hertfordshire with the major's parents and me."

"Not if I can help it."

"Annie, are you sitting on my bed?"

The shadow moved, floated around the bed hangings, and came to a stop in front of the wardrobe.

"No, Miss Elizabeth." One of the wardrobe doors opened. "And you truly must hurry now. Which gown will you wear?"

"Annie, you little fibster. I saw you — well, not you, but something that I think is you."

"Are you vexed? I didn't mean no disrespect, and I promise I won't do it again."

"Don't be silly. Sit on the bed anytime you like. In fact, if you don't mind living in Hertfordshire, you may leave the castle with the bed. "I'm certain," said Elizabeth, not relishing the prospect as perhaps she should, "I'll be the one to win the wager at midnight."

"We'll see about that. But even if you win, I cannot accept your offer. I want to go to London."

"And once you're there, what will you do then? Will you be walking in Miss Juliette's house?"

"Haunting it?" Annie's voice held a hint of laughter, but when she spoke again she was quite serious. "I cannot know what'll happen when I get to London. But I should think I'll walk no more."

Elizabeth stretched out a hand to touch the nebulous shape of Annie, the ghost. She saw, but she felt nothing.

"Annie, are you wearing a striped gown?"

"Aye. And Lord Decimus hit the nail on the head when he said it reminded him of his youth. The gown is four decades old."

Annie's giggle and her soft "Good-bye, Miss Elizabeth. Hurry now!" were all but drowned by an imperative knock on the chamber door.

"Elizabeth!" Without waiting for a reply, Juliette whirled into the room. "What, aren't you dressed yet? Aren't you going to help fetch the Christmas tree?"

"Yes, I am. But listen—"

"But nothing. Hurry up! Where's your riding habit? The children will go in the sleigh, but you'll ride with Stewart, Clive, and me."

Carried along by Juliette's whirlwind energy, Elizabeth was dressed and out of her room within the space of minutes. She pulled on her gloves while they hurried toward the stairs.

"What's the matter?" she asked breathlessly. "Did you put too much pepper on your breakfast egg this morning?"

Juliette smiled, a secret little smile full of confidence.

"It's Christmas Eve, Elizabeth. I'll have my miracle tonight. Annie and I worked it all out."

* * *

The Christmas trees, a fifteen-foot fir for the Great Hall and a smaller one for the servants' hall, had been loaded onto a wagon. A horse had been harnessed to each of the ash logs, which would be lit that night in the two fireplaces of the Great Hall and kept burning until Twelfth Night. Stewart and Juliette had ridden off, and Clive was about to help Elizabeth mount when Grace and Adam hopped off the sleigh and came tearing toward them.

"Uncle Clive! Uncle Clive! May we ride on the logs?"

"Please, sir?" Adam, trailing the muffler his anxious mama had wrapped around his throat, added his entreaties to those of his sister. "We've never ridden on the yule log. It'd be a rare treat."

Clive knew well that Margaret would comb his hair if he permitted the twins to ride on the log. But he also remembered childhood Christmases on the Shropshire estate, where he, Harry, and even Fanny had delighted in the sport.

"It sounds like fun," said Elizabeth. Sensing his dilemma, she turned to Clive. "We could tie the horses to the sleigh and walk beside the children. That would make it perfectly safe, wouldn't it?"

Sam Nutley had left his seat on the sleigh. Thrusting his chapped hands into knitted mittens, he came up to them.

"Now don't you worry none about the little ones, your grace. Haven't I always taken care of you and Master Harry? Aye, and Lady Fanny, too. I'll see Miss Grace and Master Adam don't come to no harm on the logs."

297

"I know I can depend on you. Thank you, Sam."

Clive looked at Elizabeth. "We can still tie the horses to the sleigh. Then you and I can ride in it."

Before Elizabeth could reply, Grace tugged at her sleeve.

"I hope you like Uncle Clive. My mama says sleigh rides are very romantic. She went on one with my papa, and he proposed. And if Uncle Clive proposed to you, and you don't like him, wouldn't you be in a pickle!"

To her annoyance, Elizabeth felt the blood rush to her face. She could not help but notice Stenton's amused look; it was directed straight at her. Still, she hoped it was his niece's precociousness that had brought the gleam to his eye.

"Thank you for the warning, Grace. But I think, if your uncle has anything to say to me it will be more in the nature of a scold."

"Why?" asked Adam.

Grace's eyes were wide. "I didn't think grown-ups need scolding. Have you been bad?"

"I know!" said Adam. "Mr. Ponsonby and Miss Whitlock were talking about smugglers and spies this morning. And Miss Whitlock said how brave you were to go down to the beach to talk to Uncle Clive. But I bet he didn't like it one bit that you bothered him."

Grace cut in. "I didn't hear about smugglers! You're making it up!"

"I'm not! You didn't hear 'cause you were late for breakfast, and Mama came and told Mr. Ponsonby and Miss Whitlock not to let their tongues run on like fiddlesticks. She said we're excited enough without hearing about Uncle Clive's mad adventures."

"You're making it up!"

"Am not!"

A large hand clasped each of the children's collars.

"If I hear another word," Clive said sternly, "you may neither ride on the logs nor in the sleigh. You will walk."

"Come along." Grinning from one ear to the other, Sam Nutley prodded the twins toward the ash logs strapped with rope to the horses' harness. "And mind you hold on and keep your feet well out to the sides."

The children had no trouble obeying the first part of Sam's order. They simply wrapped their arms around the front ends of the logs, which were notched to securely hold the ropes and hung about ten inches above the ground. They found it a little more difficult to accommodate their feet and, when Sam nodded to the grooms to set out, let them drag in the snow as the horses slowly plodded forward.

"Margaret will have my head for this," said Clive, looking after his squealing niece and nephew.

"She may not learn of it." Elizabeth had quite recovered her poise. "I doubt the children will last a mile. Before long, they'll be quite happy to climb back into the sleigh."

Clive reached for her mare's bridle. "You're right on one count, wrong on two."

"How am I wrong?" She followed him to the sleigh and watched him tie the reins to the rear seat. "Are you suggesting they'll stay on those logs all the way back to Stenton? Nonsense! We must be halfway to West Dean."

"Wrong direction, Elizabeth. We're closer to East

Dean than West. Although, if Chamberlain hadn't struck up a friendship with Beamish, we might have been obliged to go even beyond West Dean for the firs."

"That is neither here nor there." Accepting his hand, she climbed into the sleigh. "The fact remains, we are a good three or four miles from Stenton Castle. Grace and Adam will be tired of their bumpy ride before they have gone one-fourth of the way."

He settled beside her. "That I do not deny. But you were wrong when you supposed Margaret may not learn of their ride. She only has to look at their boots."

"They'll be scratched. I admit I did not take that into account."

He lightly flicked the reins, and the mare standing patiently between the shafts set off at a sedate walk. The powdery snow kicked up by her hooves glistened and sparkled. The small bells dangling from the arm-rests of the box seat jingled softly.

"You were also wrong when you supposed the children would happily climb back into the sleigh. There won't be a sleigh. We, my dear Elizabeth, are taking a different route."

She stared at him in disbelief. "You cannot do that! No, I'm sure you're jesting. You wouldn't make them walk!"

But the sleigh made a gradual turn, moving away from the logs and the coast.

Clive met her troubled look. "Elizabeth, I expect and, indeed, most of the time, accept without a word accusations of harshness toward Grace and Adam from my cherished sister-in-law. But I warn you, I shall not accept unjustified reproaches from you."

Suddenly she laughed. "Oh, but you do invite accusations and reproach! The way you said there wouldn't be a sleigh for them quite made me overlook that your groom has only to set them on the horses."

"Yes, I have noticed that you allow emotion to govern your sense."

"Like last night? I wondered when you'd get around to that."

"Don't remind me lest I be tempted to administer the scold you mentioned to Grace."

"I am quaking in my boots."

He did not reply immediately but guided the horse off the uneven ground into a narrow lane curving to the left.

"I believe that quite often you are afraid, but you don't allow fear to stop you from doing what you believe is right. I admire that, Elizabeth."

"You do? No doubt, then, I quite misunderstood your feelings when I bumped into you on the cliff path and later, when you saw me in the midst of your smugglers."

"You read my feelings correctly. But as you get to know me better, you'll learn that I do not harp back on what is past, especially when everything turned out for the best."

Her mind reeled with the phrase, "as you get to know me better," but she rallied sufficiently to say, "Despite the outcome of the venture, most gentlemen would still have wished to wring my neck."

A corner of his mouth curved down in a wry grin. "Believe me, when I recognized you, that was my most fervent desire. But, contrary to my fears, you did not get hurt. The spy was caught. And, I am now convinced, thanks to you, Duval is alive to identify the clerks at the Horse Guards and the Admiralty who leaked information."

"Are you, perchance, praising me for disobeying you?"

"Not at all. I disapprove of your interference, but I was trained to accept assistance from the most unlikely quarters. Whereas an officer is schooled to follow a superior's orders unquestioningly and to expect having *his* orders obeyed, an agent . . ."

He pulled on the reins, bringing the horse to a sudden stop atop a rise. Under the blanket of snow, the downs looked strangely flat and smooth, except to the far right, where the scattered cottages of West Dean clearly marked a dell.

"To the devil with government agents!" he said cheerfully. "I retired four years ago, and although I was pleased to accept this assignment, I find I have no desire for another. Spying and intrigue are for men younger than I. My interests now lie in a different direction, and that is why I brought you out here."

"Pardon me if I seem excessively stupid today. But what do I have to do with your interests?"

"I don't think I should answer that question while we still have an unresolved wager between us."

She had not liked the gleam in his eye when Grace made her ingenuous observation about the possible results of a sleigh ride. She profoundly distrusted it now.

"Then I suggest you take me back to the castle. Your sister asked me to participate in the treasure hunt, and I wouldn't like to disappoint her."

He gave a crack of laughter. "If that isn't Fanny all

over! When she isn't busy trying to foist some heiress or other on me, she's trying to find a treasure — no doubt to present it to me as a Christmas gift."

"I think it is very nice of her." Elizabeth kept her eyes on the village of West Dean. "I take it," she said diffidently, "that you could use a fortune?"

"Two or three fortunes. But pray don't tell Fanny." His voice held a hint of laughter. "She would only encourage me to commit bigamy."

She turned to face him. "How can you treat the situation with such a deplorable lack of seriousness?"

"But I don't. I merely refuse to accept Fanny's notion of a cure for my impecunious state. My father's first wife brought a large dowry into the marriage. It was used to redeem the mortgages on the Shropshire estate. And if she, indeed, owned jewels worth a king's ransom, I doubt not they were sold before the first anniversary of their wedding day."

"Miss Flora and Miss Amelia also believe that the first fourth duchess's jewels are still in the castle."

He shrugged. "Have your treasure hunt if you like. I shan't spoil sport. But in the meantime, would you listen to my problem?"

"Of course."

She'd do anything rather than speculate whether there was some special meaning behind his confidences. Why was he telling her about Lady Fanny's attempts to provide him with an heiress? And that his father had married one?

"All this is my land." His whip prescribed a full circle. "And at present, all of it is wasteland. I read what documents I could find in the muniment room and learned that in my grandfather's day a salt mine pro-

303

vided employment for the men of East and West Dean, but it ran dry more than sixty years ago. Since then, the village families depended on positions at the castle itself."

"But the castle was closed for forty years."

"Exactly. And even if I could afford to keep it open all year round, there wouldn't be work for everyone. The Seaford people are not too badly off. They have their fishing. East Dean had its share of fishermen, but several years ago a storm destroyed their boats. They do not have the means to buy a new fleet. And West Dean, situated inland, is even worse off."

"Thus, they depend totally on smuggling."

"Which makes them an easy prey to men like Duval."

"Intolerable! Smugglers must be free spirits. Proud to defy our government. But incorruptible when approached by a foreign agent."

He bit down a smile. The Home Office would not agree with at least a part of Miss Gore-Langton's philosophy.

"So what do I do about Stenton, Elizabeth? Somehow, the estate must provide for the villages."

A heavy frown scored her brow. "Have you tried sheep? They do well in East Sussex and Kent. I don't see why they shouldn't do as well here."

"By George! That's it. Not two months ago, I talked with an acquaintance who has property near Lewes. He swears the downs are excellent for sheep farming."

"Good. That'll provide for a few shepherds, and extra hands will be needed at shearing time. The women might do some spinning and weaving. But what about the rest of the men?"

"Devil a bit, Elizabeth! *I* don't know. That's why I asked you."

"I know nothing about estate management."

He picked up the reins again and turned the horse toward the castle. "But you grew up on the coast. I was hoping you'd know how I can help the people here. Stenton must be made to pay for itself and to provide for the villagers."

"Let me think about it."

But for quite a while, as the sleigh glided southward through the pristine whiteness, her mind refused to grapple with the problem. Instead, it dwelled on isolated incidents, such as his reference to the wager, his saying he admired her for doing what she believed was the right thing to do; and, once again, it lingered on the phrase, "as you get to know me better."

Finally, when Stenton Castle came into view in the distance, she told herself to stop being foolish. Picking on a few words and imbuing them with a special meaning was worse than foolish. It was madness.

She became aware of his gaze on her.

"Rather impressive, isn't it, this aspect of the castle?" he said. "The stronghold of the Rowlands. In all its history, it was never taken by marauders from across the Channel. I could not help but feel rather proud when I first set eyes on it."

She gazed at the solid outer wall, the snow-crowned towers, the Great North Gate wide open to welcome a visitor to Stenton.

"Visitors," she murmured. "Families pay fortunes for the lease of a house in Brighton and Worthing. I'll wager a pony they'd pay even more for a wing of Stenton Castle."

He stared at her.

"You'd need more staff, of course. Not only maids and footmen but a slate of gardeners to grow fruit and vegetables." She faltered under that fixed stare. "A home farm. Pleasure boats. It would mean work for the men and women from the villages."

"Great Scot!" He was visibly shaken. "Visitors? *Paying* visitors?"

"Forget it. 'Twas just a foolish notion I suddenly took into my head."

"Not a bit! It's a marvelous notion."

He urged the horse into a brisk trot, then turned his head to look at her. And the laughter in his eyes, the sudden, mischievous quirk of his mouth made her heart turn over.

"Just wait till I tell Decimus. *Paying* visitors. He'll have an apoplexy. But I'll be dashed if I won't do it."

Chapter Twenty-five

The hearths in the Great Hall were cleaned out, the ash logs ready and waiting to be lit. The Christmas tree was set up and decorated with white satin bows, with tiny carved toys and shining silver bells, and the candles were fastened to the tips of the widespread branches.

Dinner was put forward an hour so that the children might join in the meal. It was a lively affair. Grace and Adam were in high spirits, and the addition of Gabrielle de Tournier and Sylvester Throckmorton to the party proved a surprising success.

With Duval's departure, Gabrielle's mood had softened, and although at first she had been reluctant to accept Clive's hospitality, she had raised no further objections when Throckmorton wistfully pointed out that he could recover from his exertions on the beach so much more comfortably at the castle than in the Crown and Anchor. She was obviously fond of the elderly gentleman, the way Fanny and Juliette were fond of Decimus, and Lord Nicholas Mackay had soon discarded the notion that Gabrielle was Throck-morton's mistress.

She was about Juliette's age, her hair the color of ravens' wings, and her dark brown eyes sparkled with laughter when she joked with Grace and Adam or teased Sylvester about the loss of his best beaver hat the previous night, a loss the stout gentleman did not take lightly. She was vivacious without putting herself forward. Even Lady Harry, who regarded every unat-tached young lady around Clive with cold displeasure, thawed under Gabrielle's charm.

All this, Nicholas observed with a fond eye. But his gaze sharpened when he saw that Clive kept looking in Gabrielle's direction. Devil a bit! Gabrielle was not Clive's type of woman at all. Besides, he was far too old for her.

Too old. Nicholas himself was the same age as Clive. Five-and-thirty. And Gabrielle no more than twenty. Shaken, Nicholas set down his knife and fork. He *couldn't* be too old. What did age matter when a man finally fell in love? Totally and absolutely. Head over heels.

His eyes met Gabrielle's across the table. She smiled, and he suddenly recalled two lines of a bit of poetry he had read years ago. Probably in his salad days when he was still at Oxford. He had thought it rather mawkish stuff then; now the words touched him deep in his soul.

"Drink to me only with thine eyes, And I will pledge with mine. . . ." He knew then that he would marry her.

When Gabrielle resumed her conversation with Elizabeth, seated on her right, Nicholas looked once more at Clive. His friend's gaze was still centered on that part of the table where Gabrielle sat, but Nicholas realized it was not the young Frenchwoman who had caught Clive's attention. It was Elizabeth.

Great Scot! Was that the way the wind was blowing? Interesting. Only four nights ago, Clive had told him it would take an exceptional woman to make him want to give up his comfortable bachelor's existence. But that had been the day *before* Elizabeth arrived.

Nicholas became aware of a stir of activity around the table. He had eaten the meal without being aware of it, and now the party was preparing to remove to the Great Hall for the lighting of the yule log.

It had been agreed that the gentlemen would forego their port in favor of the wassail, and Nicholas politely but firmly wended his way past the Misses Rowland, past Decimus and Sylvester toward Gabrielle.

Elizabeth was there. For the first time Nick noticed that she looked different. She wasn't wearing gray but a gown of deep burgundy velvet, the perfect foil for her creamy skin and the diamonds around her throat. And for once her hair wasn't bundled in a chignon at the nape of her neck. She had piled it up high, a style that made her look like a queen wearing her crown. No wonder Clive hadn't been able to take his eyes off her.

Nicholas drew her aside. "What about my wager with Juliette?"

"You're out of luck, it seems. I am beginning to think Stenton isn't even interested in remembering."

"Can't say I blame him. Elizabeth Gore-Langton *now* is a dashed sight more interesting than was the shy, scrawny girl of eleven years ago."

"I was not scrawny!"

"Pardon me," said Gabrielle. "I could not help but hear what you said, Nicholas, and I feel strongly that I must correct you. Elizabeth is *more* than interesting. She is beautiful."

"She is more than beautiful," said Clive, appearing at Elizabeth's side. "She is breathtaking. May I have the honor of taking you into the Great Hall, Elizabeth?"

As so many times when she wanted to be her most poised, Elizabeth felt the warmth rush to her face. Her one short season had left her woefully ill equipped with ready answers to such lavish compliments.

"Thank you." She lightly placed her hand on the proffered arm.

They were the last to leave the dining room. A moment ago, the excited squeals of Grace and Adam and the chatter of the adults had filled the short passage leading to the Great Hall. Now there was silence.

Clive increased the pace. "What's amiss? I expected the squeals to grow louder. Can it be that the imps don't like their tree?"

"More likely the footman was slow and they caught him lighting the candles which, according to their nurse's tale, are always lit by the *Christkindl*."

Clutching the skirt of her gown to enable her to keep up with Clive's long stride, Elizabeth arrived rather breathlessly in the Great Hall.

At first glance, nothing seemed to be amiss. The children, the adults, all stood in a wide circle around the tree, and the look on their faces was one of astonishment and awe, not disappointment. Then she saw

310

the footman assigned to the task of lighting the candles. His hands shook. He stared up at the tall fir as though he were seeing a ghost.

Elizabeth's eyes flew to the top of the Christmas tree. Her grip tightened on Clive's arm as she watched the long wax taper held by an unseen hand move from candle to candle until the last one was lit.

"Annie," she whispered. "You little devil."

Only Clive heard. "Your ghost?"

"*Your* ghost."

The flame on the taper flickered, then died. The taper floated toward the footman, who took a hasty step backward, turned on his heel, and fled toward the kitchen wing. The clatter of his shoes on the tiles broke the spell of silence.

"It's the *Christkindl!*" shouted Grace.

She and Adam ran forward, pursued by Margaret, who ordered them to stop. Suddenly, everyone was talking and moving.

Flora and Margaret were indulging in a mild fit of hysterics. The children insisted it was the *Christkindl* that had lit the candles, then pounced on the tennis racquets and balls left by *Knecht Ruprecht* beneath the tree. Amelia, Fanny, and Gabrielle argued with Sylvester Throckmorton about ghosts and apparitions. Sir John and Lady Astley held hands. And level-headed gentlemen like George Wilmott, Stewart, and Nicholas tried to restore calm yet could not help but cast uneasy looks around the hall now and then.

In the confusion no one noticed that the taper had ended up in Decimus's hand.

"Annie, m'dear," he said reproachfully, "what a scare

311

you gave me! Could've broken your neck with a trick like that."

"Pish-tosh! I cannot possibly break my neck. But listen, my lord. I need your help."

"Anything, m'dear."

Decimus started toward the wassail bowl and the cups set out on a trestle table near the north wing. Later, pastries and pies, jellies and aspics, cold meats and cheeses would be spread on the white cloth, but for the present he'd be content with the liquid refreshment.

"When the party breaks up, I want you to detain the major. My lord, can you do it?"

"Detain Stewart?" Decimus dipped the ladle into the spicy punch. "Nothing easier. But why?"

"Miss Juliette needs a few moments, ten or fifteen minutes, to prepare a surprise for him."

"She was always one to like surprises. But mostly she liked to be on the receiving end." Decimus smiled indulgently. "Tell her she can depend on me."

Annie left him to sample the wassail and flitted off. She still had much to do, not the least of which was keeping an eye on Miss Flora and Miss Amelia, who were sneaking off just as the butler and the housekeeper led the staff into the Great Hall so they might observe the lighting of the yule log. Hesitating only briefly, Annie hurried after the duke's elderly cousins.

Fanny, too, had noticed Flora's and Amelia's departure. But when she would have followed them, George stopped her.

Raising her hand, he briefly touched his lips to her wrist. "My impetuous love," he murmured. Let them go. They can't do any harm. And how would it look

312

to the children if one by one we all disappeared?"

She stifled a sigh. "You're right. Adam and Grace expect me to lead the caroling."

Holding on to George's hand, she glanced at the fireplace where Clive knelt by the hearth and lit the kindling under the first ash log. He rose, and she saw him turn and look at Elizabeth Gore-Langton, who was in conversation with the elder Astleys.

Fanny swallowed. She could not recall ever seeing such a look on Clive's face, his harsh features softened by a smile, and his eyes—why, they positively glowed!

Feeling like a Peeping Tom, she turned away hastily. "Dash it, George! I'll never know a moment's peace if Flora and Amelia make off with the jewels. They're Clive's, and if he sold them he could afford to marry Miss Gore-Langton, who probably doesn't have a penny to her name."

George cast a pensive look at his brother-in-law. "I'm not saying you're wrong about Clive and Miss Gore-Langton, my love. But I wouldn't put too much hope on those jewels."

"But they're in the castle. I know it! Why else would Flora and Amelia—"

"Fanny," he interrupted. "If the jewels are not a part of the Rowland estate, and if the first fourth duchess left no will bequeathing them to your father, I'd be willing to wager a pony they'll have to be turned over when found—to the duchess's family."

After the lighting of the yule logs Elizabeth was aware only of Clive Rowland and the minutes ticking by and taking her closer to midnight. Sir John had told her that he was thinking of leaving already on Wednesday, Boxing Day. Lady Astley had conceived the notion to have a New Year's celebration for the tenants who wouldn't have a Christmas dinner at Astley Manor this year.

Which meant she'd have only one more day at Stenton. The words she had cherished that morning, "as you get to know me better . . ." no longer served to nourish her secret dreams. There would be no miracle for Elizabeth Gore-Langton.

But there still could be a kiss. The reason for the wager was no longer important. As the evening wore on, she cared less and less whether Clive remembered her from eleven years ago. What mattered was that he would have no reason to kiss her if he lost the wager.

She joined in the caroling and the charades. She went out onto the portico with Lady Harry, Gabrielle, and Juliette to admire the snowman built by the twins and Stewart, who had all three refused to participate in the charades and had donned coats and boots instead.

But her mind was busy plotting ways and means that would make the kiss possible. When the children said good night at eleven o'clock, she had just told herself it would be perfectly all right to maneuver Clive under the kissing bough hanging from the chandelier in the center of the hall. There was nothing awkward about it! All she needed to do was stand close to him, look up, feign surprise, and —

"Goodnight, Miss Elizabeth," said Grace, curtsying. Clutching her tennis racquet to her chest, she tilted her head and gave Elizabeth a curious look. "What's the matter? You look as if you had just been told to bathe in cold water. Don't you like Christmas, Miss Elizabeth?"

"Don't be impertinent, Grace." Clive, with Adam in tow, appeared behind his niece. He turned both children toward the west wing passage. "Off you go. And remember! No tennis playing in your rooms. If I discover a broken window or a cracked lamp, you'll have no dinner tomorrow."

"Yes, Uncle Clive," they chorused.

As they trotted off, Grace was heard to say, "He didn't say we cannot play in the corridor."

"But he meant it." Adam looked over his shoulder. "Would you save us a piece of Christmas pudding, Uncle Clive?"

Elizabeth chuckled. "I'll wager my own share of the Christmas pudding that you'll have to send for the glazier in the morning."

A teasing light sprang to his eye. "What? Another wager? I didn't realize what a little gamester you are."

"I seem to be an extremely fortunate gamester. There's no risk betting on the children playing tennis inside. And, it now appears, I am about to win a canopied tester bed."

"You can hardly take it with you." He took two cups of wassail from the tray of a passing footman and, handing her a cup, started for one of the settles by the fire. "Or do you expect Sir John to load it atop his coach?"

"Not at all. I'll have a carrier cart pick it up."

"You could leave the bed at Stenton. Ownership is an excellent reason for you to return."

She sat down on the settle rather abruptly. Lud! What was he saying? It was unthinkable that an unmarried lady visit a bachelor. Or a widower. Yet it did not sound as though he expected the Astleys to come with her.

For an instant she toyed with the notion that he was offering her *carte blanche*. But Stenton was a gentleman. If he wanted a mistress, he'd turn to a member of the muslin set not to a lady of quality.

"Elizabeth?" Stretching one long leg toward the hearth, he sat down beside her. "Is it so very important to you that I remember our previous meetings?"

All too aware of him so close beside her, she turned her gaze onto the crackling yule log.

"No."

And it truly wasn't important—except when she thought of the kissing bough.

"No," she repeated. "It is no longer important. It could only have mattered in the very beginning, when it might have influenced your perception of me. But now—"

"But now," he finished when she broke off in some confusion, "we have established a relationship quite independent of vague memories."

Though not the relationship she dreamed of. And she still had her memories. But she wondered if they had truly played a part in how she felt about him now.

"Clive!" Fanny swept around the settle. Arms akimbo, she demanded, "Pray tell Margaret that *I* shall be your hostess tomorrow night."

Margaret, too, planted herself in front of Clive. "But as Harry's widow it is *my* duty and my *right*—"

"Ladies!" Clive rose. "There's no need to squabble. It is all settled."

"*I* am the hostess," Fanny said with satisfaction.

316

Margaret glared. "Nonsense! *I* am."

Elizabeth and Clive shared looks brimming with laughter.

"Does this remind you of something?" he asked.

"Very much. I remember Adam and Grace in a similar spat only this morning."

Margaret gave an indignant sniff, but Fanny started to laugh.

"I apologize, Clive," she said. "But pray don't keep us in suspense. How have you arranged the seating at the Christmas dinner?"

"If I had a duchess to preside with me over the dinner, I would of course have the tables arranged in the shape of a horseshoe."

His gaze strayed to Elizabeth but immediately returned to Margaret and Fanny.

"Why, what can you mean?" asked Margaret. "We're not a large enough company to warrant such elaborate arrangements."

"But, yes. I was informed yesterday by no lesser authority than the innkeeper of East Dean that it has been the tradition at Stenton to invite certain families from the villages to the Christmas dinner, which is served in the Great Hall at four o'clock."

"Oh, famous!" Fanny beamed. "I get to meet the smugglers after all."

"This year," said Clive, "we shall have two long tables set up. One will be presided over by Fanny and me. The other by Decimus and Margaret."

The two ladies eyed each other uncertainly.

Taking advantage of their silence, Clive removed the wassail cup from Elizabeth's hand and set it and his own down before the hearth.

"Fanny. Margaret. I hope this answers all your questions, for Elizabeth and I will have to excuse ourselves. There is a small matter of business we must take care of at midnight."

Proffering his arm, he ushered Elizabeth across the hall. "There's a fire in one of the small salons," he said. "We can hide there until the clock strikes twelve."

She saw Juliette hurrying in the opposite direction, toward the east wing passage. Stewart was about to follow her, but Decimus tugged at his sleeve and drew him into conversation with Sylvester Throckmorton.

Sir John and Lady Astley had retired some time ago. Gabrielle and Nicholas had disappeared. Flora and Amelia, who had left the party several times that night, called good night and wandered off once again.

"I doubt there's a need to hide," said Elizabeth, wanting to be alone with him, yet fearing it. Besides, the kissing bough was in the Great Hall. "Just about everyone is leaving."

Clive stopped in the archway of the west wing passage. The salon he wanted opened off the corridor on their left. He had ordered a fire lit and a sprig of mistletoe hung from the ceiling in a strategic spot near the fireplace.

But he'd rather kiss Elizabeth in the Great Hall. Beneath the kissing bough. With the Christmas tree looking on. It could be, if Elizabeth was agreeable, the beginning of a tradition.

"Well?" said Elizabeth. "What shall it be?"

He looked back into the Great Hall. Only Decimus, Sylvester, and Stewart were there. Stewart made the attempt several times to break away from the two elderly gentlemen. Each time, Decimus detained him.

Exasperated, Stewart finally exclaimed, "It's no use asking me over and over! I tell you, I never saw a girl in a striped gown. So how the deuce am I supposed to know what's become of her?"

Elizabeth whispered, "I believe Annie wears a striped gown. Could your uncle be looking for her?"

"With Decimus anything is possible."

Faintly, a clock could be heard striking the hour. Decimus tilted his head, listening intently.

"Ah," he said. "Midnight. Well, Stewart, my boy, you'll have to forgive an old man for bowing out of a most interesting conversation. Come along, Sylvester. Time to seek our couches."

The two stout gentlemen ambled toward Clive and Elizabeth. Stewart, shaking his head, strode off and disappeared in the east wing.

"Clive, my boy." Decimus raised his quizzing glass. "And Elizabeth. Be sure to douse all the candles on the tree. We don't want another fire."

"A footman already did that," Sylvester reminded him. "More than two hours ago."

"That's all right then."

Arm in arm, the gentlemen went off. A short while later, Sylvester's wheezing marked their progress up the stairs.

Clive looked at Elizabeth. There was a light in his eyes that took her breath away.

"And now, Miss Gore-Langton, to our unfinished business."

It seemed the most natural thing in the world that he took her hand and led her back into the Great Hall. She need not have agonized over the means to catch him beneath the kissing bough. It was where he took her of his own accord.

Their gazes locked, they stood beneath the bough of greens and holly berries and mistletoe.

"You did not win the wager," Elizabeth said softly.

"But I'll get my prize. Didn't I tell you I was looking forward to claiming it?"

He swept her into a crushing embrace, which Elizabeth returned with fervor by clasping her arms around his neck. She raised her face and knew this was the moment she had been waiting for since she saw him stride toward her on that rainy day of her arrival.

His mouth claimed hers in a kiss every bit as breathtaking and magical as she had dreamed, igniting a fire that heated her blood and melted her bones. Rational thought receded, but as she was about to surrender to feelings and sensations she had never before experienced, one last clear thought whirled through her mind.

One kiss was not enough to make a miracle.

Chapter Twenty-six

Juliette brushed her hair until it shone. But tonight she would neither braid it nor tuck it under a cap. During the four days of marriage, before he had to return to his regiment, Stewart had told her he liked her hair loose and flowing.

Shivering, she turned away from the dressing mirror. She wasn't cold. She was shivering in a fever of excitement and apprehension, for tonight she would launch a frontal attack.

"Annie," she said softly, "I'm as ready as I'll ever be. Do you have the keys?"

"Yes, Miss Juliette." Two brass keys dangled about a foot above the bedspread. "Now don't you fret about me not doing my part."

"Thank you, Annie. And if I succeed, if Stewart takes me back to London with him, I swear I will take you in the carriage."

"I know you'll keep your word. Now run along, Miss Juliette. You still have the major's man to deal with."

Juliette drew a deep breath. Pulling her wrap close, she marched determinedly toward the door connecting her chamber with Stewart's.

John Piggott, the major's former batman, sat on a low stool drawn up to the fire. He was polishing the buttons on Stewart's tunic. At Juliette's entrance, he rose and thrust the tunic behind his back.

She waited until she heard the soft grating of the key in the lock behind her before she spoke.

"There's no need to hide the tunic, John. I'm glad you're taking care of the major's uniform. I'm hoping that tomorrow he'll wear it."

John's expression was frankly doubting, but he produced the tunic, shook it out, and hung it in the wardrobe.

"Is there aught I can do for ye, ma'am?"

"Yes, John. You may leave."

He gave her a long, considering look. "Yes, ma'am. But I doubt the major will like it if I'm not here. Like as not, he'll ring for me afore he's taken two steps inside the chamber."

Botheration! Her eyes flew to the bellpull dangling between the connecting door and the tall dresser. Neither she nor Annie had remembered the bell that would recall John Piggott.

"Thought I'd just mention it," he muttered, "seeing as you went to the trouble of removing *both* keys."

"Oh." Her face flamed. It was one thing to have Annie know her plan. But that John had guessed!

Blushing like a schoolroom miss and dressed in a nightgown and wrap, Juliette found it difficult to look dignified, but she did her best. She looked the old soldier straight in the eye.

"Can you remove the bellpull, John?"

In answer, he set a chair next to the dresser, climbed on it and, when he found he still could not reach the hook attaching the bellpull to the wire, climbed atop the dresser.

When he handed her the bellpull, he was smiling, a sight that struck her dumb. She hadn't known he *could* smile, for she had seen him only grim and dour looking.

"Good night, ma'am." He went off as fast as his limp allowed.

For a moment, she stared at the door he had firmly shut behind him. But she had no time to muse about this strange, gruff man, who seemed to dote on her husband but had never before shown her more than the bare minimum of civility.

She tossed the bellpull into a drawer, pushing it well to the back. She blew out the candles in the wall sconces and dimmed the lamp on the bedside table.

The covers had been turned back and a hot, flannel-wrapped brick placed in the middle of the bed. Sliding between the sheets, she pushed the brick toward the foot end.

Now to the most difficult part, the part of her campaign that would require all her courage. With trembling fingers she untied the fastenings of her wrap. Quickly, she slipped it off her shoulders. Next, the nightgown. She bundled the two garments together and tossed them as far from the bed as she could.

And not a moment too soon. She was still tugging

and pulling on the covers when the bedroom door opened.

"What the deuce?" Surprised by the near dark in the chamber he expected to find well lit, Stewart stopped in midstride.

"John? Where the devil are you?"

The covers drawn tightly against her chin, Juliette lay quite still.

Stewart slammed the door and strode toward the bed. As he reached for the lamp, Juliette heard the second key turn in the lock. Annie, bless her, had done her part.

"Juliette!"

Stewart had not turned up the lamp after all. The dim glow was sufficient to show him the blond head on his pillow.

The dim light was also sufficient to show Juliette that he was not at all pleased by what he saw. But she had known this wouldn't be easy. A tight mouth and a forbidding frown could not shake her determination.

"Come to bed, Stewart. It is late."

"Juliette, either you leave right now, or I'll leave."

"Impossible."

He turned on his heel and strode to the door. He pushed down the handle, he rattled it, but the door would not budge.

"We're locked in, Stewart."

"If this is a jest, it is not funny."

"I am in dead earnest."

He swung around, staring at the connecting door. "Locked, I presume?"

"I'm afraid so."

In a few, quick steps he reached the dresser.

"There's no bellpull," she said, sounding apologetic against her will.

He returned to the bed.

"What do you want, Juliette?"

"My husband."

She scooted up against the pillow and at the same time allowed the covers to slip until her shoulders were exposed.

He gave a groan. "Julie, don't do this to me! I'm trying hard to be noble, but it gets more difficult every day."

"I don't want you noble. I want you loving."

"I'm a cripple. You deserve a *man* to love you."

The sheets slid to her waist as she sat up in indignation. "Stewart Astley, how dare you! Horatio Nelson lost an arm *and* an eye, but he never called himself a cripple."

He could not take his eyes off her. Did she know what she was doing to him? He could not doubt that she did. She looked so proud, so sure of herself in her beautiful nakedness.

"But you, Julie! You cannot bear to look on the stump of my arm without shuddering."

"What did you expect? The papers were writing in detail about amputations. How awful they are. How painful." Her voice grew husky with emotion. "When I saw your poor arm, the still-raw skin—Oh, God! How much it must have hurt!"

He frowned at her, but it was a puzzled frown not the grim, tight look he'd had earlier.

"Julie, I believed the stump, the scars repulsed you."

325

"What?"

"Your body was racked with shudders that first night after my return. I thought it was revulsion. You couldn't bear to look at the ugly stump."

Anger flared, hot and sharp. That he believed her capable of such shallow emotions! Worse, he had refused to talk to her, had denied her the opportunity for an explanation!

Accusations, reproaches welled on the tip of her tongue. But the sight of his haggard face made her bite them back. He had suffered no less than she. And even though he deserved to be punished for his lack of faith, it was reconciliation she wanted not a renewal of hostilities.

"I cannot promise that I won't shudder the next time I see the stump. Until I get hardened to the sight, I will always picture the surgeon with his saw. I will feel the pain you suffered."

"Julie, you mustn't torture yourself. It was bad, but I survived."

The hard-won calm deserted her. "Stewart!" she cried. "They said in the papers that . . . that the stump is dipped in hot tar!"

Suddenly—and he did not quite understand how it happened so quickly—he sat on the edge of the bed and Juliette, gloriously naked, was drawing him toward her.

"Make love to me, Stewart."

Her hands tugged at his coat, his shirt, his cravat.

"Hurry, Stewart!"

Her touch, her voice, so urgent and loving, broke down the last wall of reserve. He no longer tried to resist but helped as best he could to shed his clothing. He felt alive, as he hadn't felt in weeks.

And he wanted her. Wanted her now. Wanted her forever.

"I don't know how you got rid of John," he said breathlessly while struggling with the buttons on his pantaloons. "But, maybe, next time you'll think twice about sending him away before I'm undressed. I may have to make love to you with my blasted boots on."

Reluctantly, Clive loosened his tight hold and stepped back from Elizabeth. He had seen Symes peek into the Great Hall and discreetly shut the door to the north wing again. Symes could be trusted not to spread it about that the master was kissing Miss Gore-Langton, but any moment a footman might enter the hall from one of the passages.

He had meant to claim one kiss, but no sooner had her arms wrapped around his neck and her mouth offered itself so provocatively than resolve was vanquished by desire. He had kissed her again and again until her mouth was soft and yielding and as hungry for his touch as he was for hers.

"Elizabeth."

He gazed into her eyes, darkened and hazed with the desire he had aroused. His power thrilled and humbled him; it stirred a protective instinct he had long believed dead.

"Elizabeth, we must be sensible."

Her eyes cleared. She unclasped her hands from his neck and took a step back.

A smile tugged at the corners of her mouth. "I was sensible for a very long time. But something happened to me when I arrived here. Ever since, I have had very few sensible thoughts in my head. And do you know, the strange thing is that I will find it a dead bore to return to my old ways."

"Is that an invitation to kiss you again?"

The smile deepened. "Yes."

Once more he crushed her to his breast, tasted again the sweetness of her lips.

He straightened. His hands cupped her face, his thumbs caressing the corners of her mouth. "This is madness, Elizabeth. If you won't use common sense, I must."

"Afraid I'll be compromised?"

"Afraid I'll lose my head altogether."

Her eyes widened, then fell. He wondered if he had been too blunt in his admission of ardor. Nothing in her demeanor had warned him she might be offended when confronted by his passion.

He feared she would leave without a word, but she reached up to smooth the hair at the back of his head, where her fingers had earlier wreaked havoc.

"Good night, Stenton," she said softly.

He turned her in the direction of the east wing. Walking beside her, he said, "Do you think you could bring yourself to use my Christian name?"

She hesitated, then said lightly, "It shouldn't be too difficult. In my mind I've called you Clive more than once."

He accompanied her down the passage, but stopped at the foot of the stairs. He could reach his chamber from the east wing, but prudence told him to leave her right here.

"Merry Christmas, Elizabeth. Sweet dreams in *your* bed."

He resisted the impulse to draw her close once more. Turning on his heel, he strode off to use the stairs across the hall.

"Merry Christmas, Clive," she said to his retreating back. She said it softly so he wouldn't hear the quiver in her voice.

One of the footmen, carrying a snuffer, came down the stairs as Elizabeth started up.

"Best take a candle, miss," he said, removing one from its holder on the wall. "I've just doused the lights in the corridor."

"Thank you."

Shielding the flame with her hand, she ascended swiftly to the first floor. She did not want to think about Clive's kisses, but with the taste of his mouth still on hers, she could not help but dwell on them and on the feelings they aroused in her.

She had floated in a bubble of happiness, believing that her miracle was about to happen. A man did not kiss a woman the way Clive had kissed her unless he had serious intentions. That was what she had believed.

Until he told her they must stop lest he lose his head altogether.

She did not doubt the nature of his feelings for her. His kisses had been tender as well as ardent; they had held sweetness as well as passion. But while she had been lured into dreams of a life and love shared forever after, he had struggled to keep a cool head.

The Duke of Stenton could not propose marriage to Miss Gore-Langton, a penniless lady's companion. He had tried to warn her that morning during the sleigh ride. He had confessed his own impecunious state, and even though he seemed to have scorned his sister's attempts to provide him with an heiress, it was obvious that, if he married, he must take a bride with a dowry. As his father had done.

Hurrying along the dark corridor in an effort to reach her chamber before composure could wholly desert her, she almost did not hear the soft voice calling to her as she passed Stewart's room.

"Psst! Miss Elizabeth!"

She swung around. The flame of her candle flickered wildly, but it did not go out. The dim glow fell on a slight form in an old-fashioned striped cotton skirt with an overdress of some dark blue material. A huge mobcap all but hid a thin little face framed by wisps of dark curls.

"Annie! Is something wrong?"

"Quite the contrary!" Annie executed a dance step. "Miss Juliette and the major, they're both in there. Making up. There's going to be no more talk about having the marriage voided."

"Juliette's miracle!"

"Aye, that it is. A miracle. With just a little help from me." Annie touched the key in the door of Stewart's room.

"You locked them in?"

At Annie's nod, laughter bubbled inside Elizabeth but just as quickly died. If only her own miracle could

330

be brought about by something as simple as being locked in.

Annie's shrewd eyes rested on Elizabeth. "We don't want to disturb anyone. Let's talk in your room."

As Elizabeth followed Annie around the corner to her own chamber, she thought how strange it was that she felt no surprise at seeing the ghost as clearly as she would see Juliette. Neither did she have to get used to that thin little face with the large eyes. It was as though she had known all along what Annie looked like.

Annie disappeared through the closed door. Elizabeth, distracted by her musings, realized only just in time that she must use a more conventional method of entering a chamber.

"What about *your* miracle?" Annie asked bluntly when Elizabeth had shut the door. "Didn't you get your kiss?"

"Oh, yes." Elizabeth paced the room with quick, impatient steps. "I was kissed several times."

"But it isn't enough, is it? You want his grace to feel the way you feel. You want him to fall head over heels in love and ask you to marry him."

Elizabeth looked at Annie, perched on a corner of the dressing table. "That's the most disconcerting thing about you. That you know exactly what's in a person's mind. It made me wonder if I'd gone mad and was talking to myself that first time you spoke to me."

"It has come in handy to know what people are thinking." Annie toyed with the lid of Elizabeth's jewelry box. "Take the old ladies who're looking for the

331

duchess's jewels. The plump one, Miss Flora, now she'd make off with the lot if given a chance. She doesn't say so, but she's thinking it."

"But that mustn't happen!"

"You want the duke to have the jewels, don't you?"

"He certainly could use them. He could buy a herd of sheep and a fleet of fishing boats for the villagers."

He could also forget about the heiress.

Elizabeth shot a look at Annie to see if the little ghost had picked up the thought that had come unbidden into her mind. But either Annie did not want to embarrass her, or she was caught up in her own train of thought.

"Well, there's no need to worry about Miss Flora," Annie said gaily. "Miss Amelia will keep her sister in line. Besides, they're still convinced the marquetry chest is in Lady Fanny's room, but they'll never find it there."

"Annie! Do you know where the jewels are?"

"But of course." Annie gave Elizabeth a wide-eyed look of astonishment. "I put them in their new hiding place, didn't I?"

Chapter Twenty-seven

When the fire was discovered, Annie had run to rouse the duchess, who had snatched the marquetry chest from the secret compartment and thrust it at the young nursery maid. "Keep it safe, Annie. We may need this if Stenton is gutted," she had said and hurried off to the nursery.

"And I did." Annie slid off the dressing table. "Shall I show you where, Miss Elizabeth?"

"Please do." Feeling rather dazed, Elizabeth picked up the lamp on her bedside table. "And having put the jewels in a safe place, you followed the duchess into the burning nursery?"

"But, yes. I couldn't just stand by, could I now?"

"You're a brave girl. I don't know if I'd have had the courage."

"All of us come to a point when we must show pluck," Annie said sagely. "For me it was the fire. For you, perhaps it was when you went down to the beach last night. Or, perhaps, your time to show your mettle hasn't come yet."

Annie led Elizabeth down the corridor, past Miss Flora's and Miss Amelia's chambers, toward the south wing. But she did not go into the south wing. She stopped at the last room this side of the stairs.

It was a small sitting room. A ladies' room. Elizabeth remembered peeking into it during her tour of exploration. A half-dozen chairs and an oval table with a marble top stood in the center of the room on a large Turkey rug. A pigeonhole desk and two glass-fronted cabinets lined the wall adjoining the stairs, and the fireplace filled a large portion of the opposite wall. A sewing table, two tambour frames, workbaskets and workboxes, and several straight-backed chairs were placed by the windows, where at least during the early part of the day sufficient light would make the use of working candles unnecessary.

Elizabeth raised her lamp and studied the wainscoting with the richly carved and bossed frieze at about shoulder height. She did not know about Miss Flora and Miss Amelia, but Lady Fanny and Lady Harry had thoroughly examined the bosses in this section of the castle to see if one would twist to open a secret compartment.

"I trust your memory is good, Annie. If we must test every one of these carved rosettes, we'll be here all night and day."

Annie giggled. "You're making the same mistake the other ladies made. The chest is *not* in a secret compartment."

"Then where—"

Elizabeth drew in her breath sharply. Her gaze

334

flew to the tambour frames, the workbaskets and workboxes. One of the boxes was in the shape of a miniature sea chest, the rounded lid richly decorated with marquetry work.

"But that's impossible! Incredible!" she said. "Someone must have noticed it before now."

"Who? Did any of you ladies sit in this room and work your embroidery, your crocheting, your tatting?"

Slowly, Elizabeth crossed the room toward the sewing nook. "Mrs. Rodwell . . . the maids who clean and dust. Surely they would know it wasn't a workbox."

"Look at it!" Annie flitted past her. "If you didn't know exactly what you're looking for, would you have taken it for a *jewelry* box?"

"Even knowing what I was looking for, I looked right past it." Elizabeth dropped to her knees. Setting down the lamp, she picked up the marquetry chest. "It's locked, Annie."

"Aye, and that's what almost caused trouble when the village women came to clean. One of them wanted to break it open to see if there was thread in it that she might use. Thank goodness the others reminded her that none of them would be asked back if anything was discovered broken or missing."

Elizabeth gently shook the box. There was no sound or rattle. If jewels were inside, they were securely cushioned.

With the box tucked beneath her arm, she rose. In the morning, she'd give it to Clive.

"And you'll let him kiss you again," said Annie.

Elizabeth shot her a startled look. "I wish you wouldn't always read my mind."

"But you will?" Annie insisted.

"Certainly I will," Elizabeth said briskly.

She picked up the lamp. Something was happening to her throat. It felt tight and prickly.

"I am twenty-eight years old, Annie. Surely I am entitled to snatch a bit of happiness before I turn into a crotchety old maid!"

"Happiness?" said Annie. "Then why are you crying?"

Elizabeth gave a defiant sniff. "It's the smoke from the lamp. It bothers my eyes."

Annie did not dignify such a bouncer with a reply. Following Elizabeth into the corridor, she said, "I'll be off, then. Good night, Miss Elizabeth."

"Where are you going?"

But Annie had disappeared.

Elizabeth returned to her chamber. She looked at the bed with its gilded posts and the beautiful canopy and drapes of ivory velvet. *Her* bed. And Clive had wished her sweet dreams.

She sat by the dying fire, the jewelry box in her lap. The clock on the mantel showed it was almost three. She must wait at least five more hours before she could think about seeking out Clive.

A long wait. Not as long as she had waited for his kisses but long enough to give her the craziest notions.

She convinced herself that the jewels, which Lady

Fanny believed to be worth "a king's ransom," were the key to her happiness. They were the miracle that would bring about Clive's proposal of marriage.

Just when her spirits lifted, they were dashed again. She was certain the treasure wouldn't make the slightest difference in his approach to matrimony. He was still the Duke of Stenton, above the touch of Miss Gore-Langton, daughter of a mere baronet.

And then she wished she hadn't found the jewels at all. If the miracle should happen, if he should tell her he loved her and ask her to be his wife, she'd rather have him do so in the face of impecuniousness.

She must have dozed finally, for when Annie spoke to her, she was quite startled. Her head jerked back and it took a moment to recognize where she was.

"Miss Elizabeth, didn't you hear me? His grace is in the library. You can take him the box now."

Elizabeth straightened in the chair. She rubbed her fingers, which were stiff with cold or, perhaps, from clutching the marquetry chest.

She glanced at the clock. "I cannot see him now! It's not yet six."

"Six! Gorblimey, I almost forgot to unlock the major's door!"

Elizabeth was getting quite used to Annie's sudden appearances and disappearances. But she would have liked the chance to ask why Clive was up at this ungodly hour. On Christmas Day.

As though it mattered.

337

She rose. It probably wasn't what Annie meant when she had talked about showing pluck, but she'd go to the library now.

Once again clutching the jewelry chest under her arm and carrying a lamp, she hurried along the corridor. If she slowed down, she might change her mind. She did not even pause for breath at the library door, but knocked and entered.

He stood by the window, his back to the door. He still wore the dark blue coat and champagne-colored pantaloons he had worn for the Christmas Eve celebration. But, then, neither had she changed out of her velvet gown.

He did not turn but said, "It's snowing again and the wind is kicking up. If we're lucky, you won't be able to leave tomorrow."

"How did you know it was me?" Heart pounding, she crossed the room to stand at his side. "Oh, the reflection in the window. But you weren't even surprised."

Taking the lamp from her, he set it down on the desk. He did not smile, but there was a warm light in his eyes when he looked at her.

"I was expecting you. After sending me to the Great Hall where Grace and Adam were playing tennis, your little ghost informed me that you wished to speak to me."

"I did not send her."

His look turned quizzical. "But I sent her to you to be sure you knew I was here, waiting for you."

She did not know what to say and wished she had Annie's ability to read minds.

To break the silence, she asked abruptly, "Did they break something? Grace and Adam."

"Knocked the mistletoe off the kissing bough."

They stared at each other.

"I want to kiss you again, Elizabeth."

"First let me give you this." She thrust the marquetry chest at him. "Take it. It's the jewelry box of the first fourth duchess. Annie showed me where it was."

"Annie has been busy."

Without taking his eyes off Elizabeth, he set the box beside the lamp.

"Aren't you going to look inside?" she asked. "It's locked, but I think a paper knife would do the trick."

"Elizabeth, will you marry me?"

"Those jewels can buy—*what* did you say?"

A rueful look crossed his face. "I knew it was too soon to speak."

"Too soon?" She struggled to keep her voice calm and even. "Not at all. It seems as if I'd been waiting forever."

"I almost spoke last night, but we've only known each other a few days. Then Annie said you might leave Boxing Day—"

"Sir John won't travel in a snowstorm."

"Elizabeth, I love you."

She glanced at the jewelry box, sitting unopened on his desk. Her heart filled with happiness.

"Elizabeth." Placing a finger beneath her chin, he

gently tilted it so that she faced him again. "I think you're not indifferent to me. But if you need more time . . . I shan't enjoy the waiting, but I'll understand."

"Lud, Clive! I don't need more time. I've known for years that I love you, although I told myself I had quite gotten over my youthful infatuation."

He clasped her shoulders and stared intently at her.

They started to speak at the same time.

"You're Lizzy—"

"You met me at the same ball you met Rosalind—"

"Rosalind's friend . . . that child they sent along to play chaperone!"

"I wasn't a child! I was seventeen. And I was a bridesmaid at your wedding."

He shook his head. "You cannot blame me for not recognizing you. You're so unlike that . . . shy little kitten everyone called Lizzy and who hardly exchanged a word with me."

"You hesitated." She gave him a suspicious look. "You weren't, perchance, thinking of calling me a *scrawny little girl?*"

"Of course not," he said just a bit too quickly. "What gave you that silly notion?"

"It's the term used by your friend Nicholas."

His hands dropped from her shoulders. He frowned. "Are you saying Nicholas recognized you?"

"He did. But he had the advantage of having seen me once or twice over the years."

"The knave! I recall that first night when you came into the Crimson Drawing Room with him and Juliette, something was said about introductions being unnecessary." The frown deepened. "Nick was grinning. I remember thinking that mischief was afoot."

She decided to make a clean breast of it. "When Lord Nicholas learned that you did not recognize me, he wagered—"

"Say no more. Nick will bet on anything." Clive cocked a brow. "Was the bet with you?"

"Juliette."

"The deuce! Who else knows of my lamentable memory?"

"Annie."

"I should have known."

"You have no grounds for complaint. If I must live with the epithet of scrawny kitten, you ought to be able to bear a bit of teasing about your memory."

His brow cleared. A smile, starting in his eyes, lit his face. "I can find no fault with that. Elizabeth, I ask you once more since I do not recall a clear answer—my lamentable memory. Will you marry me?"

"I will."

She was in his arms before the words had quite left her mouth. And then she had no need or opportunity to speak. He kissed her ruthlessly and thoroughly until she thought her bones would melt in the fire he ignited.

Finally he raised his head. "How soon can we marry? I must warn you, I'll be six-and-thirty next

341

month. Too old, if my sister is to be believed, to wait much longer before settling down and filling my nursery."

"As soon as you can lay your hands on a special license?"

She had said it half teasingly, but the gleam in his eyes warned her she would have a difficult time backing off. And in truth, she did not want to wait any longer than she must.

"I'll have a license by tonight."

"Clive! It's Christmas Day."

"Tomorrow, then."

"Tomorrow," she promised. But tomorrow seemed an eternity away. Her arms tightened around his neck and a slow, inviting smile curved her mouth. "At least we need not wait for a license to kiss."

Epilogue

She stood at one of the window slits in the northwest tower and in the gray morning light gazed down onto the carriages lined up at the castle's imposing entrance. It was the second day of January, 1811. The day she would leave Stenton Castle.

Annie did a little skip, but the attempt fell woefully short of the bouncy, spritely skips she used to do. For some reason, on this remarkable day when her most fervent desire was about to be fulfilled, Annie felt blue-deviled.

She looked at the drizzling rain and leaden sky which made the morning even darker than it would ordinarily be at seven o'clock. That was it, no doubt. The dismal grayness made her movements drag and her heart heavy.

But, at least, the rain wasn't turning to ice as had happened the past four days. The weather had been so bad that Sir John and Lady Astley and the Misses Rowland, who had not planned to stay over New Year, were obliged to postpone their departure.

From her vantage point in the tower, Annie could

see the lower three of the steps leading from the courtyard to the portico. Lord Nicholas was there and the young French lady, Mam'selle Gabrielle. They didn't seem to mind the rain but smiled at each other in quite the same way Miss Juliette and the major did now.

However, Lord Nicholas would be better advised to hustle his lady into the carriage, or he'd have her sneezing and sniffling all the way to London. They'd be traveling in Mr. Throckmorton's coach with its brand-new left front wheel. And Mr. Throckmorton would ride with Lord Decimus so Lord Nicholas could take mam'selle to her parents in Mary-le-Bone.

As a child, Annie had once attended a fair in the village of Mary-le-Bone. But, apparently, it wasn't a village anymore, and a great many French lived there now. And from all she'd gathered, even the French king had taken up residence in England while their own king, dear Farmer George, was locked up at Windsor Castle.

Whatever was the world coming to? She could only hope London hadn't changed so much that she wouldn't recognize it when she got there.

Now his grace was coming down the stairs. And Miss Elizabeth — no, *her grace,* the Duchess of Stenton.

The heaviness of Annie's heart lifted as she remembered the morning of Christmas Day when his grace announced his forthcoming nuptials. What a to-do there had been! What excitement. Lady Astley had cried a little at the thought of losing her dear

Elizabeth, but she had talked no more about leaving on Boxing Day, because, of course, Sir John must give Elizabeth away.

Before dawn on Boxing Day, his grace had set out for Lewes in his racing curricle. He had returned in the early afternoon with the special license and with the vicar from Seaford.

Emotion threatened to overcome Annie. It had been a lovely wedding in the Great Hall, with the candles lit on the Christmas tree and Miss Grace and Master Adam singing. And Miss Elizabeth so beautiful in the old silk gown and lace veil from the trunk on the second floor.

Annie had remembered the trunk just in time and told Miss Juliette about it. True, the silk was brittle and yellowed, but in the candle light it looked like pale gold. The skirt, meant to be worn over hoops, had to be shortened. But the bodice with its inset of lace across the bosom, and the long sleeves which were not unlike the leg-of-mutton sleeves fashionable in Annie's day, fit to perfection.

With a little sniff, she turned away from the window slit. She slipped into the north wing and from there to the strip of landing beneath the oriel window. She looked out at the Great North Gate and saw Lord Nicholas and Mam'selle Gabrielle bowl away in their borrowed coach.

Annie remembered the thrill of watching the Great North Gate open. Well, if his grace's plans worked out, it need never be closed again. The duke and duchess were staying on at Stenton, at least until they had engaged a man-of-business to oversee the leasing of the east and west wings, and a bailiff to run the home farm. They would also place orders in Bournemouth for the building of fishing and pleasure boats.

"Yes, indeed," whispered Annie. "Stenton Castle has come alive again."

She turned and looked down into the Great Hall. The duke and Miss Elizabeth had come inside and were bidding farewell to Sir John and Lady Astley and the Misses Rowland. Sir John had offered to convey the sisters to London, for they had arrived in a hired chaise. It'd be no trouble he had assured them. He planned to stop in Hans Town to pick up the elderly cousin who had served as Juliette's chaperon while Stewart was abroad. The lady had been hoping for years to replace Miss Elizabeth as Lady Astley's companion.

Annie floated down into the hall. She could not see the sapphire brooch Miss Flora had received from the first fourth duchess's jewelry chest, but Miss Amelia had left her pelisse unbuttoned and the string of pearls gleamed softly against the gray of her gown.

The contents of the marquetry chest had, in a way, been a disappointment. Besides Flora's brooch and Amelia's necklace, which had both been labeled and marked in an elegant, spidery hand, the chest had contained only an emerald necklace and matching earrings.

Lady Fanny had started to cry when she saw the many empty compartments. But Sylvester Throckmorton, an expert, assured her that the emeralds were worth, if not a king's ransom, at least a small fortune. And both Throckmorton and Lord Decimus confirmed that the duchess had been the last of the Veryans; there would be no one of her family to question the Rowlands' right of ownership.

His grace had lifted the necklace off its bed of velvet and placed it around Miss Elizabeth's throat.

"I said to you once that you should always wear emeralds, didn't I?" He had smiled at Miss Elizabeth in a way that made Annie feel warm all over.

"Annie!"

Miss Elizabeth's urgent whispers recalled her to the present.

"What are you waiting for? Go to Miss Juliette. The major is impatient to leave."

Annie saw that the elder Astleys, the Misses Rowland, Lady Fanny and Lord Wilmott, and even Lady Harry and the twins had left. Only the major and Miss Juliette remained. And Sylvester Throckmorton.

"Miss Elizabeth—your grace! Where is Lord Decimus?"

"I don't know. I don't recall seeing him after breakfast. Do hurry, Annie. Miss Juliette won't be able to wait much longer."

"I must see Lord Decimus."

Annie did not wait for Elizabeth's reply but flitted off to the south wing, to the former nurseries where Lord Decimus had his chamber.

Swiftly, she entered.

"There you are m'dear!" Decimus's face brightened. He rose and came toward her. "Knew you wouldn't let an old man leave without saying good-bye to him."

"No, I wouldn't do that," she said softly. "Especially since we shan't see each other again."

"But of course we will. Now that Clive's a tenant for life, he'll spend time here at Stenton every now and then. He'll have more house parties, and he's bound to invite me."

"I'm leaving the castle, my lord. I'm going to London."

"Stap me! That's where I'm going!"

"I know. That's why I made your acquaintance in the first place. If Miss Juliette couldn't take me, I wanted to apply to you for help."

"Any time, m'dear." He bowed in a very courtly manner that made her feel like a great lady. "So you'll be in London, eh? With Juliette. In that case, we'll see each other sooner than you think."

"No, my lord. Once I reach London, I'm afraid I shall be no more." Again, she felt a heaviness descend on her. Her voice trembled. "You see, my lord, I am a ghost."

He peered at her, even raised his quizzing glass to get a clearer view.

"Fustian," he said, but he sounded a little uncertain. "A ghost, you say?"

"Yes, my lord."

"Then why the deuce won't you stay here? Aren't you comfortable?"

"I am. But I was born and bred in London, and I always wanted to return."

He pursed his mouth, puffed out his cheeks, and

from the deep crease on his brow it was obvious that he was thinking hard.

"You don't want to do anything hasty, m'dear. It never pays off. *I* should know. I'm always just a trifle too hasty when it comes to discards at whist or raising the stakes at faro."

"But I've had forty-one years to think about it. You cannot call that a hasty decision. Only now . . . now I don't know anymore what I want."

"Tell you what. Go for a visit. Spend several weeks, a few months with Juliette. She's got a snug little house off Russell Square."

"A visit?" Her heart raced at the possibility. "But I'm not sure that I can. Merely visit, I mean."

"Why not?"

"Because I don't know what'll happen to me once I get there. Whether I'll simply cease to be—"

"Poppycock! A body does not simply cease to be."

Annie smiled sadly. He did not understand. Or, perhaps, he did not want to understand.

"And if you don't like it in London, which is quite possible—I'm not sure *I* like all the changes, the renovations and innovations—and I'm a man who cannot bear country living!" He frowned. "Now what was I going to say? Ah, yes. If you don't like London, say so. I'll take you back to Stenton."

Annie's mind whirled. If it were possible. . . !

She did not understand herself. She had waited for this day such a long time, and now that it was time to go she felt torn. She'd had such fun flitting in and out of the lives of Miss Juliette and Miss Elizabeth, trying a hand at peacemaker and matchmaker, giving Miss Grace and Master Adam a candle-lighting they'd never forget.

She still wanted to go to London. But she also wished she could go on being Annie, the ghost. At the castle, she'd not be lonely again.

A knock fell on the door.

"Decimus!" Wheezing, Sylvester Throckmorton stuck his leonine head into the chamber. "We'd best get going if we want to make the King's Head by luncheon."

"We'll be down in a moment."

Misunderstanding the "we," Throckmorton said, "Come along, Decimus. Your man's waiting by the chaise, not up here."

When Throckmorton's stentorian breathing receded in the corridor, Decimus said, "Run along, Annie. Stewart's carriage is ahead of mine. You don't want to hold up traffic."

"No, my lord." Her voice quavered. "Good-bye and God speed."

"We'll meet again, m'dear."

He held out his hand. Hesitantly, she stretched out her own. To her utter astonishment, he raised her hand and kissed it, then turned and ambled off.

Annie stood motionless. London . . . she did want to see it again. Didn't she?

Avoiding the corridor and stairs Lord Decimus would walk, she slipped straight into the Great Hall. No one was there.

Never before had she stepped outside the castle walls. She did now and stopped just outside the front door.

The last two carriages stood waiting. His grace was talking with Mr. Throckmorton. The major, splendid in his light blue tunic with gold facing, his pelisse draped over one shoulder, assisted Miss Juliette into the coach. He climbed in after her. John Piggott put up the steps, shut the door, and took his seat on the box.

"Annie!" Elizabeth stared at the little ghost on the portico. "Have you changed your mind?"

"I want to see London," Annie said grimly. "But I also want to be a ghost."

"And you cannot be one in London?"

The carriage started to roll.

"Miss Elizabeth, if only I knew!"

Hearing the agony of indecision in Annie's voice, Elizabeth said, "When you followed the duchess into the burning nursery, you did not know if you'd come out alive. But you went ahead."

"I did, didn't I?"

The thin little face beneath the huge mobcap assumed a look of determination. Annie started to move, slowly at first, then, seeming to fly, swift as a swallow, caught up with the coach and disappeared inside.

Briefly, Elizabeth saw the mobcap again as Annie stuck her head out the window.

"I'll find out what happens, Miss Elizabeth! All it takes is a bit of pluck."

THE BEST OF REGENCY ROMANCES

AN IMPROPER COMPANION   (2691, $3.95)
by Karla Hocker
At the closing of Miss Venable's Seminary for Young Ladies school, mistress Kate Elliott welcomed the invitation to be Liza Ashcroft's chaperone for the Season at Bath. Little did she know that Miss Ashcroft's father, the handsome widower Damien Ashcroft would also enter her life. And not as a passive bystander or dutiful dad.

WAGER ON LOVE   (2693, $2.95)
by Prudence Martin
Only a rogue like Nicholas Ruxart would choose a bride on the basis of a careless wager. And only a rakehell like Nicholas would then fall in love with his betrothed's grey-eyed sister! The cynical viscount had always thought one blushing miss would suit as well as another, but the unattainable Jane Sommers soon proved him wrong.

LOVE AND FOLLY   (2715, $3.95)
by Sheila Simonson
To the dismay of her more sensible twin Margaret, Lady Jean proceeded to fall hopelessly in love with the silver-tongued, seditious poet, Owen Davies—and catapult her entire family into social ruin . . . Margaret was used to gentlemen falling in love with vivacious Jean rather than with her—even the handsome Johnny Dyott whom she secretly adored. And when Jean's foolishness led her into the arms of the notorious Owen Davies, Margaret knew she could count on Dyott to avert scandal. What she didn't know, however was that her sweet sensibility was exerting a charm all its own.

Available wherever paperbacks are sold, or order direct from the Publisher. Send cover price plus 50¢ per copy for mailing and handling to Zebra Books, Dept. 3582, 475 Park Avenue South, New York, N.Y. 10016. Residents of New York, New Jersey and Pennsylvania must include sales tax. DO NOT SEND CASH.